GALAXY'S EDGE

LEGIONNAIRE

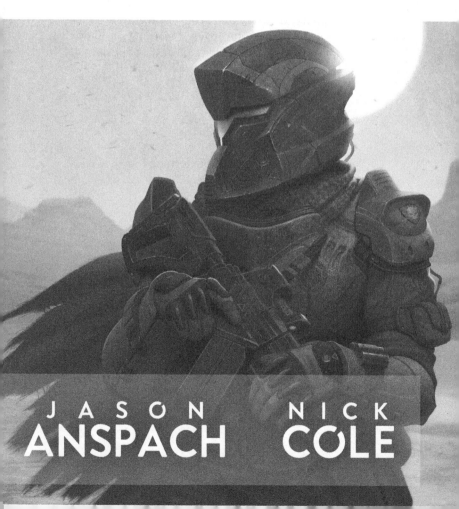

J A S O N
ANSPACH

N I C K
COLE

Second Edition

Edited by David Gatewood
Published by Galaxy's Edge Press

Cover Art: Fabian Saravia
Cover Design: Beaulistic Book Services
Interior Design: Kevin G. Summers

Website: InTheLegion.com
Facebook: facebook.com/atgalaxysedge
Newsletter (get a free short story): InTheLegion.com

OTHER GALAXY'S EDGE BOOKS

Galaxy's Edge Season One:
- Legionnaire
- Galactic Outlaws
- Kill Team
- Attack of Shadows
- Sword of the Legion
- Prisoners of Darkness
- Turning Point
- Message for the Dead
- Retribution

Tyrus Rechs: Contracts & Terminations:
- Requiem for Medusa
- Chasing the Dragon

Stand-Alone Books:
- Imperator
- Order of the Centurion

A LONG, LONG TIME FROM NOW
AT THE EDGE OF THE GALAXY...

IMPERATOR

ORDER OF THE CENTURION

REQUIEM FOR MEDUISA

CHASING THE DRAGON

IRON WOLVES

LEGIONNAIRE

KILL TEAM

GALACTIC OUTLAWS

ATTACK OF SHADOWS

SWORD OF THE LEGION

PRISONERS OF DARKNESS

TURNING POINT

MESSAGE FOR THE DEAD

RETRIBUTION

CONTRACTS
& TERMINATIONS

ORDER OF
THE CENTURION

SEASON 1

PART ONE

01

The galaxy is a dumpster fire.

That's not the way the Senate and House of Reason want you to hear it. They want me—or one of my brothers—to remove my helmet and stand in front of a holo-cam, all smiles. They want you to see me without my N-4 rifle (I'm never without my N-4) holding a unit of water while a bunch of raggedy kids from Morobii or Grevulo, you can pick whatever ass-backward planet garners the most sympathy this week, dance around me smiling right back. They want me to give a thumbs-up and say, "At the edge of the galaxy, the Republic is making a difference!"

But the galaxy is a dumpster fire. A hot, stinking dumpster fire. And most days I don't know if the legionnaires are putting out the flames, or fanning them into an inferno.

I won't clint you. I stopped caring about anything but the men by my side, the men of Victory Company, a long time ago.

And if you don't know how liberating it feels to no longer give a damn, I highly recommend you find out.

Four years ago, when my Legion crest was so new the ink hadn't dried all the way, I would have cared. I would have sat in this combat sled and chewed the inside of my mouth until it bled. I see LS-95, so new he hasn't proven himself worth a nickname, doing it right now. He's sitting on the jump seat across from me, perspiration glistening under the red light, as the sled speeds toward some village on the dark side of who cares.

I lean across the divide that separates us and punch his slate-gray armor square on the shoulder. "Hey. KTF."

He nods hesitantly. It's obvious the kid's embarrassed that his nerves are showing. He puts on his helmet. The bucket hides his emotions from his comrades.

"KTF. Why do you leejes always say that?" The question comes from the sled's turret gunner. Regular Republic Army, black and tan fatigues and a one-size-fits-all woven synth-steel helmet, polarized goggles pulled up on the top. We call these types "basics." We made his Repub-Army butt take seat six the moment we entered the sled.

Twenties, LS-81 to Leej Command, took over on the twins. Combat sleds are quick and agile, and that doesn't allow for heavy firepower. Their only defense is a twin medium-heavy blaster turret manned just aft of the cockpit, capable of a 360-degree field of fire. If a gunner is skinny enough, the twins can be pulled back to shoot straight into the air, too.

All we see of Twenties are his legs slowly rotating as he moves the turret in deliberate, sweeping patterns. He's looking to open up on any native even thinking of springing an ambush.

This may surprise you, but we rolled out of Camp Forge without the heavy armor of our MBTs. Legionnaires aren't supposed to need that kind of support on a Joint-Force (JF), low-contact, diplomatic mission. Legionnaires are too good at what they do. Save the MBTs for the brass at CF.

Ooah.

Truth is, there is no safe op. A well-executed ambush always has a chance to cause some damage, even if we spot 'em early. Unless we KTF.

Unlike the Repub-Army gunner, Twenties won't lock up. Won't miss.

Maybe that's not fair to the basic sitting in seat six. He looks like he just transported from academy yesterday, but maybe he's a dead shot. He ain't a legionnaire, though. And for us, that's three strikes in itself. He's looking at me with those wide and innocent eyes. Eyes that haven't seen war except through a holoscreen or an FPS arcade sim. He's sincere in his question, so I answer him.

"You survive our trip to market, Basic, I'll let you know."

The sled fills with laughter, some of it clean and organic, guys with their buckets off. Just like a regular night at the barracks. Other laughs are filtered through the micro-comm speaker of the legionnaires already wearing their buckets. Those guys sound like a bunch of bots laughing at a joke about fluid changes.

Exo, LS-67, acts like he's got the chills, rubbing his arms. Helmetless, he makes his teeth chatter and pulls up his synthprene undersuit as high as it will go on his neck. "That's ice cold, Sarge. Straight Parminthian."

I shrug.

A buzz emits from the onboard comm speakers. Each sled has two drivers, with room for a field commander in the front section. The tail end fits six men and the turret gunner. Right now all eyes are fixed on the relay screen built into the wall separating us from the drivers. The red cabin lights dim to near non-existence as a gray-haired legionnaire flickers on screen from the cockpit. He's cradling his helmet in one arm, gently rubbing an old scar on his neck as though he'd just stepped out of a tightened noose.

LS-13, rank major. The CO of Victory Company. To us, he's Pappy. His holo transmission is going to the back of each combat sled in real time.

"Victory Company, this is Pappy. Listen up."

The major's voice is always strained and hoarse. Not from yelling. He brushes a hand across the scar, still pink and angry from a CQ scrap in some dusty shack two decades ago. Word is it still *hurts*, too. Enough that he cuts away the regular synthprene suit so it doesn't touch his neck. The major probably should have died back then, but Pappy don't die.

"We're still speeding through the plains and are about three clicks to the hills. Moona Village is what passes for a major town on Kublar. According to Republic intelligence, the village elders are supportive of Kublar's newly appointed Republican senator."

Kublar.

That's where we are. I'd almost forgotten. The past eight months have been nothing but a series of rotations between a planet in galaxy's edge and *Chiasm*, the capital-class destroyer we're jumping all across the edge in. Jump in system, drop shuttles to clean up whatever mess the locals have made for themselves and the Republic, jump out, repeat.

Pappy's hoarse briefing continues.

"Republican intel says that the Mid-Core Rebels are working hard to establish relations with the Kublarens. Trying to find an ally. No signs of MCR supplying the koobs with arms, but expect at a minimum small-arms fire and maybe some old-tech heavy battery emplacements.

"But I *do* mean old-tech. Savage Wars era. Central Command decided that speed and overwhelming blaster power would carry the day if the koobs get stupid, and Pappy agrees. Rep-Int says to expect an open-arms greeting, but we know better, don't we, boys? Be ready, and if things go south, KTF. Pappy out."

The display goes dark. I move to the control console and key in the forward holocam. The combat sleds are in convoy formation, carefully spaced to avoid catastrophe should a tac-bomb detonate beneath us. I rotate the cams. Moona Village is another thirty-minute drive, but we're already passing a few of the small dwellings in its orbit, scattered among the foothills of the mountain. Kublaren herders wearing tattered black and brown robes watch the convoy pass, their frog-like neck sacks expanding with each breath and flashing a sudden deep purple that contrasts with their dust-colored skin. Three-fingered hands clutch herding staffs, and every other koob has a decrepit hard-matter projectile rifle strapped to his shoulder.

That won't do much against legionnaire armor, but I don't expect it'll keep them from trying if they've got a mind for a fight.

Koobs love fighting. It's in their DNA. They allied themselves with the Republic in the Savage Wars, centuries ago, and were used to great effect throughout the conflict thanks to the tactical genius of men like General Rex.

Some koob kids are doing their peculiar run/hop alongside the combat sleds. I hear a request to "dust 'em" come from a leej up on the twins. Apparently I wasn't the only one who preferred a legionnaire take the place of the basic assigned to the twins.

"Negative. Do not engage."

The voice belongs to LS-33, a newly appointed captain, his commission straight from the House of Reason. These guys are the worst. They're not soldiers, just politicians seeking to climb the ladder. But they love giving orders. Wouldn't you know that Captain Devers is the OIC for Magnum and Doomsday (that's us) squads. At least he's riding in Magnum's CS today.

Small victories.

"Copy," the legionnaire answers.

Unwilling to pass on an opportunity to elaborate, Captain Devers adds, "Kublar is a type-VII planet identified as a potential R-1. This world will bring substantial revenue and stability into the Republic once they've fully embraced Republican ideals. Do not aggravate. It would be better if—"

Pappy breaks in. "Maintain L-comm discipline."

There's a pause, and all anyone can hear is the static hum over the L-comm.

"Copy."

The hurting ego in Devers's voice is palpable. I'll bet my last ration pack he records a whiny holo for Colonel La-Donna to be sent the moment long-range comms clear up.

"Pappy shut that point *down!*" Exo shouts, his voice jovial.

My legionnaires, none of them government appointees, all share the sentiment. It's a beautiful thing when a *real* leej officer shuts down a point, short for appointee. I should maintain respect for rank, but screw those guys. Surest way to die in the legionnaire corps is to be placed under the command of a point. It's no secret.

There's a rhythm to life at galaxy's edge. Long bouts of inactivity.

Boredom.

Routine.

And then, whether you want it or not, whether you're ready or not, things go sideways. But sideways is where legionnaires earn their pay.

The comm spikes with a shout. "Those koob kids got something!"

A thundering boom sounds.

Strong enough to cause the sled's repulsors to hop and send vibrations along the interior hull. The forward cam catches a ball of flame engulfing the command sled. Pappy's sled. I see the vic jump into the air, spiraling like a football, right before a storm of dust and rocks obscures the cam and the feed cuts out.

"Buckets!" I scream.

Those of us without helmets on quickly pull them snugly over our heads, watching as our interior displays boot up in .08 seconds, plugging us into the legionnaire battle network. It's a special net just for us. Rep-Mil has no access no matter how much the Fairness in Combat

Committee begs and complains. It's untraceable and an impenetrable fortress to any code slicer dumb enough to risk messing with it. The moment my helmet is online, I'm hearing chaos over the legionnaire and Repub-Army bat-net, with commands and counter commands coming fast and furious. Someone from the L-SOC attachment is issuing an override, requesting a command update. I'll leave that to one of the captains.

"Doomsday squad," I call through my helmet's mic. "Switch to local channel Fear-Beta-Nine. We need to drown out this chatter and focus."

Without hesitation, the four legionnaires sharing the back of the sled send hands to the sides of their buckets, keying their transponder frequencies. A legionnaire's helmet is the most expensive part of our kit. Each is custom built and costs about the same as a luxury sled, though that's mostly due to the requirement that they be produced by Repub contractors who have a forty percent profit margin built into their figures.

I'm in the wrong line of work.

Still, the filtration system, clear-vision visors with instant thermal or UV optic overlays, bone conduction headsets, exterior interface, tongue toggles, DSK AI, and voice enhancers aren't cheap.

Twenties screams from the turret. "One of those koob kids put a charge on the CS! Sket! Incoming fire!" I can see his legs while the turret moves in spasmodic motions as the twin repeating blaster barrels search for targets.

Dat-dat-dat-dat-dat-dat!

The twins open up as Twenties finds hostile targets. He's crouching and bouncing on his legs with every burst. "Get some! Get some! I see you, koob! I see you, *too!*"

Dat-dat-dat-dat-dat-dat!

The outside of the sled is alive with the spewing of pressurized, explosive rapid-fire bolts, red streaks of energy sizzling through the air.

A sound like heavy fists pounds across the sled's hull like a drumbeat. A momentary cry comes over my helmet's local channel and then Twenties goes limp, his body slowly snaking its way down from the turret like ice melting down a mountainside. My men, anxious to get in the fight and protect the wounded, pull him out. His chest and helmet have black scorch marks. So much for koobs only having slug throwers.

I open my mouth for LS-75, Doc Quiggly, to check Twenties's vitals, but Quigs is already removing the helmet while two other legionnaires hold the wounded's shoulders up. The leej is burnt up and gonna need some skinpacks, maybe some grafting, but the armor did its job.

"I'm going up top!" I call, climbing into the turret and making my way to the top. The Repub-Army kid in seat six is frozen in fear, his eyes fixed on the large blisters covering Twenties's face.

The scene outside is unreal. I've been in combat multiple times, but I've never seen anything like this. The air is thick with blaster fire and my bucket's ventilators are working overtime to keep the smoke and hot smell of ozone from overpowering me. Bodies from the command sled are strewn all over the place, and the sleds behind it, blocked in the road, are getting pelted with small-arms fire while their twin guns blaze at koobs. The aliens are firing from behind stone and mortar huts, rock walls, berms, you name it. An old-model tank, the type that still fires explosive projectiles, is laboriously rotating its main gun toward the convoy.

To prepare an ambush and not be zeroed in already is a sign of amateurism. Not that I'm complaining. Obvious mistakes aside, the place is still danger hot, and it's going to take some hard fighting to regain control of the situation.

I'm not worried, though. The *Chiasm* is still in orbit—I can see its massive bulk in the sky, pale like a moon in daylight—and a wing of tri-bombers will be down in short order. The guerrilla positions will be vaporized, and we'll check Pappy's sled for survivors, clear the wreckage, and continue on to Moona Village.

I don't know why, but I keep watching the *Chiasm*. There's thick blaster fire everywhere, and my focus should be on the koob threats surrounding us. But I just... stare at the destroyer. Almost transfixed. Call it a premonition.

I see a flash erupt in the center of the *Chiasm*. Moments later, I hear a sharp crack. I watch, frozen in place, at the turret, as the *Chiasm* splits in half and slowly sinks into the atmosphere, its sharp prow glowing red as it burns in reentry.

We're all going to die.

02

Knowing you're a dead man living impacts everyone differently. Legionnaires are always the last to lose heart. We don't stop fighting, ever. But I've worked on enough joint operations with Repub-Army basics and PNAs (planetary national armies) to see the varied reactions to lost causes.

Some men collapse into themselves like a rotten pumpkin. They see the reaper coming for the harvest and they're overwhelmed with existential dread, thoughts of loved ones, regrets, you name it. I've seen these guys literally curled up into balls, pulling on their hair with their blasters tossed to the side.

Others develop a "take as many with you as possible" mentality. Obviously, that's much better tactically than those made ineffectual in combat—fighting is preferable to whimpering on the ground. But these types are prone to risk. They'll charge heavily fortified positions head on with only a rifle and a few grenades, or hole themselves up trying to kill as many targets as possible until the inevitable, final boom comes for them. While a spontaneous charge can sometimes take the enemy by surprise and even turn the tide of battle—not to mention look great in holofilms—tactically speaking, it usually results in substantial casualties and defeat.

I said at the start that legionnaires don't lose heart and don't stop fighting. We survive. We constantly refresh our tactics so the optimal battle plan is always in action. And we do it well. With every shot, every motion, we optimize our results for battlefield victory.

So when I say we're all going to die, I don't necessarily mean right now.

The *Chiasm* is the only Republic warship in this system, and Kublar is so remote that it'll be a good month before another can arrive. That's assuming the Republic even *knows* about or notices the *Chiasm*'s destruction; add whatever time it might take for missed status cycles to get flagged in our government's bloated bureaucratic quagmire. Our convoy has eighty effective fighting men, including basics. Camp Forge has another two hundred, but they aren't getting here before morning. The koobs... well, this is their planet. They've got more than enough time and manpower—*koobpower*—to wipe us out.

And yeah... we're all dead.

Eventually.

But if the koobs don't suffer a minimum thirty-to-one loss for each legionnaire they dust, I'll die one pissed-off sergeant. Granted, we're not outnumbered thirty to one right now. It's maybe two to one. Maybe. But it's a long trip back to Camp Forge. We've got time to run up the score.

Attention! LS-55, Sergeant C.Chhun.

My helmet's AI has something to say.

The visor is alive with a HUD that indicates the location of my squad, green dots on a blue circular grid. Enemy combatants spotted by a legionnaire show up as red dots until they disappear as a confirmed kill. If we lose sight of a target long enough for the computer to no longer accurately predict its location, the dot turns yellow and stays fixed at its last confirmed location.

I'm seeing a corvette-load of red dots. Too many yellows for my taste, as well.

Assessing Threats.
Assessing Threats.

The message blinks in the upper left corner of my visor, superimposed over the optical scans of the ambush zone. Our buckets all run a software programmed by Republic scientists dedicated to keeping legionnaires the most fearsome warriors in the galaxy. It sounds great in theory, but it ends up being more of a distraction than a help. Still, the House of Reason loves it, and the contractors who make each bucket *love* the House of Reason. So we deal with it.

Primary Target: Model M6 Heavy Tank.
Manufacturer: Industrious Equipment.
Planet of Origin: Unknown.
Registration: Unknown.
Manufacturer's Recommended Crew: 5 humans/
near-humans.
Actual Crew: Unknown.
Display Technical Schematic? Y/N

That right there? That's the problem. My visor is full of garbage text when "Tank!" would have done just fine. I flick my tongue across a sensor inside my helmet to turn off the message display. I wish that would do the trick permanently, but all it does is prevent any more updates for fifteen minutes. No time to be upset about it. This is how it is, and there *is* a tank out there.

I look at the convoy behind me. The sleds in the rear are backing down the narrow, high-walled alley that winds through a farmer's village on the way to Moona. The koobs fighting nearest are all hiding behind walls or in buildings. They've learned that when a legionnaire sees a koob in the open, he doesn't miss. A few of them are sticking a rifle over the top of a wall and shooting blindly. But then I see a leej gunner on his sled's twins blow off a three-fingered hand, and that practice seems to stop as well.

The tank is on top of a ridge about a thousand yards away. That might be in range for the personal anti-armor missiles each squad carries, if it were a clean shot, but this tank is behind a wall of rock with thick branches from two spoonja trees further obscuring it. We'll have to get closer to disable it. Time for a little mountain climbing.

I drop down from the twins into a waiting group of leejes, all of them jumping for a chance to get in the fight. Twenties has come around, but massive blisters crowd his eyes, making him effectively blind. I send the basic up to take a turn on the guns and brief my guys. The kid hops right up without hesitation. If he's afraid, he's not showing it to the rest of us. He soon adds to the cacophony of noise.

I give an impromptu briefing. "Hostiles are concentrated south of the caravan. Most have been suppressed by the twins, but there's an old-model MBT on a ridge that's going to pick the sleds off one by one if we don't take it out. L-comm is still flooded with noise, too much talking from the basics out there. I want you to find Sergeant Powell and tell him we're taking that ridge. He should be in the sled immediately behind us. Ready to lower ramp?"

"Yes, sir."

"I'm going to inform the point about what we're doing. Form up with me when you've got Powell and his guys. Ooah?"

"Ooah!"

The men prime their N-4s and begin to take up formation at the rear of the sled, waiting for the order to disembark. I pull Quigs aside. "How's Twenties?"

"He'll live. Out of the fight, though."

"The hell I am," Twenties calls from his jump seat. He unstraps the vibroknife from his shin.

Quigs is on him instantly, holding his wrist tightly. "What're you doing, Twenties?"

"Just need to see. Gonna pop these blisters."

Quigs sighs. "That's... don't do that."

"I'd prefer if *you* did, Doc."

I break in. "Will he be able to see well enough to shoot if you bust open those blister sacs?"

"Possibly," Quigs answers. "Could be some permanent scarring, potential vision trouble down the road."

I nod. "Your call, Twenties."

"Do it."

I can't help but smile behind my helmet. What a beast. "Carve him up, Doc. Twenties, you're on overwatch."

Using a sterilized scalpel from his kit, Quigs slices open the blisters. Water spills out onto the deck, and Twenties grits his teeth in pain. Quigs stands back to examine his work. "Can you see?"

"It's blurry, but good enough to drop a koob if it puffs up its purple throat sac."

Twenties gets in line behind Exo and the rookie, Quigs on his heels.

I again pull the medic aside. "I want you to check on Pappy's sled. See if there's any chance..."

"Roger."

Quigs gets behind me, taking the final place in line usually reserved for the sled master. It's still on me to call for the ramps to open. Sleds have one main ramp that drops down and another that opens upward, so the back of a combat sled looks like a pair of jaws opening to spew out squads of sleek legionnaires in their gray combat armor.

I put my hand over the sled's ramp button. "Final check!"

Each squad member calls his number.

"LS-67! Go!"

"LS-95! Go!"

Twenties grunts out his call sign, still in pain. "LS-81! Go!"

"LS-55!" I shout. "Go! Go! Go!"

The ramp drops with a thud the moment I press the button. The cracking of slug throwers and sharp *kewps* of blasters fill our audio sensors. The loudest noises are canceled out to keep from drowning in ambient noise, which can be critical in battle. You never know when someone might be sneaking up behind you. Also, fun fact, loud noises can cause permanent hearing damage.

Polarized lenses automatically eliminate the glare of the outside sun, and I watch my guys fly outside like they've got rockets on their backs the moment they see open air. They're a bunch of cooped-up dogs making a break for it when the front gate opens.

We've practiced sim disembarkations hundreds of times and have rolled out from live combat sleds onto the field almost as often. By the time a legionnaire undertakes his first CS storming, the motions are all muscle memory. From my vantage point at the end of the line, it's a thing of beauty. Exo and the rookie move in quick step, each peeling off at the base of the ramp and covering a side of the sled. Exo takes a knee on the soft side, scanning our rear and flanks for any yellow dots that our HUD might have missed. Rook takes a knee on the hot side, his extremely heavy, rapid-fire automatic blaster hoisted higher than human arms could manage thanks to powerful servos built into his armored sleeves. Never agree to arm-wrestle a SAB user unless he's only wearing his synthprene.

Twenties is out next, moving quickly and burying his pain somewhere deep inside. He takes his place behind Exo and places his hand on his shoulder. At this point Exo will identify targets that Twenties will help engage. Exo gives the all-clear and moves to join the rookie, leaving Twenties to cover the cold zone.

As man four, I move to whichever side has an odd number. I put my hand on Twenties's shoulder. It all happens in seconds.

"What looks good, Twenties?" I ask, though I have a decent idea where he'll want to go.

Twenties points two fingers at a stone building with a flat roof not far from our sled. "Right there. Help me clear it, Sarge?"

This is where being down a man hurts. Time is of the essence, and we can't take that ridge until I've called in to Captain Devers. But leaving Twenties to set up and secure his long rifle in overwatch alone is unacceptable. So we'll have to do it quick.

KTF.

"Let's go," I order, before leading the way.

There's a three-foot-high stone wall on the side of the road. I hop over it in stride, taken aback by the extra couple of feet I fall before landing in some sort of garden. I scan the surroundings through the open sights of my N-4 while Twenties makes his way over somewhat more gingerly.

Our target building is a squat, square house constructed almost entirely out of the abundant rocks that cover Kublar. The doors are solid enough, but they don't have anything on modern automated pneumatic portals. They're built from a dense, perennially green wood found near water supplies. The windows are just holes in the rock facade. Fancy koobs try to arch them; most just go with another square. A few have shutters, but that's hit or miss. The one we're moving toward is the simple type.

Twenties and I move on either side of the door in breaching position. I reach down and try the handle.

It's barricaded. No surprise.

With his helmet destroyed, Twenties pulled out his conduction set prior to disembarking. He whispers into his external mic, hoping only the two of us can hear each other. With buckets, we can just mute external speakers, but... "I've got an entry charger, Sarge." He reaches into a thigh pouch and removes the small, sticky explosive.

"Save it. We'll go through the windows after clearing." I produce a fragger from my chest bandoleer. "There's a window on the other side—you go in that way. We'll clear corners and get on the roof."

"Probably koobs in there."

"Probably should've warned us about the ambush."

That ends the discussion.

I move to the edge of the window, careful not to expose myself. Bone conductors in my helmet amplify the sound of someone shifting around inside. I hesitate for a second, wondering if maybe another legionnaire had eyes on this hut first. Then I hear the telltale wheeze-croak of a koob air sac inflating.

I toss in the grenade, shouting "Frag out!" into my L-comm. I roll back and brace myself against the exterior stone wall of the building. My armor is able to absorb all the kinetic energy of a fragger, but the little monster shoots out so many minuscule projectiles that some of them will find their way to the seams and shred through my synthprene undersuit.

The grenade explodes, and a cloud of black smoke shoots from the windows and beneath the door. The boom is loud enough that I can feel it in my chest, but my bucket's audio dampers reduce the volume to little more than a muffled *whoomp-whoomp*. The first *whoomp* is the fragger detonating an outer shell that sprays outward as two-millimeter-thick shrapnel. The second *whoomp* is the four compact balls that shoot upward and provide a second detonation, sending even more shrapnel at every angle. This secondary explosion lacerates anything organic to such a degree that severing or puncturing a major artery is all but certain.

Smoke is still drifting out of the window as Twenties and I climb into the hut. My bucket filters away the acrid odor while my visor switches on its IR filters, allowing me to better see through the haze. No such luck for Twenties, who coughs from the smoke.

Three koobs are on the floor. Two are dead, and one is writhing in pain, its air sac ruptured. I step over the body of the survivor, its phosphorescent yellow blood pooling on the wooden floor. I'm content to let the koob bleed out.

I take hold of the single-rung ladder that leads to the roof. Halfway up, I hear Twenties's blaster discharge a single shot.

Whatever helps him sleep at night.

Topside, the battle is raging on. The koobs nearest the sleds are still hiding behind whatever cover they can find, but the ones on the ridge are firing down at us defiantly. The tank's main cannon is still traversing, seeking out a sled near the rear of the column. The gunner probably was overwhelmed by such a target-rich environment and spent all this time second-guessing himself until he saw that sleds were hitting reverse and getting away from the jam.

Twenties begins to unpack his sniper kit with practiced efficiency. He stacks a pile of lumber against the parapet and takes up position, his N-18 long-barreled rifle resting on its bipod on the roof's edge.

Exo and Rook are crouching between our sled and a rock wall with men from Hammerfall and Specter squads. I signal to LS-52, Sergeant Powell, to send up relief to watch Twenties's back. He nods and sends a leej running. Then I call for Captain Devers over L-comm.

"LS-55 with priority message for LS-35 on channel Fear Beta Twelve. Over."

Static hums and the point's voice comes up. "Uh, this is Captain Devers. Go ahead, Sergeant."

The fool is hailing me over the L-comm for all to hear. I wait for some cross-talk between drivers coordinating their retreat to subside before saying, "Captain Devers, sir, requesting message on channel Fear Beta Twelve, over."

"Just spit it out, Sergeant."

I mute my comm and give a brief, profanity-laced discourse on the value of House appointees. "Sir, requesting permission to lead joint assault with Hammerfall and Specter Squads. Requesting additional support from Gold Squad."

"Negative, Sergeant. Gold Squad is waiting this thing out in here with me. The sleds are... we should be clear of the road soon. Over."

"Sir, with all due respect," I'm careful here, aware that I'm broadcasting on L-comm for all to hear, "that tank isn't going to let every sled squirt out. We need to take it down. Requesting permission to go without Gold Squad."

"Sergeant, it's fine. We should have Camp Forge on the comm soon. There's some residual interference, but then I'll request an artillery cannon barrage. I'm ordering all units to return to their CS and await… wait for their turn to get off the road, over."

I open my mouth to reply when the sensational *krak-bdew* of the N-18 ruptures the air around me, followed by the hiss of super-heated gases escaping the rifle's barrel. My eyes go to the ridge, and I see a koob tumbling down like a rag doll. The HUD on my visor shows one less red dot.

Twenties found his mark.

And from the looks of it, the old MBT has settled in on one of its own. My visor traces the potential trajectory. The gunner is looking to blast one of the sleds at the end of the column, still locked in place. I call out the danger on L-comm. "Silver 6, Silver 6, this is LS-55 on overwatch. Do you copy?"

Whoever is in that sled is going to be lit up if they don't disembark right now.

"What is it now, Sergeant?"

Of course it's Captain Devers's sled. If there weren't basics and leejes in there with him, I might well keep my mouth closed. "Silver 6, Silver 6, confirmed hostile MBT zeroed on your location. Disembark! Disembark!"

"Belay that order," Devers says with all the postured regality of an admiral of the Core. "These koobs don't have munitions for that thing or they would have fired by—"

The MBT's turret spews out fire. A shell blasts into the rock wall, saving the sled from a direct hit. The tank begins to compensate, raising its cannon.

"All units, disembark! Disembark!" The order is called in by Lieutenant Ford, LS-33. His men call him Wraith due to his penchant for appearing undetected, commenting on conversations you didn't know he was there to listen in on. Wraith oversees Hammerfall and Specter Squads, and I can see the red bar painted on his shoulder plates as he stands with Exo and Rook at the marshaling point.

Doors drop, and legionnaires begin to spill out of the immobile sleds. But something is delaying Silver 6. Captain Devers isn't opening the door. The tank makes a final adjustment. Having overcompensated, it ratchets back down. Whoever's sitting behind the gun isn't comfortable, thankfully.

The cannon belches a booming fire. I suck in a breath as Silver 6's drop door flings down. A single leej stumbles out seconds before a high-explosive shell pierces the sled's armor.

An eruption of flames issues from every conceivable opening in the sled. It comes out of the port leading up to the twins like a funnel. It blows through the front windshield and billows out the open ramp. A couple more leejes stumble out, both of them engulfed in flames.

I can hear them screaming until their bucket comms short out from the heat.

Legionnaire armor will save you from a lot of things, but burning alive ain't one of 'em. Other than the lone survivor, the entirety of Gold Squad is wiped out.

Oba, what a way to go.

The silvene lining, if there is one, is that the senior leej, in this case Captain Devers, is always at the back of the line. The last one off the sled. Looks like we'll take that ridge after all.

03

When I was a kid there was nothing I loved more than watching the Galactic Fighting Championships. I knew the name of every fighter in every species index and weight class. For a while, I thought I'd *be* a GFC champion. I would "train" by punching and kicking our domestic bot, D2O (Ditto) while it attempted to clean. I still have a holopic somewhere of six-year-old me holding Ditto in a rear naked choke, its shining gilded arms waving helplessly. Good times from our family apartment on Tiamu City.

Yeah, I'm a Teema boy. Born and raised.

Anyhow, when Republic aptitude testing consigned me to the Legionnaire Corps, my GFC dreams tapped out. But I still love combat sports. We even have something we call "LFC"—Legionnaire Fighting Championships—on board the *Chiasm*.

Did, anyhow.

Of all the fighting formats, my all-time favorite is tag team. You've got four equally classed fighters, two on each team. One man per team starts the fight and can tag in their partner at any time, provided they can reach them. Those fights have a strategy that you don't see in one-on-one bouts. There's a thing called the hot tag that always causes the ampistadiums to erupt. A fighter will get isolated, and the opposite team just works 'em over while his partner desperately stretches out a gloved hand to tag himself in. Usually these guys don't have the stamina to keep going, and tap or get knocked out. But sometimes they hold on and make it across the octagon to tag in the fresh fighter.

Right now I feel like the partner waiting to be tagged in. I'm watching the leej assigned to watch Twenties's back run up to the house we've occupied. The moment that leej, a kid from Magnum Squad, reports for duty, I'm gone.

He makes his way in through a window. Time to go. Stairs take too long, and every second counts. I hop over the side and drop fifteen feet or so into what passes for a koob front yard.

It's that kind of stuff that'll force me to get cybernetic knees before I'm thirty. But hey, what old soldier *isn't* a cyborg?

I sprint straight to the marshaling point and slam into the rock wall as a rough and ready group of legionnaires awaits the order to move out. An order that should come from the senior officer on site, even though the plan was orchestrated by me.

"LS-55 reporting, ready to execute battle plan," I say, slightly winded, to Lieutenant Ford—Wraith.

The lieutenant looks at me a moment. "Still no comm connection to Camp Forge, so let's not pretend we've got air or artillery. It's all on us. Initial plan was yours, Sergeant Chhun. Give the word and we move."

I wish every officer was more like Wraith.

"Roger," I say, struggling to control my breathing so the other leejes don't get the feeling I'm panting in their audio receptors like Uncle Creepy. "We push straight up and don't stop until we reach the base of that ridge. Magnum takes left, Hammerfall right, and Doomsday up the gut. We'll climb up on either side in a pincer maneuver and hammer them inward."

Twenty-three helmets nod in understanding. A comment comes on our mission channel. "We move too fast and the koobs'll be firing at our backs."

Exo chimes in. "We don't move fast enough and we're going to lose the last five sleds bottled up here."

As if in confirmation, the tank booms again, missing its target high. The tank's gunner has finally managed to make up his mind. He's no doubt realized by now that the fast-moving sleds in open ground are too tough to hit, and can't penetrate his armor with their twins. So he's ignoring the sleds that were able to back out and is focusing on picking off the immobile vics one by one. The way they're all lined up… not good.

I offer the assault team clarification. "The tip of the spear—I need a sprinter to volunteer—will draw them out, eliminating targets of opportunity as they appear on the HUD. It's up to the rest of us to drop those koobs before they have a chance to send a slug or a blaster charge into our runner's back. Most of us will be able to keep moving, but I want Hyena Squad to stick around and verify clear all buildings and trenches while the main force continues to the ridge."

Wraith stands and checks his N-4. "That's settled, then. I get my run in today after all. See you up top."

Before I have the chance to object to Lieutenant Ford assuming the most dangerous position in the assault, he's up and over the wall without so much as an "Ooah!"

The remaining legionnaires are stunned for perhaps a half second, but quickly follow, not wanting to leave him isolated.

Wraith runs like he's alone on a yellow sand beach somewhere in a subtropic system, the only sentient being for miles. His form is perfect and upright, and he's moving at a pace that seems impossible to maintain all the way to the ridge. The idea was to move quickly but deliberately, making sure not to get too far behind enemy lines that we could be encircled. But Wraith has pretty much overrun the koob position singlehandedly.

They just don't know it yet.

Between us and the ridge lies a small crop of stone huts and three-foot-high rock walls. Beyond all that is an open plain leading to the ridge, peppered throughout with craggy boulders.

The tank fires again and hits its target, incinerating an empty CS.

Impossible as it seems, Wraith is putting distance between himself and the rest of the legionnaires. He's easily fifty yards in front of us now, approaching a low stone wall with yellow dots on the other side, signifying that koobs were spotted in that location before legionnaire suppressive fire made them one with the dirt. He hurdles the wall without breaking stride.

I can see a trio of koob heads pop up in astonishment and turn to watch Wraith sprinting past them and toward the stone buildings.

"Dust 'em!" I scream.

So many legionnaires score head shots on these koobs that there isn't much left of them except shredded air sacs and drooping shoulders. They didn't even get close to bringing their slug throwers—and at least one PK-9A blaster rifle—to their shoulders.

Legionnaires are expert marksmen.

The run for the ridge continues at breakneck speed. I hear a loud *krak-bdew* a millisecond after seeing a blaster bolt strike a koob on a distant rooftop. Those blisters don't seem to be bothering Twenties too much.

Two koobs spring from around the corners of adjacent huts, looking to light up Wraith in convergent fields of fire. Effortlessly, Lieutenant Ford double-taps his N-4 and hits each koob center mass, dropping them. He continues unabated in his loping stride, clears the final field wall, and streaks across the plain toward the ridge.

Men from Hyena fan out and make sure every last koob is eliminated while the rest of us do our best to keep up after Wraith. I can hear the booms of fraggers and blaster fire from the Hyena leejes behind me. Twenties is busy from his spot, too. Every single shot he takes removes a dot from my HUD.

I reach the field. Wraith has stretched his lead to over sixty yards.

"South wall is secure!" comes the call over the mission channel.

Boom.

That fast.

Most beings in the galaxy aren't going to stand up well against legionnaires in an open fight, even a species as warlike as the koobs.

Running in the craggy field is difficult. Snaking beneath the wind-whipped sea of ankle-high grass is some kind of an old riverbed. It must have zigzagged quite a bit, because I can distinctly feel my boots curve around the smooth river rocks, like they can't quite get a firm footing and are always slipping just a little bit. It's definitely slowing me down, and by the number of green dots on my HUD, it's slowing down the rest of the force, too.

Except for Wraith. He's going to storm the ridge by himself if this keeps up.

Just in case I couldn't *tell* that I was a step slow, my visor issues a stream of text, the temporary block I'd placed earlier now expired.

LS-55, Sergeant C.Chhun.
Advisory: Suboptimal speed.
Legionnaires of DOOMSDAY squad are moving 7.82% slower than their last standardized PT stress run.
Log for infraction review? Y/N

"Combat override DS8-RV6!" I shout into my mic. Thankfully, these sorts of messages don't pop up on every leej's visor, otherwise our armorer would need a kip shuttle full of assistants to fix all the shots we'd absorb while barking cancellation codes. No, Repub-Tek just installed the software in the buckets of rank sergeant and above. The joys of being a squad leader.

> Combat override acknowledged. A record will remain on file for 15 days. This log to be transmitted to your OIC, Captain S. Devers.

Joke's on you, technological embodiment of meddling bureaucratic overreach. Point is dead.

I expected we would lose at least two combat sleds before we reached the ridge. As I get within four hundred yards, I realize that the tank hasn't fired a shot since it scored a hit on the empty sled just before the assault. Maybe Devers wasn't far off and the koobs used all the shells they had access to.

Or maybe…

I flick open the Doomsday comm with my tongue. "Twenties," I say between panting breaths, "tell me about that tank."

"On it, Sarge."

There's a pause as Twenties looks through his scope at the archaic MBT, shrouded behind rock and branch. "Yeah, it ain't interested in the sleds no more. Be advised, trajectory forecasts show that the main gun is looking to fire on advancing legionnaires."

"Roger."

I switch back to the assault comm channel. "That koob tank is looking to send some heat our way! Don't group up!"

The green dots on my HUD spread out. Still, I see a concentration of about three legionnaires, all with the laughing skull of Hyena Squad painted on the sides of their buckets. I turn around for visual and see they're bottlenecked by a series of boulders. Evidently the koob tank gunner sees the same thing. The tank rocks backward from the massive blast of its cannon, and the ground around the Hyena Squad trio explodes. It looks like a portal just opened up from the hells of the Arcturus Maelstrom. A grim rainfall of dirt, rocks, and pieces of legionnaire falls back to the ground.

The tactical L-comm floods with shouts.

"Stay spread!"

"Get some pressure on that ridge!"

"Who has mortar bots?"

"Mortar bots were on that last sled that blew."

"Oba!"

The tank is looking for targets in the field of legionnaires, but there aren't any groupings of leejes as sweet as that first one. As I move closer, I can see that the tank is equipped with a coaxial MG—slug thrower of course—but they must not have the needed caliber of ammunition. The gunner is trying to snipe us with high-explosive incendiary shells.

The main gun booms again, and I can feel the force of the air as the shell blisters above me, exploding much too close behind me. I feel the ground shake. The heat from the torrid blast penetrates my armor's cooling system. I feel like a skillet left out over a fire.

That was too close.

"This is Specter-1, I've reached the base of the ridge." Wraith doesn't even sound tired.

Twenties's voice comes up on the L-comm. "Copy, I have eyes on you, Lieutenant Ford. Looks like the koobs know you're down there, too. They're looking for an angle to engage."

"Copy."

The koobs don't seem to be able to find a good line of fire on Wraith. But they're right out in the open, croaking orders at each other, looking for that magic view that will kill them a legionnaire. These muck buckers have been pinned down for most of the assault by our rear line and sleds, but once our assault force got close to the ridge, the suppressive fire slowed for fear of leej-on-leej casualties.

Unable to get a clean shot at Wraith, the koobs unleash a hellish volley of PK-9A blaster fire and slug-throwing machine guns on those of us still advancing. Red blaster bolts sizzle overhead, and bullets fly thickly. I've gotten used to the sensation of a nearby blaster bolt—the air sort of sizzles as the burning shot scorches by you. But having slugs flying around you is a totally different experience. The air seems to snap and crack each time a bullet whizzes past. More than the blaster bolts, this gets my adrenals fired up, and I run even faster to join Wraith at the base of the ridge.

"Be advised," Twenties says calmly from his position in overwatch. "I see a pair of koobs climbing a tree fifteen degrees left of Specter-1."

Krak-bdew!

Twenties fires his N-18. "One koob eliminated, Specter-1, but I can't get a shot on the other."

"Copy," Wraith answers. "I'll see if I can spot him."

Wraith rolls out away from the ridge's sheer base and drops to a knee. His N-4 points upward in a fluid motion, graceful like a ballet dancer at Uynora Hall. He fires two blaster bolts into a part of the tree thick with green, triangular leaves, and spins back against the cliff. Koob counterfire kicks up the dirt where he stood only moments before. A koob corpse falls out of the tree all the way to the bottom of the ridge.

Wraith puts another round in it. Just to be sure, I suppose.

I'm the third legionnaire to reach the base of the ridge. We found out later that the koobs call it Kr'kik Ridge in their language. I had no way of knowing that this was the beginning of an onslaught endured by Victory Company of the 131st Legionnaires. No way of knowing that the cost we would pay in blood and lives would make us famous throughout the galaxy.

04

Most of the assault team has reached Kr'kik Ridge and spread out around its base. But the koobs above us are keeping up a steady stream of suppressing fire. We're pinned with our backs against the sheer rock wall.

This poses a number of difficulties.

First, our presence at the foot of the ridge prevents the legionnaires back at the line from firing on the koobs. The only exception so far has been Twenties and another sniper who set up inside a cleared stone hut, firing from a window. Most of the clean shots have already been taken. This ridge was prepared ahead of time for the ambush and for a defense. The koobs stacked rocks and laid trees over their blaster nests. Twenties and the other sniper are all scoped up with no one to shoot.

And we're pinned down. If the koobs were to descend the ridge and flank us, we'd be in a tight spot. I'm talking total team kill levels of tight. We can't just sit here.

And let's not forget about the tank. Unable to stop our advance, it is once again focused on the trapped repulsor sleds. Another goes up into flames as we watch impotently from our place at the bottom of the ridge. We need to break out and shut that MBT down, or there won't be enough operable sleds to return us to Camp Forge. That would mean hunkering down with limited supplies and no air support in hostile country while the remaining sleds speed off to send the relief message. I've stopped counting on getting any sort of reliable transmission to CF.

Another day at the office.

The men are doing their best to return fire and keep the koobs at bay, but stepping out and leaving the safety of the ridge isn't exactly safe at the moment, so we keep our butts glued to the cliffside.

"Sergeant Chhun, let's get these men moving." The voice is calm but authoritative.

"Yes, sir, Lieutenant Ford." I pull an ear-popper from my grenade belt. These detonate with a blinding flash of light and a truly deafening boom. The hearing loss is often permanent, and the flash can render some species blind or dazzled for up to five standard minutes. I don't know how koobs will react to it, but their eyes are pretty large. I'm sure it'll hurt.

Wraith looks at the grenade and then at me. "That's a hell of a throw you're planning, Sergeant."

"I don't have that kind of an arm, sir." I switch on my comm. "Doomsday-4, this is Doomsday-1. Where are you, Rook?"

The rookie's voice comes back. "Western edge of the ridge, sir. I've deployed my SAB and I'm laying down suppressive fire."

"Well, I need you back here at center mass."

"Yes, sir."

Rook weaves his way through entrenched legionnaires, ducking his head instinctively as bullets chew up the ground. Each time he has to move around a dug-in leej, the hostile fire intensifies. They're salivating up there at the merest glimpse of gray armor. Like sailors too long away from port.

"Sergeant?" Rook reaches my position and rests his SAB against the rock.

"Here," I say, placing the grenade in his hand. "I want your servo-enhanced arms to chuck this thing up the side of this ridge and into the koob position."

"Ear-popper?" Rook looks to the heavens. "That's about fifty meters, straight up."

"You think you can do it?"

Rook pauses, looking at the top of the ridge. At the sky. "Never tried, but I think so, yeah."

"Here." Wraith digs out his own ear-popper. "Throw this one in right after that. It'll be a climb, and I want to make sure the koobs are still disoriented when we get up top."

Rook takes hold of the grenade in his other hand.

The lieutenant points to the legionnaires spread out behind me. "Sergeant, I want you to go to the west side of the ridge with them. I'll take the remaining force up the opposite way. Is there a heavy with you?"

I turn and spot a leej from Hyena Squad with an ae-ro-precision missile launcher strapped to his back. "Yes, sir."

"Good. I saw Exo from your squad make it to the ridge; he's positioned to move up with me. As long as one of us gets a heavy to the top of that ridge, we can destroy the tank."

I nod.

"Get moving the moment the ear-popper goes off." Wraith begins to move toward his assault position, hugging the rocky side of the ridge. He stops to clap Rook on the shoulder. "Oh, and Legionnaire?"

"Yes, sir?"

"Don't let that thing drop back down on top of us."

"Yes, sir."

I swap out a charge pack on my N-4 and give orders that the rest of my team do the same. "Freshen your rifles up, boys!"

A flurry of *clacks* marks the legionnaires' assent.

I look at Rook, visor to visor. "Okay, Rook. Let's let those koobs know we're coming up for dinner."

Rook pulls back his arm and hurls the first grenade in the air. It goes up like it was launched from a mortar bot. For a moment, it looks like it doesn't have the proper angle and is liable to tumble back down on our heads. My visor's display calculates the trajectory a moment before the grenade reaches the peak of its ascent. It'll land just inside the koob position.

"Now the second!" I call out as the first succumbs to gravity and begins its descent.

Rook tosses the next grenade a little farther in.

BRAP! ... BRAP!

The ear-poppers erupt within a few seconds of each other. The noise is so substantial that I can hear a whine inside my bucket's transceiver as it dampens the decibels. The base of the ridge shields us from the flash, but the extreme brightness has enough power that even the ambient light blast we get causes our visors to darken.

All koob gunfire has ceased.

"Go! Go! Get up that ridge!" I scream.

The legionnaires with me have already started moving. We fly around the side of the rocky formation, six men in front of me and Rook, plus our heavy on my tail. An uprooted tree has fallen across the path. Legionnaires go over, around, and under it, then begin the desperate climb up the rock. Everything hinges on time right now, and these men know it.

As I reach the log, something in its root system catches my eye. Several of the roots look cleanly severed, like they were cut with vibro-axes. The tree's top end rests on a ledge.

The bulk of my team have sprinted ahead and are already climbing. I make a split second decision and throw out my arm, stopping Rook and the leej with the missile. "Hold on."

The two stop. "What is it, Sergeant? UED? Mine?"

"No. This tree. I think it leads somewhere. Somebody cut the root system so it would fall in a specific direction. See how it rests on top of that ledge?"

"The three of us check it out?" Rook asks.

I hop on the log and hurry on up it. "The rest of the group will reach the top eventually, but if this path is set up as a means of flanking, we need to block it and prevent our guys from becoming targets while they're in mid-climb. Even koobs'll be able to hit a legionnaire clinging to rocks."

We move up the log and step off onto a narrow trail, just wide enough for a standard human or near-human.

It's sheer, though—a big drop straight down. Turning around, I can see the rest of my assault team still climbing, about a hundred yards away. If the koobs came this way, they *would* dust every one of us, no matter how bad a shot they were.

The trail leads up, but the incline isn't steep. We aren't following long before we're easily twice as high as the climbing legionnaires. A switchback puts the rest of our team out of view, but I can tell that this thing goes all the way to the top. Probably into the midst of the koobs' fighting positions. About two hundred standard seconds have passed, and I still haven't heard any koob gunfire. The double shot of ear-poppers must've done a number on 'em. Still, as the trail reaches its apex, I find myself wishing I had another one with me.

Natural gray stone gives way to the tan square slabs used to build the koob walls and huts below. We're now flanked by a stone wall one either side. The path is leading us into something made by koob hands. It's like we're climbing out of a cellar and into the open light. I can see the swaying of leaves above me. We're going to come up right in the middle of Koobville.

"This is it," I say after double-checking that my external comms are muted. "Go in hard and KTF."

We burst through the trailhead. I'm acutely aware of the fact that we've made a time to the top that climbers won't match. It's just us and the koobs, and Oba, there are a sket-ton of koobs up here. Most are still shaking off the effects of the ear-poppers. I can see trails of phosphorescent blood trickling from the ear holes on the tops of their craniums and the slitted nostrils above their mouths.

One of them seems to have come around enough to realize that we're in his midst. We stare at each other for a split second, then the koob lets out a bellowing croak from his air sac and jerks up his PK-9A blaster rifle.

"Dust 'em!" I hear Rook shout. My trigger finger has squeezed out two blaster bolts by the end of the second syllable, dropping the koob in a heap.

We're standing in the midst of probably one hundred and fifty koobs. There's nothing to do but open up on them. If the warning croak of the koob I shot didn't alert the others to our presence, assuming they can even hear, the deluge of blaster fire will do the trick. I discharge my N-4, and in this target-rich environment, I go through two charge packs in less than a minute. Rook's SAB does the real grunt work, sending an unrelenting torrent of blaster fire into the massed guerrillas. Powered by a specialized pack carried on his shoulders, Rook can keep this up for a long, long time.

The leej from Hyena puts his aero-precision missile on his shoulder and flips open the targeting reticule. The clear screen locks in on the koob tank and gives a beep, indicating that the intelligent rocket inside will find its way to that tank no matter what direction the operator fires, unless it's directly into an obstacle. Of course, with the tank only twenty yards away, the leej would have to sneeze inside his helmet to miss.

I won't clint you. At this point I thought the three of us were going to take the entire ridge on our own. In disarray from the ear-poppers and the blaster fire thrown against them, the koobs are breaking into a full retreat in the opposite direction. They must've thought an entire RRE—rapid relief element—had arrived.

But there are always a few who stick it out and fight. Like I said before, creatures all act differently when they realize they're dead beings walking. A few koobs just stand there and discharge their weapons. I take at least three hits from the slug throwers. My armor absorbs the impact, but it still hurts like Stage's Blazes. If you're trying to get a sense for what it feels like to be hit by an old-fashioned hard-mass projectile while in full legionnaire kit, imagine being struck by a seamball from a big league thrower. Repeatedly.

Any leej'll tell you: Just because you wear armor, doesn't mean you don't get hurt.

The heavy weapons specialist from Hyena, Kravetz, isn't as lucky. A bullet strikes the armor protecting his inner calf and ricochets straight up, finding a gap between his protective pieces. He drops like a rock and I just know he's gone. The sheer amount of blood pumping out of gaps and down his armor, staining it red, makes it obvious. His femoral artery was severed by the bullet. Out of the fight, Kravetz is not much longer for this life.

There's a proverb that gets repeated around all branches of the Republic military machine. "Expect the worst and you won't be surprised." It dates back to the Savage Wars. Probably longer than that. The reason this little adage has withstood the entropies of time is because of how true it repeatedly proves itself to be. I'm disappointed but not surprised when we lose the one member of our three-man advance team who can pop open that tank. And I'm not surprised when said tank swivels its turret to point directly at Rook and me.

"Get down!"

We drop to our stomachs just as the tank fires a shell that would have cut us in half if we were still standing. Eager to turn us to mist, the gunner must've made the mistake at aiming at us instead of the ground beneath us.

I'm not complaining.

The blast impacts the rock wall behind us, and the explosion hurls us several feet forward. We land with a crashing thud, tangled up with one another. Absent, thankfully, is the incendiary fireball that has taken the lives of too many legionnaires already. The koobs must've had a limited number of high-explosive incendiary shells. Rook and I benefit from a standard shell without the extra burn.

My diaphragm spasms. The wind was knocked completely out of me. There's a persistent ringing in my ears that renders all other noise muffled or mute. I know weapons are being fired, but their sound barely registers. Someone is speaking to me over the L-comm, but it only sounds like murmuring. I have no idea how Rook is doing, but my HUD shows his designation as green. Kravetz has slipped into black.

And then the display itself flickers. There's an electronic pop, and my bucket's fan stops working. The smell of hot conductors, smoke, and blaster fire hits me. It's a struggle to push myself up on hands and knees. I can see my N-4 lying on the ground a few feet in front of me. I crawl toward my rifle, vaguely aware of the bullets kicking up dirt around me. The koobs must've rallied when the tank fired.

Everything is in slow motion.

A bullet strikes my N-4, causing it to do a half spin. All I can think is, "I hope my rifle still works."

I check on the tank and see that its 120mm barrel is pointing down at my position. Seems like a waste of ammunition, but then again, legionnaires are hard to kill.

There's a sudden flash of light, and my visor goes black.

05

In the seconds before death, all I had to say was an uninterested, "Huh."

My life didn't flash before my eyes. I didn't suddenly recall my father's laugh or some forgotten face from primary school. No first kiss, first drink, first... anything. Maybe that stuff only happens in the moments you're *actually* about to die. But how could your brain tell the difference?

When the explosion came from the tank, I certainly *thought* I was going to die. Did my mind somehow know better?

Chalk it up to another mystery of the galaxy.

My HUD flickered, then went offline altogether. As the polarized lenses of my bucket cleared, I had the distinct feeling that I was still in one piece. I saw the tank, still pointing its smoothbore cannon at me. But it wasn't a threat. Flames and thick, black smoke billowed out of every vent and opening. I could see the heavy metal hatch lying next to a dead koob about thirty meters away.

Turns out, the blast didn't come from the tank.

The blast *was* the tank.

Wraith's team had found a similar trail on their side of the ridge, and every one of Wraith's leejes had taken it. They'd blasted past a few disoriented koobs and poured out in full force on the top of Kr'kik Ridge. If Wraith's legionnaires were surprised to see a wave of frantic koobs running away from us and straight toward them, they didn't show it. With expected professionalism and calmness, they opened up on them. This second barrage of blaster fire sent the guerrillas even further into disarray.

While the koobs scrambled for a safe place to run and hide, Exo armed his aero-precision missile. He thumbed the switch next to the trigger guard to manual fire. I don't know if he saw the tank aiming at Rook and me, or if he just didn't want to wait the extra few seconds it would take for the missile to lock on. But the decision to go manual saved two lives.

I was out of it at the time, but the missile would have flown through the air at four hundred meters per second. An aero-precision missile makes a sound like a repulsor speeder whooshing past you in top drive at the Hendahl Raceways. It comes and goes so quickly that all you really see is the white vapor trail and the burning wreckage of its target.

And, man, did that tank burn. The missile shot through the MBT's impervisteel armor and detonated inside. Secondary explosions in the tank's magazine pretty much blew its treads off (I said it was an old tank) and just about severed the deck from the rest of the machine.

At that point even the staunchest koob fighters had their flight instinct take hold. They threw down their weapons and croaked frantic cries of retreat as they dispersed, all of them running in search of at least one place on Kr'kik Ridge free of legionnaire blaster fire.

They wouldn't find it.

Wraith's legionnaires cut through the koobs with cold precision. Double-tap. Kill. On to the next target. That's how we're trained.

Overwhelmed with battlefield terror, several koobs, their purple air sacs expanding and contracting as rapid as a heartbeat, scrambled to the edge of the ridge and jumped eighty feet down. A last, desperate hope that gravity would be more merciful than the legionnaires. For the most part, it wasn't. The ones who broke their legs, hips, shoulders, and ankles, but otherwise survived, we killed with the koobs' own slug throwers. Best to save our blaster charge packs. But that was later. After the fight on top of the ridge. After the descent.

Most of the fleeing koobs, perhaps twenty survivors, made their way to the back of the ridge. Their timing and placement could not have been worse. The rest of my detachment of legionnaires had climbed to the summit just as the koobs began to move in their direction. The aliens' flanks were exposed, and our nimble company of leej billy goats wasted no time in opening up on them. With legionnaire fire coming from their side, courtesy of my element, and their rear by Wraith's, the koobs were completely dusted.

"You all right, Sarge?"

I look to the sound of the voice and see Exo holding out his hand. I take it, and he hoists me to my feet. I don't have my bearings well enough yet to stand on my own. My knees are wobbly. "Yeah, I'm good."

We're both yelling. Maybe the boom got through Exo's noise dampers, too.

"Yeah, you good." I can hear the smile in Exo's voice. He removes his helmet, revealing his sweat-soaked head so I can *see* the smile, too. "You good thanks to Exo. Shot like that? No comp guidance, full manual? Under fire? Squad leader in the big bad tank's crosshairs?" Exo chuckles to himself, laughing at the situation. "I don't care if he's a legionnaire or not. *No one's* making that shot... 'cept me."

I take off my helmet. The breeze on the top of the ridge feels invigorating, but it's offset by the acrid smell of black smoke billowing from the tank and the peculiar fishy odor of the dead koobs. It's easy to forget how sterilized the battlefield becomes to your senses with a legionnaire's helmet over your head. I look behind me and don't see the rookie. "Rook make it?"

Exo points his head at a grouping of legionnaires. "Yeah, he's over there fawning over the koobs' old slug throwers with some guys from Hammerfall."

"Good." I open my jaw wide to pop my ears, rubbing my temples in an attempt to make the ringing subside. "You did the Republic a great service, Exo, saving your squad leader. Expect medals. Parades, even."

Exo laughs incredulously. "Just be glad you ain't point. I'd let the tank fire first and *then* I'd open it up."

I nod. He probably isn't joking.

Exo looks back at our distant line of combat sleds. "You see when Captain Devers's CS got hit?"

"Yeah." Images of the Gold Squad legionnaires burning alive flash involuntarily in my mind. "I saw it."

Exo spits. "Only good thing 'bout today."

I'm not so sure about that.

I pat Exo on the shoulder. "Well, I owe you one. What's your drink, Exo?"

"You know me. I just can't decide, Sarge. I'll have to sample five or six strains of core-world bourbons on the *Chiasm.* And then when I find a favorite, you can buy me that one, too."

It dawns on me that most of the legionnaires were inside the sleds when the *Chiasm* exploded, and everyone else was focusing on the battle itself. Am I the only who saw?

"Sergeant." The voice is coming through the external speakers of another legionnaire. Evidently I don't find the source quickly enough, because the speaker repeats with further specification, "Sergeant *Chhun.*"

I follow the sound and see Wraith, Lieutenant Ford, standing on top of the smoking, blackened tank. The flames are out, and there's a powdery white residue around the hatch. Wraith must've thrown in an inferno quencher—a chem grenade that removes all flammable gases and completely extinguishes just about any fire. One won't put out a building, but it will put out a room.

"Yes, sir?"

"Come over here, Sergeant. I want your opinion on something."

I motion with my head for Exo to follow me. We climb up the tank and stand over the blown-out hatch. I can feel the heat of the impervisteel through the bottoms of my boots. "Sir?"

He flips on an ultrabeam mounted to the side of his bucket. The clean, blindingly bright light shines into the darkened hatch. It stops on the dismembered and charred remains of the tank crew. "Those look like koobs to you, Sergeant?"

I squat down and peer into the macabre cavern. The crew is burnt up pretty badly. I suspect that Wraith saw something out of place or he wouldn't have asked for a second opinion. I take it as a challenge to spot whatever his LOA—Legionnaire Officer Academy—educated brain discovered.

A koob's most distinctive feature is its air sac, but those would have burned away. I decide to count fingers. The first corpse has only one arm, along with the expected three digits, same as any koob. My eyes scan the next body fragment. This one must have lost its hands from the blast, because there's nothing there, shoulder down. But the frame seems... large. If this was a koob, it was a strapping one. The village tough guy. I squint. The shoulders seem to have... spikes. Like a horn pointing downward, armor-like. Puzzled, I look at what's left of the neck and face. More spikes are protruding from the cheekbones.

"One of them's a koob, but the other has spikes. Looks almost like a Kimbrin. That's a Mid-Core species." I look up at Wraith, squinting from the light shining down just past my head. "What would Kimbrin be doing on Kublar, sir?"

Wraith doesn't provide any speculation. "Look at the third one, Sergeant."

I have to slide over a bit to get a better view. The body is lying supine on the floor, its hands across its stomach and chest like it was sleeping. I can't see the head from this angle.

Exo is looking over my shoulder. "What d'you see?"

I count the blackened and charred finger bones.

Five. Five fingers.

I stoop down to get a look at the head. The cranium and dental structure... it's unmistakable. I stand up abruptly, my stomach doing flips.

"Human."

"Whaaaat?" Exo hisses the word, a long breath.

"Thank you, Sergeant." Wraith looks me straight in the eyes, though his helmet is still on. "That was my assessment as well." He hops off the tank, N-4 in his hands, and begins to walk away.

"Sir?" Exo calls after him. "Why are there humans and Kimbrin placing ambushes with the koobs?"

Wraith stops and looks back at us both. "I don't know."

Exo and I exchange a look. Things have been hot through galaxy's edge for a while now. The Mid-Core Rebels have talked a big game, but to this point haven't done anything planetary police couldn't handle.

Sensing our uncertainty, Wraith says, "We'll have some basics pull out the bodies. For now... get some rest." He places his hand to the side of his helmet, as if listening to an incoming L-comm transmission. "Sergeant, I want you to take one of those incoming sleds back to the caravan once they empty out. But still, try to rest up, okay?"

"Yes, sir."

I turn and look out over the edge of Kr'kik Ridge, stepping over the tank's cannon to get the view the gunner must've had. Smoke from the blown-out combat sleds drifts heavenward like some ancient animal sacrifice burnt on the altar. Pappy's wreck of a repulsor still blocks the front of the road, but the vehicles at the back of the column have been pulled out of the way. I see a pair of sleds moving easily over the rocky plain toward our position on the ridge, their repulsor engines delicately lifting the vehicle just high enough to avoid scraping its belly.

The legionnaires who didn't rally for the charge are moving along the roads, checking the dead. I pull out my field mags and zoom in. Twenties hasn't moved from his overwatch position, and leejes from a mix of squads are traveling in pairs, making sure the dead koobs really are deceased. Koob women and children are peering out of windows, afraid to come outside.

I scan to the head of the column, the point where the ambush first broke out. Quigs looks to have made a temporary hospital in one of the koob houses. He's ordering basics around, converting them from Repub-Army soldiers to Rep-Med orderlies. There are enough medical supplies in the caravan to do alright for most combat wounds, though the skinpacks won't last forever. With no med-drop shuttles (because no *Chiasm*), we're not in a position to fight a protracted battle unless it's to the last legionnaire.

I chew the inside of my mouth. If we're going to survive, our best bet is to scrub the visit to Moona Village and head back to Camp Forge. Some point somewhere probably won't be fond of that decision, especially with us already on Moona's doorstep in the foothills.

They'll live.

The sleds have stopped beneath the ridge, and a cadre of basics in their black and tan fatigues hop out. Legionnaires are positioned to show them the easy way up. The regular Repub-Army troops are carrying up repulsor gurneys to remove the dead and wounded. Thankfully, they'll only need one for Kravetz, the leej who got caught by a bullet with a bad bounce.

I hop down from the tank. The crunch of Exo's heavy boots hitting the ground behind me reminds me that he's still there. He stood in silent vigil on that tank. It's not like Exo not to talk.

"Grab Rook and let's catch a ride back to Twenties. I want to know how his eyes are holding up."

"Yes, Sergeant." Exo bounds away to find Rook, who lopes over to us carrying some sort of koob slug thrower with a carbon-fiber stock and iron sights.

"You ever see one of these, Sarge?" Rook asks.

"In museums, maybe. That's the kind of stuff the colonists used during the Savage Wars."

"I know, right? Badass. You think the duty officer onboard the *Chiasm* will let me stow it in the barracks?"

I see a glimmer in Exo's eyes. "*I* can tell you where the duty officer will tell you to stow it," he says.

How do I break it to the boys that the *Chiasm* is a wrecked hulk burning itself out somewhere on Kublar right now? I decide to keep quiet until I've had a chance to speak in private with Lieutenant Ford, who's probably the highest-ranking officer we have left.

We file past a row of basics on our way down. Mixed among them is the gunner from our combat sled. Most Repub-Army use the less compact NS-2 blaster rifles, but the kid's carrying an N-4. If you ask me, the NS-2's additional blaster charge capacity and range don't make up for its loss of power relative to the N-4. But then, Repub-Army troops don't get in close like us legionnaires.

The kid and I lock eyes, and I can tell he's worried I'm going to call him out for carrying a legionnaire's rifle. His appearance is different now. Gone is the youthful, fresh-out-of-the-academy look. There's dirt commingled with sweat on his face, and his eyes are distant, devoid of any sort of a twinkle. He's just survived the nastiest ambush I've ever had the displeasure of fighting in. He should be a walking ball of gratitude. But all this kid can think about is being called out. We both know where he got the rifle.

But the legionnaire who dropped it isn't going to pick it up again. His fight is over.

I nod, and the kid looks down. He walks past me, his flush face showing relief. I turn around, watching him go. "Hey."

The gunner pauses as the other basics with him continue onward. "Sergeant?"

"KTF—it means Kill Them First."

He stammers a moment, unable to get his mouth to work. "Oh."

I think of the two koob kids who waltzed right up to our line and destroyed Pappy's sled. "You saw why today."

06

It takes the repulsor engines of two sleds plus the pushing power of eight legionnaires to cajole Pappy's wreck of a command vehicle out of the lane. I hop out of my transport, back from Kr'kik Ridge. I'm just in time to see the destroyed sled tip on its side and tumble over a partially demolished section of wall. The combat sleds release their magnetic cables and swing back around to take up predetermined perimeter positions.

My ride raises its ramp and shoots off back toward the ridge. Rook says something about showing his slug thrower to Twenties, then he leaves Exo and me on the road.

The only koobs I see now are dead, and most of those have been lined up in a neat row by the basics. The fish-left-out-in-the-summer-sun scent of their blood has me wrinkling my nose. For his part, Exo is handling the smell in stride, with his helmet pushed up so it's resting on the top of his head like a hat cocked back. But I'm tempted to put my helmet back on. Only, with the HUD inoperable, it really is a bucket with a viewport at this point.

I take out the comm assembly. It's shorted out, but I should be able to fix it or find a replacement. These, at least, are a helmet component that can be reused on the outside.

A Repub-Army basic jogs over to us. From the patch on her uniform's left arm, I identify her as a sled co-pilot. She stops in front of me and reads the decal on the chest plate of my armor: *LS-55, Chhun.*

"Sergeant Chhun?" she asks, as if she's not sure she read the name correctly.

"That's him," Exo answers on my behalf, propping his N-4 on his shoulder. "The sarge you want in charge."

"What is it, soldier?" I ask.

"I've been looking for you, Sergeant. The OIC wants to see you."

I look back toward the ridge. "Lieutenant Ford? I just spoke with him, he's back on the ridge."

The driver shakes her head. "No, not Lieutenant Ford. Captain Devers sent me to find you when he couldn't reach you over L-comm."

Exo stiffens. "What in the actual kelhorn? Did more of Gold Squad make it out of that sled?"

The face of the driver falls slightly. "No... no, just the captain."

Of course. The stinking space rat must have pushed himself to the front of the queue once he realized the sled was in the tank's sights. I feel a tightness in my chest and become aware that other legionnaires are watching for my reaction. My helmet is off, so I force my face to relax and quell the urge to let loose a salvo of expletives. My jaw tight, I ask, "Where is Captain Devers right now?"

"He's set up inside the third Kublaren hut to your left."

"Thank you." I read the name on her uniform. "Thank you, Specialist Grant."

Grant jogs to a nearby sled and jumps up on its side-board to talk with the driver inside.

As I begin to make my way to the appointed building, I notice Exo matching my stride, placing the barrel of his N-4 from one hand into the other. "What's eating you, Exo?"

"I'm gonna go ask Point how he got out of the CS first from his position as sled master."

I stop walking, forcing Exo to stop as well. "No, you're not, because we both know how that will turn out."

"Damn right we do, with a blaster bolt through the 'House of Reason' he calls a brain."

I shake my head fractionally. "That's not going to help things. What *will* help is if you round up Twenties and Rook. Quigs is busy, so let him be. Then get Wraith on the comm and have him come down here."

"Yeah," Exo says, the acceptance coming reluctantly. "All right. What do you think Point wants to talk to you about?"

"Probably chew my ass for not sitting in the sled and waiting my turn to get barbecued. But let me worry about that, ooah?"

"Ooah."

Exo pushes his bucket down over the top of his head and takes off for Twenties's overwatch position. I look up to the heavens at the last place I saw the *Chiasm*. There are just a few white clouds against Kublar's pale blue sky. As my boots crunch along the road, past combat sleds undergoing hurry-up maintenance checks, I wonder whether the whole of Victory Company wouldn't be better off if I walked into Devers's office, pistol in hand, and sent him to join the rest of Gold Squadron. The outside chance that Pappy might have survived, that I might have to see the disappointment in his eyes, keeps my sidearm in its holster.

I reach the squat, stone building commandeered for use as a temporary command center. The door is missing, blasted off its hinges. Black scorches outline pockmarks of blaster fire in the rocks. I strap my N-4 over my shoulder and step inside the darkened space. As my eyes adjust, I see Captain Devers sitting at a makeshift table—the missing door—going over a datapad. I walk crisply and stop in front of his desk. My salute is precise as a scalpel, textbook and flawless, the legionnaire way.

"LS-55, reporting as ordered, sir!"

Devers pretends not to have heard me and continues to swipe and tap at his datapad while I hold my salute. Finally, and without looking away from the screen, he speaks. "Why aren't you wearing your helmet, Sergeant Chhun?"

"Sir, my helmet was damaged in the assault."

"It looks fine to me."

"Sir, overlay optics and HUD are nonfunctioning, cooling and filtration systems are nonfunctioning, comm systems are nonfunctioning."

Curling his lip, Devers brushes his temple with the paltriest of salutes. I let my arm down in a controlled motion, my muscles—not gravity—returning it to its place at my side.

"Sergeant, explain to me why you assaulted the ambush position instead of continuing on with the exfiltration as ordered."

Called it.

I look straight ahead, staring at the opposite wall. "Sir, when I saw the tank score a direct hit on your command—"

"You know what? Never mind." Devers waves away the discussion. "I already know what you're going to say. You thought I was dead, so you followed through on your own course of action. But as you can see, I'm not dead."

"No, sir."

"Had you waited only a few moments, I would have been in a position to coordinate your assault."

I don't know what to say about that, so I keep my mouth shut.

"You lost legionnaires in the attack."

"Yes, sir. Four KIA during the assault."

Devers makes his hands into a steeple and taps his chin in a practiced contemplative look. "That will need to be logged for review upon our return to Camp Forge."

Somehow I'm sure the three Repub-Army soldiers and four legionnaires incinerated under his orders will escape the same level of scrutiny. Having friends in high places seems to do that for you. "Shall I have Doomsday Squad prepare for our return to CF?"

"No." Devers gestures to his datapad. "We're not going to Camp Forge."

"Sir?"

"We're continuing on to Moona Village."

Before I have a chance to register my surprise at this, Lieutenant Ford enters the hut. He salutes. "Captain Devers."

The captain returns the salute. "Lieutenant."

"What's this about going on to Moona Village, sir?" Ford asks as he leans his N-4 against the legs of the makeshift desk.

Devers seems eager to explain. "The mission to secure support for the newly appointed Kublaren senator is too important to the Republic to fail. Our success here will yield significant gains. A type-VII planet at this stage of development hasn't been seen since the Savage Wars. Blue skies, abundant natural resources, optimum gravity and temperature, and all of it untouched. With Republic guidance, the galaxy's edge could have an R-1 world in less than ten standard solars."

Translation: The koobs were not only sitting on a gold mine of natural resources, they also sat along a premier hyperspace lane as the Republic expanded ever farther to the edge. And the Republic fully intended to use that to its advantage.

Wraith waited patiently for Devers to complete his speech. His every move exuded calm and coolness. "Understanding that, sir. Our effective fighting force has been reduced by thirty percent, and our commanding officer is incapacitated. We are in hostile surroundings and unable to raise Camp Forge on any comm channel. Legion doctrine demands we scrub the mission."

Devers looked to me with drawn lips. "I'm aware of protocol, Lieutenant Ford."

I doubt that.

"However, *I* was able to reach Camp Forge." Devers raises his eyebrows. "These orders are direct from Colonel LaDonna. The mission will continue as planned."

"Sir," I say reluctantly. "Sir, I have to question, respectfully, the decision of Colonel LaDonna to continue on with the loss of the *Chiasm*. We're in Indian country," I say, surprised that the ancient term was the first to come to mind. "With no capital ship support, we should consolidate forces at Camp Forge. It's our best hope for survival on a hostile planet."

The look of confusion on Devers's face is almost comical. "What do you mean, 'loss of the *Chiasm*'?"

Wraith folds his arms. "What are you talking about, Sergeant?"

Was I the only one who saw it?

"At the start of the battle, I could see the *Chiasm* in orbit. It... erupted. I saw it explode and begin a descent into the planetary atmosphere."

Wraith is speaking in hushed tones through his helmet. "You're sure about this?"

"Positive."

"No," Devers says, shaking his head. "You're mistaken. A trick of the light or... or... battlefield hallucination. You did *not* witness the *Chiasm,* a battleship of the Republic, explode."

"Sir, I—"

Devers holds up a hand. "Sergeant, I received a transmission from the *Chiasm* only minutes before you arrived."

Minutes? How is that even possible? I saw the ship blow apart. I've been in combat before—this wasn't some hallucination brought on by stress.

"Sir, I'm not sure how that would have happened." I give the first plausible explanation that comes to mind. "Maybe a communication relay was bouncing on repeat until it could get through the atmospheric obstructions? But I assure you, the *Chiasm* is destroyed."

The captain stares at his lap. I can hear his feet kicking the legs of his chair. Wraith is examining me from behind the shrouded secrecy of his bucket, I can feel it.

Finally, Devers stands up. "You're under a lot of stress, Sergeant. The action started swiftly and overwhelmed your senses to the point where you imagined the destruction of a capital-class destroyer and subsequently led a reckless charge that resulted in an unacceptable *four* legionnaire deaths. I'm giving you two orders. The first is to no longer mention your delusion about the *Chiasm*. It will be bad for morale and may impact mission success. The second is to report to the medical staging point to see if the medic can help. He's busy with severe casualties, Pappy chief among them, but your mental health is important to the legionnaires, too."

Devers puts his hands on my shoulders like a concerned father with that last part.

My jaw clenches, and it's everything I can do not to lash out. "Yes, sir."

The captain smiles. "Good. Dismissed."

I turn and begin to walk away, leaving Ford and Devers to discuss the next move. I stop short at the door and turn. "Sir, you've made contact with the *Chiasm*. When will the med-drop arrive?"

"The... med-drop?" Devers looks as though he'd never heard of the term for an emergency medical dropship. When the wounded are hurt in the field too severely for the medic to treat with skinpacks, a dropship from the supporting destroyer is sent. These come in fast and take the injured soldier back up to the capital ship in orbit or to the nearest field hospital. We call them doc drops, informally.

"Yes, sir. With the severe casualties we've suffered, especially Pappy, a doc drop needs to happen. We don't have enough supplies in the sleds to give proper treatment. I have a legionnaire with facial wounds who may well need more than skinpacks."

"Oh. Right. The *Chiasm* is having some difficulties with their hangar shielding and aren't able to launch or receive any craft. In fact, that's probably what you saw. The malfunction."

"That's unfortunate, sir," I say as I leave the building. "Given what we've seen from this koob attack, I suspect more than just Pappy will need a doc drop before the mission is completed."

"That might be so," Devers says, a mirthful grin tugging at the corner of his lips. "So you'd best wear your helmet. Hadn't you?"

"Yes, sir." I put the bucket over my head, and the world goes a little duller.

I walk toward the makeshift field hospital, a wide koob building with a corner of its roof partially collapsed. Broken and crumbled stones lay scattered outside. What caused the damage, I couldn't tell you. Maybe an errant blast from the MBT. I lost track of all its shots.

Combat sleds are revving their repulsor engines into a whine as basics do system checks. It should all sound a lot louder. With my dead helmet, every noise sounds as if I'm under a blanket. Like a scared kid hiding beneath the covers.

A pull at my elbow arrests my progress. I turn and see Lieutenant Ford. He's alone.

"Sergeant Chhun," he says, looking over his shoulder for a moment. "The *Chiasm*. You're sure?"

"I was until Devers—"

Wraith taps the side of his helmet and cuts me off. "I can barely hear you, Sergeant."

I pull my helmet up until it rests on the back of my head, exposing my face. Now the lieutenant's audio sensors can pick up my voice unimpeded. "I was sure until a few minutes ago, Lieutenant. I don't know what to say except that it *wasn't* a trick of the light. Lieutenant, you know this isn't my first campaign for the Republic. I know what I saw. And if it was some sort of koob trick, it was better than even Rep-Psyops's work. It wasn't just what I saw. I *heard* it, too."

"That seems beyond the koob's tech reach," agrees Wraith.

I search for something that will explain how a capital-class destroyer simply blew apart. "Maybe the koobs did it with the help of Mid-Core Rebels. Like the ones we saw smoking inside the tank."

Wraith considers this for a moment. "We've had a lousy time reaching Camp Forge, let alone the *Chiasm*, since we moved out. Devers is the only person who's been able to bring either of them up. Could be his bucket. It's got newer tech. Prototype stuff. Or, it could be..."

The magnitude of what Lieutenant Ford is hinting at hits me in the chest like a round from an N-18. "What are you saying, sir?"

"I'm saying I trust the report of a legionnaire more than the report of a point. As far as I'm concerned, the *Chiasm* is no longer a tactical consideration."

I see over Wraith's shoulder that Captain Devers is walking toward us. Wraith follows my eyes and turns to look for himself. He lowers the volume of his helmet's external speaker. "Keep the *Chiasm*'s fate quiet. I need Victory Company to stay focused. We'll deal with the ramifications of the situation after we're done with Moona Village."

I clench my jaw and nod my approval. There's nothing to be gained from telling the men that not only will help not soon be coming—it *can't* come. Legionnaires can fight their way through a tough situation, but we're still human. For now, we can only complete the mission and return to the safety of Camp Forge. *Then* we can share the lousy news and figure out how to hold tight until a relief ship is sent.

Not for the first time, I think about how it would be nice to have a few MBTs along for this op.

"Sergeant Chhun," Devers calls as he joins us. "I specifically instructed you to keep your helmet *on*."

Before I can reply, Lieutenant Ford steps in. "I asked him to remove it. He's inaudible with it on."

Devers tugs at a fingertip of his synthprene gloves. He takes on a professorial tone. "Lieutenant, legionnaires are a collective. A force of nature, like a hurricane. The enemy, when caught in such a storm, feels overwhelmed and help-less by it. But a legionnaire without his helmet is no longer part of a raging storm. He becomes an individual drop of rain. The enemy will rally at the realization that the storm is only so many drops of rain, and brush it aside."

All I can do is stare blankly at the captain. I finally blink. Reincarnation must be real, because no one could get that stupid in one lifetime.

"Captain Devers," Wraith says, letting me know with a slight wave of his palm that he's got this, "Sergeant Ch-hun's helmet is *non-functional*. It serves no purpose be-yond making him less efficient in battle."

"It's clear to me, Lieutenant Ford, that you don't fully understand the role of psychology in warfare. Thankfully, the House of Reason *does*. And so do I. These MK-100 suits will be phased out in favor of a new type of reflective ar-mor that costs a tenth as much to produce." Devers moves his arm as if showing off an invisible soldier in the new gear. "It will dazzle the enemy and excite the Republic, and I'm quite sure you'll find you've won your battles before the fighting even begins."

"Captain Devers," I interject, "all due respect, but I don't think the koobs would've skipped the ambush just because a bunch of leejes showed up wearing shinies."

"You're not paid for your thinking, Sergeant. You're paid to follow orders. Now put your helmet back on."

Lieutenant Ford holds out his hand. "I'd like to inspect your helmet before you do, Sergeant."

I hand the bucket to him. He turns it over in his hands, looking at it thoroughly.

"I'll join you," Devers says. He has the smug tone of a man who believes himself to have the upper hand.

The captain taps on the helmet's black-screened visor. "Sergeant Chhun can see through the visor, and the plasteen will still serve as protection against projectiles, blunt force, and galactic-legal blaster fire." He clasps his hands behind his back and assumes a triumphant parade rest. "That's all in *addition* to the advantages gained by maintaining a solid, *uniform* appearance. We legionnaires are an incomprehensible, indecipherable storm."

Without uttering so much as a word in reply, Wraith tucks the helmet under his arm and pulls his vibroblade from the sheath in his chest-webbing. The sudden appearance of the humming weapon causes Devers to take a step backward. Wraith drives the blade into the top of the helmet and proceeds to cut straight through, nearly severing it in two.

Wraith tosses the helmet at Devers's feet. "This helmet is inoperable. I won't tolerate *anything* that might jeopardize the mission... sir." The lieutenant turns on his heel and continues on toward the field hospital.

I've never heard a term of respect like "sir" spoken in such a cutting way. It was as if the word's meaning had transmogrified so as to mean "you privileged bureaucratic Kelhorn scum-sucker who plays with the lives of legionnaires for your own career."

And Devers knows it. He stands in stunned silence.

I'm just as surprised. But not so surprised that I forget to catch up to Wraith. The area near an upstaged point is a dangerous place to be.

07

Pappy is propped up, sitting against a wall, his legs splayed out and his feet forming the peaks of two sharp mountains beneath a koob blanket. I've seen the meter-high lizards that provide the wool, and judging by the smell in the room, the beast's stink doesn't go away after shearing and looming. But then, most koobs smell like their livestock, so maybe it's not just the blanket. Pappy is still in his armor, with the exception of the entire right sleeve. Every protective piece from his shoulder on down has been removed, and the synthprene bodysuit cut away.

Skinpacks cover his neck, chest, arm, and half of his face. Whatever flesh isn't hidden behind the white membrane-like healing wrap is raw and red like a sunburn. His lone uncovered eye, blue-gray, is on high alert.

Tough SOB hasn't taken any pain meds.

"Ford. Chhun. I'm glad you're here. Come visit an old man in the infirmary." Pappy's voice is even hoarser than usual. He seems aware of the fact. "I breathed in the better half of a fireball, and this is about as loud as my volume will go."

"It's a wonder you can speak at all," Doc Quigs says from his place across the room. He doesn't look over at us, keeping his attention on a sedated basic with a nasty-looking hole in his shoulder. The medic is using carbon-steel forceps to dig something out—a bullet, or maybe shrapnel from an MBT shell. "You sucked in more smoke than a fleet yard carbon scrubber."

Pappy grunts at the joke as Wraith and I squat down beside him.

"How you feeling, sir?" Wraith asks, the electronic resonance of his voice bouncing around the stone interior.

"Like a still-smoldering pile of twarg crap." Pappy manages a smile, but it instantly transforms into a wince. I can actually see the skin around his mouth and lips crack and split open. "Ah! Kel, that hurt."

"Sir, Captain Devers just informed Sergeant Chhun and me that he made contact with Camp Forge. Orders are to press on and meet with the chieftain at Moona Village."

"News to me, but I'm confident you can do it. We took the best shot the koobs had in them and gave it back a hundredfold. They likely won't do much more than harass the caravan, and that only until we hit the plains and put some distance between us and them on the way back to CF."

Wraith and I exchange a look. "Sir," Wraith says, "I'm not entirely sure that's correct. We ID'd two non-Kublaren species fighting with them in the ambush. A Kimbrin and a human. Unconfirmed, but we suspect they were Mid-Core Rebels."

Pappy closes his eyes for a long while. It's the first I've seen him show any signs of fatigue since I walked into the medical quarters.

"I had Doc Quigs pump me with stims until I could get a clear picture of our situation." Pappy sighs. "Maybe I'm just coming down. I *hurt* a lot more. Listen, I'm not surprised that Colonel LaDonna wants the mission to continue on. Even at half strength. He's got the sector admiral breathing down his neck to get this warlord's support for the koob's new senator. Supposed to make all the difference. But if the MCR has augmented the hostile koob locals, or stirred up some tribes against the Republic, that presents a major complication." He lets out a dry cough and grimaces from the effort. "Once we clear these foothills and reach Moona Village, hailing the *Chiasm* will be easier. Tri-bombers will be able to provide the support necessary to spring us from anything too hot."

Only there are no tri-bombers. I decide to tell Pappy what I saw. "Sir, I—"

Wraith shoots out his hand and cuts me off. "We'll continue on in the mission, and we'll do it successfully."

Pappy nods. "That's what I expect to hear from a legionnaire. Now, up to this point, the rules of engagement have been joint force, and you know the limitations the Rep-Army puts on combat. After what you've told me, the political garbage ends now. I want the rest of this mission run like a full-leej op. KTF."

"Yes, sir," Wraith and I answer in unison.

Hell yeah. That's what's going to get us back alive to Camp Forge. Not worthless House of Reason rules of engagement designed to make local scumsack aliens happy, even if it gets basics and legionnaires shot.

Quigs rinses blood from his hands in a wooden bowl. The basic he'd been working on is stitched up and numbed up, somewhere deep in happy land. "Sir, best to wrap things up. I've already waited longer than I'd like to inject that cycler in you. The bot's got to get in there to take care of the internal damage from the blast. Before complications arise."

Pappy furrows his brow. "So shoot the damned thing in me, Legionnaire."

"Without sedation? I'd be guilty of a Republic war crime—torture. You *don't* want to be awake while that thing does its work on the inside."

We stand waiting for Pappy's reply. If anyone could handle the microscopic bot moving through their insides with a nanotorch and chem-scalpel without sedation, it would be the major.

"Just a moment longer and you can do whatever you want, Doc." Pappy locks eyes with me. "I had Doc Quigs show me the footage our TT-16 bot captured on his data screen. My screen was blown to hell. Victory Company owes its survival to your charge, men. I understand you were pivotal in formulating the plan, Sergeant Chhun."

"Thank you, sir."

Pappy nods. "We took a licking. Lost a lot of men. Most of the officers left are basics… or the point."

I catch myself shaking my head in disapproval, but stop before Pappy notices. Or, if he did notice, he isn't letting on.

"I need *legionnaire* leadership in the field if we're going to finish the job and get to CF. Lieutenant Ford, I'm awarding you the brevet rank of captain. Sergeant Chhun, I'm awarding you the brevet rank of second lieutenant. And you can believe I'll fight Colonel LaDonna through the six storms of the Andular Nebula to get those made permanent."

I wasn't expecting this. Me. An officer. I don't know what else to say, so I rise to my feet and salute. "Thank you, sir. I'll make every endeavor to live up to your expectations."

And I mean every last word. Being a legionnaire is like that. You spend ninety percent of your rotation hating every last second of your life, and then it all washes away in an instant. Because we're brothers. Because fighting for each other—not the Republic—is what it really boils down to.

Pappy looks at me while I stand there saluting. He's stock still. Just when it starts to get awkward, when I'm questioning whether I should still be holding my salute, he says, "At ease. I can't raise my arms."

I drop into parade rest.

"I know," Pappy says, "that you and Ford both will do fine work."

Wraith nods. "Thank you, sir." He turns to me. "Sergeant—*Lieutenant* Chhun, let's have a brief word with Quigs and prep to move on to Moona Village. Rest well, sir."

Pappy breaths out a long exhalation in response and rests his head against the wall, looking up at the wooden timber ceiling. His eyes are closed by the time we walk away.

The only man in the room with his bucket on, Wraith keeps his speaker output turned down to barely a whisper. "How's he look?"

Quigs looks at the reposing major, as if he needs to examine him again before being ready to answer. "He'd look a lot better to me if a med-drop were inbound."

"Count on zero support from the *Chiasm*," Wraith says. "We've got no comm connectivity with anyone but Camp Forge, and that's spotty at best."

"Can't CF relay the request on our behalf?"

I join the conversation. "If it can happen, we'll make it happen."

"I guess that's as good as it'll get," Quigs says, shaking his head and staring at the floor. "What's the plan for the wounded?"

"Can they be moved?" Wraith asks.

Quigs looks back at the wounded basic he just operated on. "Can they? Yes. *Should* they? Probably not."

I scratch my chin. "If we pack in the sleds to standing room only, we can use two for transport of the wounded. Other than Kravetz, there were no casualties on the ridge. Sleds already recovered the bodies of the leejes KIA in the field."

Wraith agrees quickly. "That's the plan, then. Quigs, have some basics do a full med-sled strip-down on two of the vics. Preferably ones with weapon malfunctions. I heard at least one sled can drive but got its guns blown to hell. I want as many twins as possible for Moona Village. Make it absolutely clear that we only strip out a sled with working twins if nothing else is available."

A med-sled strip-down involves removing all of a combat sled's jump seats and taking out the swivel stand for the twins' gunner. Repulsor litters are then magnetically anchored to the walls so the wounded can be loaded in like Republic marines on the subdeck barracks of a Republican corvette. I do the math in my head—there are enough sleds to pack in those fit for battle and transport the wounded. That's about it, though.

"What about the fatalities?" I ask.

Quigs lets out a sigh. "What's the last count?"

"Too many," Wraith answers. He looks over his shoulder to see if Pappy heard the comment, but the major remains in repose with his eyes shut. "Nordic funeral is about all we can do."

"I'll gather up some thermites," I say. "What about the koobs?"

"Leave 'em." Wraiths' voice is cold as an ice moon. "Koobs started this, koobs can clean it up."

Quigs finds a basic visiting a wounded buddy and relays Captain Ford's orders about converting two of the combat sleds. The basic jogs off, but I see him stop just outside the door to salute before hurrying away.

The doorway darkens as Captain Devers steps inside. He doesn't say anything, just sort of looks around, inspecting the room. He examines himself in a dirty and clouded mirror, then picks up a rag, dips it in a bowl of (mostly) clean water, and with short, swift strokes, cleans his armored shoulder protectors. You can tell a legionnaire's rank in a couple of ways, but the easiest is the paint on the shoulder. Evidently Devers didn't think his captain's bars were quite visible enough, and he's taken the opportunity to wash away the Kublaren dirt.

"*Lieutenant* Chhun," Wraith calls to me, emphasizing my new rank for Devers's benefit. "I want everything ready to go in the next sixty. Find Sergeant Powell and reorganize squads as needed."

"Yes, sir, *Captain* Ford," I say. I jog out the door, but not before looking over to Devers. He's standing perfectly straight, as if someone just stuck the barrel of an N-4 up—

Well, he doesn't look happy.

Deceased legionnaires and basics are stacked on rough pallets constructed from the peculiar green lumber the koobs use in their dwellings. All the leejes on the funeral pyre have their helmets on. That might sound strange, since Twenties and I are both without a bucket, but legionnaire helmets are custom-fitted to perfection. Tongue toggles, eye height and spacing, cranial circumference, everything is exact. It's rare to find anyone whose helmet you can comfortably wear, and an imperfect helmet is just as likely to get you killed as it is to deflect a fatal blaster shot. So the buckets stay on the dead.

Their kits don't. We need ammo and supplies for what's coming. Most of the guys have clipped on as much as their webbing and muscles will allow. The rest is crammed into the waiting sleds.

What extra N-4s and N-18s we have were set aside for the basics to use. Every soldier of the Republic on this op needs to be armed with more than just a prissy driver's sidearm. The Repub-Army standard blaster is woefully underpowered, with a nine-pound trigger pull. I guess to avoid accidental discharge? The point is, they suck. They'll kill if the attacker is right outside the sled's window, but if a swarm of koobs gets that close, we'll have already lost.

The pyre is a good eight feet high. I've got four thermite grenades stashed inside it at various levels to make sure everything burns completely. The fifth, the igniter, is in my hands.

Word has already gotten out about Captain Ford's field promotion. Mine, too. The feeling among the legionnaires is one of agreement. And relief. No one wanted to be under the sole command of a point. Both Ford and Devers are captains, and technically Devers has seniority by date of rank. But leejes have a tradition for when an op's CO is taken out of action and there's no way to get a formal order from Command (no one can reach Camp Forge since Devers got through): they take a vote on their acting CO. The squad sergeants have already surveyed their legionnaires and reported the results to me, since I'm the only leej lieutenant still alive.

Eighty men rolled out of Camp Forge. Forty-six remain. Basics and legionnaires alike are gathered around to hear the results and receive their orders to move. Twenties and other leej sharpshooters are stationed on overwatch, but the koobs aren't going to come for another visit. Not yet. We killed every last hostile out here, and any non-combatants are locked up in a hut under guard until we roll out.

Wraith is standing by my side. Devers is nowhere to be seen. No surprise. He has to know he's not being voted Victory Company CO.

"Captain Ford," I call out, loud enough to be heard clearly by all. "I've received all twenty-nine legionnaire votes. By a margin of twenty-nine to zero, Captain Ford has been elected acting CO of Victory Company."

A cheer goes up from the legionnaires. A few basics join in as well.

Wraith nods and raises his hand for silence. His helmet's external mic is set high, giving the effect of speaking through an amp-horn. "Thank you, men. I won't stop fighting for you. I ask in return you fight for me and the Legionnaire Corps I represent. The Corps *we* represent. Now, I understand from Doc Quigs that Pappy is under sedation and a cycler bot is patching him up on the inside. We're set to speed into Moona Village, complete our mission, and get back to CF. We do that quickly, and Pappy should be just fine."

Wraith moves in a slow semicircle, looking at the helmet or face of each and every legionnaire. "Nothing has changed, gentlemen. The mission is on. Full green. If the koobs want to try something, they'll find that a company of legionnaires at half strength is no less deadly. Especially when we go in with KTF as the directive. And per Pappy, *and* me, that *is* the directive. Any questions?"

A Repub-Army second lieutenant raises his hand. He's a point, but must not be as connected as Devers because he's a basic instead of a legionnaire. "Why isn't Repub-Army given a say in the mission CO? This is a joint-force operation."

Exo adjusts the heavy APR launcher on his shoulder. "You know what koobs did in the Savage Wars to the battlefield dead? Chopped 'em up and turned 'em into koob stew. You basics are only gonna survive if the *legionnaires* lead the way back to CF. And we ain't fightin' under the command of no point."

There's slight murmur at this. Wraith raises his hand. "That's enough, LS-67. Lieutenant, this is now a legionnaire-run operation. You don't have to like it, but you need to accept it." He puts a hand to the side of his helmet. "I'm informed that the last of the wounded have been loaded onto the med-sleds. Let's give these soldiers the proper honors and then load up. Sergeant Powell?"

The sergeant of Specter Squad steps forward smartly. "Ten-shun!"

A cadre of legionnaires and basics snap into a rigid attention. The sound of their feet stamping on the ground reverberates off the stone walls. I make my way to the funeral pyre, thermite grenade in hand.

Wraith speaks words every legionnaire has come to know by heart. "These that lay at rest have sacrificed themselves so their brothers may live. They have sacrificed themselves for the Republic under which we all stand. May their names be synonymous with the honor of our great Republic. Sergeant."

Sergeant Powell holds out a datapad. "LS-65. Kravetz, Byl!"

"Ooah!" we shout in reply.

"LS-43. Davish, Nateen!"

"Ooah!"

"LS-61. Granite, M—"

"This ceremony is out of order."

I turn to see Captain Devers walk into the midst of the ceremony. "If I'm not mistaken—I am, after all, only a *point*—it is the job of the company commanding officer to hold the memorial service."

I grit my teeth. "Captain Devers, sir! Legionnaire vote between Captains Ford and Devers resulted in Captain Ford being granted the position of Victory Company CO."

"I understand that to be the case, Lieutenant Chhun." Devers flicks a speck of dirt, visible only to him, from his armor. "However, the vote was premature. Colonel Hilbert—*Pappy*—made me brevet major shortly before he underwent sedation for the cycler bot insertion."

Every soldier stands in stunned silence. There is no way this could be true. Pappy wouldn't...

"Therefore, I am *very much* in command of Victory Company."

08

"Oh, hell no!" Exo shakes his rifle menacingly at Captain Devers. His helmet is on, but there's no mistaking the anger in his voice. "Ain't no way—*ain't no way!*—that Pappy made this *point* a major."

A wave of approval at Exo's words ripples through the legionnaires. But the basics aren't so sure; they're speaking quietly to one another, and their unease is on display in the way they awkwardly hold their arms and shift from one foot to the other.

Captain Ford holds up a hand, indicating his desire for Exo to stop talking. "You know the protocols, Captain Devers. A field promotion requires at least two officers or NCOs as witnesses, excluding the soldier promoted."

"The major will of course validate my claims once the cycler does its work and he's awakened."

"Sergeant Quigly!" Captain Ford shouts, calling for the medic to appear from the crowd.

Doc Quigs runs from his place at the back of a medical sled. "Yes, sir?"

"Did you witness Major Hilbert awarding the rank of brevet major to Captain Devers before you induced a medical coma?"

"No, sir. Captain Devers was in the room at the time of the administration of the narco-port, but I did not hear such a conversation."

Wraith nods. "Was there any time you were not present in the room?"

"I was there the whole time. Not at Pappy's side, mind you, but in the room."

"That's when it happened," Captain Devers chimes in. "While LS-75 was tending to other duties and Major Hilbert was slipping under sedation. He must have realized at the last moment that in promoting you to captain, he had not identified a clear commanding officer. Not desiring this, he awarded me the rank of major."

Exo leaves his place among the men and strides into the fray. "This is a load of twarg dung!"

"Stand down, LS-67!" I shout, doing my best impression of a legionnaire drill instructor.

Perhaps surprised by my calling him by his serial tag, Exo takes a step backward and shuts up.

Captain Devers is nonplussed. "I was in complete control of the situation, Lieutenant Chhun."

"Listen, Captain," Wraith says. "Without a witness, there's no way I can cede command of Victory Company to you."

"What are you insinuating, Captain Ford?" Devers's voice is menacing, but he keeps a safe distance between himself and Wraith. "That I'm *lying*?"

"No insinuation." As always, Wraith's voice is completely calm and even. "Just acting based on the facts of the situation. A field promotion without a witness is not valid."

"*Major* Devers was appointed to the Legionnaire Corps by one of the most prestigious delegates serving in the House of Reason." The comment comes from somewhere in the back, among the basics. It belongs to the Repub-Army point. "To suggest the major is lying is tantamount to calling Delegate Orrin Kaar himself a liar."

Exo spins around to confront the basic lieutenant. "Another point with something to say. No surprise there. We ain't speedin' out with Devers in command!"

The point crosses his arms in defiance. "These sleds won't move until Major Devers's rank is acknowledged. I'll employ an auxiliary lock that will keep them grounded."

"Nah." Exo is getting worked up, pacing back and forth. "It ain't happenin'. You wanna shut down the sleds? Won't be the first time leejes have walked. We'll even complement eyes right when we march past y'all on the way back. You'll be chopped up and served on a koob dinner table by then, but we'll acknowledge you for sure."

Things are getting out of hand.

Exo's speech is punctuated with "Ooah!" by most of the leejes present. He's giving voice to what they're all thinking. Hell, he's giving voice to what *I'm* thinking. Legionnaires have always bristled at Republic interference. Though we serve the Republic, we were designed to have a certain… independence. Tell us *what* to do, not how to do it.

We were founded at the start of the Savage Wars. A time when the galaxy and the Republic needed a win at all costs. Win or die. The legionnaires were run by those who fought, those who knew the terrible cost of losing. Those who did what was needed. Freed from the interference of politicians undertaking their favorite hobby—playing general—the legionnaires deployed throughout the galaxy and turned the tide of the Savage Wars.

All that's changed now. The Republic can't get the legionnaires into a bureaucratic-made quagmire fast enough. Every point placed in our ranks, every time Repub-Army, Repub-Navy, or even the Repub-Marines saddle up on a joint op and tells *us* how to run it, the Legionnaire Corps falls a little more under the full control of the Senate and House of Reason.

Rumors of point-heavy legionnaire squads being used to *collect taxes* or serve as personal bodyguards have spread from ship to ship like space lice. Victory Company almost lost its most storied commander, Pappy, because of a joint order not to KTF. The men are hot, and if they wanted to, they could dust every single basic out here before they could remove blaster from holster in self-defense.

But that can't happen. We can't break that code. I can't accept a commission from Pappy and then let that unfold.

"Everyone needs to calm down," I say, putting a hand on Exo's armor and attempting to push him back into the line. Rook and Twenties step in to help hold him back. I leave Exo with his squadmates. "There are more than enough koobs on this planet to scrap with. We don't need to fight each other."

"Indeed," Devers says. He rubs his thumb and index finger together as though he were inspecting for dust. "Lieutenant, I understand that you're new to your rank, so I'll grant some leeway on how you're handling your legionnaires. But let's not waste any further time. I desire only that we complete the mission. This isn't something I'd lie about. Think about it. Pappy—*the major*—would reveal the truth the moment he came to. I'd face a *court-martial*. There's no compelling reason not to believe me... or to follow my orders."

"*I've* got a compelling reason!" Exo breaks free from the grasp of Rook and Twenties. Or maybe they let him go. I don't know, because what happens next is so fast that it feels like reality just skipped a beat. Like we jumped forward in time. Exo busts loose, and not a second later his N-4 is out and he's pointing it at Devers's head.

"Sket! Exo!" I shout.

"Nah!" Exo pulls off his bucket and drops it on the ground. "Take off your helmet, Point. I want everyone to see the look in your eyes."

"Put down your weapon," I say to Exo.

"He said no compelling reason," Exo growls. "Well, I got a reason. A whole stack of 'em lying dead on that pallet. And a *court-martial*? Ha! We all know points don't pay the price for their screwups. Friends in high places, you know? Now, take off your damn helmet!"

Slowly, Captain Devers lifts his helmet from his head. He's covered in perspiration, and his eyes are wide with fear. They dart around wildly. With an effort, he meets Exo's gaze and calms himself. When he speaks, there's a confidence that straddles the line between resolve and false bravado. Years of political training are put to use against a deadly threat. "You'll be sent to the mines of Darus for this."

Exo's finger is on the trigger, ready to fire. He shakes off the threat with a fractional motion of his head. "It'll be worth it. Why don't you explain to us how you got off that sled? Sled leader is last out. *Last out!* Last in line. But you, you were the first one off. The *only* one off! How the hell'd you get to the front of the line, Point?" He's working himself into a frenzy, jabbing the barrel of his rifle toward Devers with every sentence.

In an instant, I see hell start to break loose. The basic point reaches for his sidearm, and I think the shooting is sure to start.

Wraith pulls his own service blaster pistol with such speed that I can't believe my eyes. He's covering the point even as some of the other basics move for their own blasters. "Don't!" Wraith yells. "Don't."

The basics hold still, but we're rapidly devolving into a standoff.

"Answer me, you kelhorned space rat!" Exo backs up a few steps, still pointing his N-4 at Devers.

"C-Captain Ford." Devers, pretender to the crown, is frozen in terror. "Captain Ford!"

Wraith speaks calmly to Devers. "Devers, follow the protocol."

Devers gives a slight shake of his head, unwilling to back down from his claims. There's *no way* Pappy promoted him, so he's either crazy or he's bluffing.

Exo is having none of it. "Forget protocol, this point *deserves* to be dusted!"

"Lieutenant Chhun," Wraith says, just as easy as though he were asking for the morning headlines, "calm your man down."

I shout, "Lower your weapon, Exo!"

"How'd you get clear, Point? You jumped out and left Gold Squad to die!"

"Dammit, Exo! Stand down!"

Seeing that Exo and I are yelling past one another, Wraith speaks softly to Devers. "We won't survive this. We have to maintain a unified front. Hurricane. Hurricane."

Exo's focus is singular and lethal. "I said answer me, Point!"

"Lieutenant Chhun..." Wraith implores me to defuse the situation. He doesn't need me to, though. He could drop Exo in the blink of an eye if that's what he wanted.

At this point, I'm convinced that Exo is going to dust Captain Devers whether he speaks or not. His gloved finger is twitching on the trigger so rapidly I'm surprised—no, *amazed*—that the N-4 hasn't already discharged. So, I just... act. I step in front of Devers and into the line of fire. I half expect a blaster bolt at center mass.

It doesn't come.

"Out of the way, Sarge."

"*Lieutenant*," I correct.

This causes Exo to pause a moment. "Out of the way, Lieutenant."

"Can't do that. Pappy gave me a job to do, and I'm going to do it. You're thinking of crossing the line. If you do, it's gonna start with shooting a fellow leej."

I can see Exo hesitate. Behind him, Twenties slyly pulls his blaster pistol and points it at Exo's back. He's watching me, waiting for my signal.

Exo takes his hand off his rifle's forward grip and jabs a finger at Devers. "That point will get us dusted just like the rest of Gold Squad."

"We won't let that happen. Now drop your weapon."

After a brief hesitation, an inner dialogue playing out its parts, Exo lowers his N-4. Rook and Twenties step forward and take the weapon from their squadmate's hands. I exhale.

Devers's mouth curls with bitter enmity. "I expect that soldier to receive fifty lashes and await court-martial!"

"One problem at a time," Wraith says. "We won't acknowledge you as a major without the appropriate witnesses. But we need to get going. I'll take combat command and control, and you can handle logistics and negotiations with the chieftain. Take it or stay here and leave it, because we're speeding out now."

Wraith walks past Devers and calls out to the men, "Sergeant Powell is going to finish the memorial roll, then I want every sled full within five minutes!"

He turns to look back at Captain Devers. "You taking it or leaving it, Devers?"

The look of contempt on the point's face is unmistakable. "Very well."

I move past Devers to ready the fire at the funeral pyre. He calls out after me. "Lieutenant, I expect that you enforce corporal discipline on that legionnaire as soon as is practicable. I further expect *you* to dole out the punishment personally."

Stopping to look the point in the eyes, I say, "We aren't going to be anything close to 'practicable' until we get back to CF. We need every fighter we have at our disposal, and Exo is one of our best."

Devers doesn't seem to have a reply, and I'm not waiting around for one. I walk in somber cadence to the pallet of the dead as Sergeant Powell calls out the names and numbers of the legionnaires to lose their life that day.

09

The ride to Moona Village is uneventful. It's what the entire trip was supposed to be like. I spend most of it in the back of a sled with that tight feeling, like all my abdominal muscles are flexed so hard that my insides feel compressed. Just waiting for hell to open back up on us.

Exo, Twenties, and Rook hopped in another sled. Nothing personal. Exo needed the time to cool off, and I needed to have some time to talk with the newest members of Doomsday Squad. Given the casualties from the ambush, Captain Ford determined to combine all remaining legionnaires into Doomsday or Specter.

"Exo wasn't wrong, sir." The comment comes from a leej named Aaldon Masters, LS-316. Young kid, maybe twenty standard years. He was already in Doomsday, riding second sled at the time of the ambush.

I expected this. Devers may not know it, but the only thing that saved his life was Captain Ford's and my unwillingness to allow him to be summarily executed for what he let happen on that sled. While the point is probably safely daydreaming about Exo getting lashes—I noted that he made sure to get on a sled full of basics—the facts of the matter are that he's going to come under investigation for leaving his place as CS sled master with Gold Squad.

Of course, him being a point, it'll all get swept under the rug. He'll get reassigned someplace cushy and fade into military obscurity, drifting from memory until he shows up on a holofeed pushing some invasive law that tears yet another tiny piece away from the Constitution of the Republic. He'll recall his military service while he does it, too. I can see myself in a cantina somewhere, knocking back a taza of mithryne and mumbling, "Shoulda let him get dusted," to the bartender.

No sense worrying about the future now though. Maybe Pappy will find a way to make Devers pay for his neglect of duty. Maybe the captain won't make it back to CF alive. Maybe none of us will.

It's all fluid.

"Sir?"

I've been sitting here lost in my thoughts, not replying to Masters's remark.

"I was saying Exo wasn't wrong."

I nod. He's not challenging me, just pulling me into a discussion among brothers.

"He wasn't wrong, Masters. I agree. But sometimes you can be right and do the wrong thing."

The kid thinks on this pearl of wisdom for a moment before straightening in his sled seat and snapping his fingers. "Yeah, I get it, LT. It's like this time a couple months back, when *Chiasm* was in port at Pendrex. I was at a pub having a few drinks when this girl takes a liking to me..."

This elicits laughs from the other legionnaires. A guy near the holoscreen up at the front, LS-130, leans forward with a big smile on his face. "Don't listen to him, Lieutenant. I *know* this is a lie. Any girl would sooner get in bed with a hool than talk to Masters's ugly ass."

Masters is actually a good-looking kid. That doesn't stop the sled from erupting with laughter, though. I laugh, too, and then instantly wonder if that's appropriate. As a sergeant, I would have...

I pore over memories, trying to recall the various lieutenants I've served under and what they did in similar situations. Problem is, most of the time I served under Wraith. He never laughs.

If my laughter bothered Masters, he doesn't show it. Instead he holds up his middle finger to LS-130 and continues his story. "Like I was saying, this girl, she was torrid, you know? Half human, half Sataar, and you *know* how good they look. So she wants me to come back to her place, and there's no way I'm gonna turn her down. Only while we're getting up to leave, her comm goes off and her datascreen lights up. Her lock screen is a photo of her and some guy, and a kid."

He holds out both hands. "I'm all like, whoa! Who's that? She shoves it back in her bag and says, 'He's not home and I don't love him.' Like, she's trying to close the deal. But, I dunno, it's like you said, right thing but the wrong way. She was really something to see... so that was right. But she had a family, so... I went home alone."

"Tell the truth," LS-130 calls out. "She was gettin' paid by the hour and you ran outta money."

The sled breaks into laughter again. I lean toward Masters and say, "You made the right call."

"Thanks, Lieutenant. You did, too."

"Thanks."

There's a chime from the joint-force comm channel just before Wraith comes on screen. It's strange seeing his image just the same way Pappy's was. I don't think I'm the only one who sort of puckered up wondering if an explosion was about to engulf Wraith, too.

"Victory Squad. This is Captain Ford. I'll be assuming Pappy's designation of Vic-1 for the remainder of the op. Advance sleds have arrived and safely disembarked. The village appears to be friendly as Repub-Intel advised. That said, I want each sled's twins manned, and I want two legionnaires anchored outside.

"Vigilance, men. We're not letting any koob get close enough to cause the sleds any harm. Now, Doomsday Squad is to set up a perimeter watching the road down the mountain. Nobody gets to come visiting until we've left town. Farmer Koob complains about his lizards needing to cross and graze? I don't care. Give anything that tries to pass our perimeter a warning shot, then dust 'em if they keep coming. Specter Squad will provide a security detail for the meeting with the koob chieftain. Lieutenant Chhun, you're in on that meeting. Make your way to the front of the column once your sled arrives. Vic-1, out."

I feel the CS slow and then come to a stop. The comm light switches to blue, indicating an internal communication. The driver's voice fills the sled's cabin. "All right, leejes, this is your stop. Exterior cams show all clear. You're free to disembark. Welcome to Moona Village."

With the driver advising no imminent threat, we're in a stand down situation. That means I can lower the doors and the leejes can just hop out of the sled, like a heavily armed family arriving at a shopplex.

But I call out from my point at the end of the line, "You heard from Jeeves that it's all clear outside, but we're not taking any chances. When the door drops, roll out hot until you get the okay from me."

"Ooah!"

The men call out their numbers, and I drop the door. The sled empties in seconds. I follow, the last out, moving low in a mobile shooting stance. The stock of my N-4 is pressed into my shoulder as I peer down its holographic open sight.

Nothing. There's nothing that sets off the "danger" ping in my legionnaire brain. A few koobs are milling about, watching us with indifference. A little off-world amusement on this slow and backward planet. "Okay," I call, standing up and relaxing my muscles. "All clear."

The squad follows suit, but only slightly. Their guard is still up. N-4s are at the ready as each man continually scans his surroundings.

Moona Village is carved right out of the mountainside. The predominant color is tan from some sort of sandstone. Steps, walls, plazas... everything is carved from the rock. While most of the dwellings are little more than koob-made caves with a door and a window, there's some impressive masonry work. Hewn rocks form massive squares and arches that seem to grow in size and detail the higher up the mountain they're carved. The sleds are hovering on a winding road that began way down below at the site of the ambush. I can't see the front of the column, and I wonder how much farther up it goes.

A small group of male koobs are gathered at the top of a staircase built into the mountainside. They're in conversation, gesturing at us. Even though I don't speak koob, it's clear they're talking about us, and it sounds a little heated.

"I don't like this, man," Masters says from behind me.

That makes two of us.

"Lieutenant," calls down a basic gunner from his place behind the twins. "Major Devers just called on the Rep-Army comms. He wants you up front so he can start the parlay with the chieftain."

"*Captain* Devers," I correct. "Doomsday, listen up. Maldorn and Guffer, stick with the sled. The rest of you make your way down to the rear of the column. Masters, you're with me. Let's go meet the head koob."

"Ooah!"

Masters and I push up the road. The clicking and croaking of the koobs fills the air, along with an odd, primitive music played on some sort of stringed instrument with plenty of tinny percussions. Cymbals, probably. A group of legionnaires hail us as they move down the opposite lane of the road.

"Hey, Lieutenant. Enjoy the climb!"

"Masters? You get made brevet sherpa?"

I smile as they walk by. I see that Twenties is mixed in with the group. "How're the eyes?" I ask.

Twenties stops and rubs the back of his wrist across his face. Like me, he's without a helmet. At least we're plugged into the L-comms, as each of us was able to fit a bone conduction comm unit. Mine is original, and Twenties salvaged his from a dead brother's helmet.

"I figure my eyes are good enough to pick off any koobs who think about sneaking up behind us," he says.

"Who's sticking with your sled?"

"Exo and Rook."

I nod. "Check in on Quigs when you pass the med-sleds and see if he needs anything." I raise my eyebrows. "Maybe the head koob'll have some medicine for us."

Someone from the group calls out, "Koobs probably just piss in the dirt and rub the mud on it."

"Hey, a little mud-pee cured that rash I told you about," says another soldier, a sardonic grin on his face. "Don't knock the ancient healing, man."

The group chuckles as they pass us by. It's funny how easily you can go from being in the thick of it to cracking jokes. Keeps you from going crazy, I guess.

We arrive at the next sled in the column. Rook and Exo are watching a cluster of male koobs while the sled's gunner leans lazily against the twins.

"Gunner!" I call. The basic snaps out of whatever daydream occupied his thoughts. "When you feel safe, you get dusted. Stay focused."

"Yes, Lieutenant."

I cross my arms and look at Exo. "Hey, we good?"

Staring at the ground, Exo nods his head. "Yeah, we're cool. I know you were looking out for me. Just got caught up in the moment thinking about that point sonofa—"

"What's the story with those koobs?" I say, pointing my head at the group of aliens looking us over.

"Yeah…" Rook stretches the word out. "Pretty sure these guys are waiting to shoot us as soon as our backs are turned. Bet all their koob cousins were the ones who sprang the ambush."

"Hey, koob!" Exo calls, amplifying his voice through his helmet. "You speak Standard? What's the story, just want to get a look at some *real* soldiers out saving the galaxy?"

A koob wearing tan and crimson robes steps forward. Arrogantly, almost. He still has a few faded spots on his frog-like face, signifying that he's only recently reached adulthood. The older koobs' skin turns a solid color somewhere in the brown spectrum. His throat sac inflates and lets out a series of clicks.

"Yew… *klik-klik*… lejundayeres…" He hops down a few stairs, his entourage of fellow koobs croaking and twisting their faces to express what passes for a smile.

"Speaks Standard," Masters says to himself. "Holy strokes, I didn't know koobs did that."

"Some of 'em learned from the Savage Wars," I say. "Must've passed it down. Poorly."

The koob stops in the middle of the winding stairway, looking down on us like we're his subjects. "Yew lejundayeres… *klik*… you see some… *klik-klik*… big die, ya? *Real* soljahr big die?"

Exo steps forward. "What'd you say, koob? You wanna see something big, let me take off my armor." I hold him back, pushing him toward the sled in an attempt to diffuse the situation, but he keeps yelling. "You stinking koob! You shoulda seen what we did to your koob buddies back there. Big die! Big die!"

"Exo, that's enough. He's trying to goad you, and you're just giving him what he wants. Keep it professional."

Sure enough, the koobs are rattling off their peculiar laughs as their air sacs rapidly quiver and deflate. The koob who did the talking swaggers up the stairs back to his compatriots, a smug look of satisfaction on his face. "Go home, lejundayere. *Klik-klik-klik.* Or mebbe home big die too, ya?"

"What the hell is that supposed to mean?" asks Masters.

"Ignore it," I say. But I know exactly what it means. We can't finish this op and get back to CF fast enough. "Rook, Exo, you two cool here?"

"Yeah," Rook says, hoisting up his SAB. "Words against blaster bolts. It ain't no thing."

It's a short hike to the front of the column. The air is crisp, with a slight chill. Typical subalpine conditions. The thinness of the air has me breathing heavier than I'm used to. Usually our buckets compensate for this by cycling in a reserve from a tiny oxygen tank that refills when needed. I make a mental note to increase my phys-con intensity.

We reach a clearing just past the final sled in the column. It's a sort of market or town square, lined with stalls like a bazaar. Kublarens croak and click for the attention of passing shoppers, selling bundles of grasses and cuts of yellow-hued meats. One Kublaren is twirling gleaming curved swords in front of a makeshift table. She shouts to us as we approach.

"*Leejuh! Leejuh! Cloo-kikkik kik cachi!*" She waves, entreating us to examine her wares. "*Cloo-kik cachi!*"

"Lieutenant," Masters says, staring longingly at a wicked-looking ebony dagger, "you think I can check some of those out?"

I see Captains Ford and Devers ahead in the distance, consulting with Sergeant Powell. The koob chieftain and a gathered band of Kublaren elders are standing opposite them, leaning on their staffs.

"Yeah, go ahead," I tell Masters. "But stick around the command sled when you're done. That's where we'll link up once this little chat comes to an end."

Captain Devers notices me from the other side of the square. "Lieutenant Chhun," he calls over the comm, "where's the translator bot I ordered you to bring?"

I press my comm receiver into my ear to better hear over the buzzing crowd. "Sir?"

Devers clears his throat. "I ordered you to bring a translator bot up from one of the sleds, Chhun. Remember?"

No, he didn't. And even if he had, there's no translator bot out here.

"Captain Devers," Wraith says coolly, "the translator bot was destroyed when Pappy's sled was hit during the ambush."

"Well, that's *great*," Devers says, holding his arms out and dropping them to his sides like a breakball player upset with a referee's ruling. "A little hard to finish the mission with a chieftain who doesn't speak Standard. So what now? I can't just stand here and wave my hands around."

"Maybe they have a koob who speaks Standard well enough to convey the message," Sergeant Powell offers.

Devers shakes his head. There's no way he'd follow the advice of an NCO.

The koobs hold a discussion in their language, and one of them calls for a young hatchling. The elder croaks in the kid's ear and watches it bound off into the crowds.

"There," Devers says, holding out his hand plaintively. "They're on it. Probably have a villager who speaks Standard before us by the end of next week. Wonderful."

"Has there been any luck communicating with CF at this higher elevation?" I say into my comm. I'm still a good walk from the meeting. "They could probably shot-drop a translator bot if we reach them."

A shot-drop is when Supply & Quarter delivers necessary items to units in the field. Sometimes it's a pod shot down from a ship in orbit, sometimes it's blasted like artillery from forward command. In this case we're looking for the latter, a pod containing a translator bot. It can be here in as little as two minutes.

"Haven't had any luck," Wraith says.

"Try it again," orders Devers.

"Silver-3, Silver-3, this is Specter-2," Sergeant Powell calls over the joint op comm. "Request from Captain Devers. Attempt contact with CF and request translator bot shot-drop."

"Acknowledged, Specter-2," comes the reply from the sled's driver.

For a while, all I can hear are the sounds of the bazaar and my own breathing as I close in on the parlay. Then a burst of static issues from the comm.

"This is Silver-3. You'd better hear this."

The comm is filled with the whining, thin sound of a strained transmission. Like a warbling voice physically stretched to the point of being too gaunt to hear.

"Put it through," Wraith says. "This is Specter-1, are we go for the translator bot?"

The reply is broken, cutting out so that barely a completed word comes across.

"Vic... ...ny? Is tha... ... ...med all were ...lled."

"You're breaking up, CF. Repeat, this is Specter-1 requesting shot-drop of a translator bot."

"Thi... ... post... ...ulu ... eed ... ... eed immed... ... ..."

The feed cuts out, leaving empty static.

"Did anyone catch that?" Devers asks.

I'm close enough to Devers, Ford, and the chieftain that they could hear me if I spoke loud enough. Instead, I talk quietly into my comm. "I think... I think that was Outpost Zulu. And I'm pretty sure they said they thought we were all dead."

10

There's a sudden surge of koobs passing by me, arresting my progress. They give me and my N-4 a respectable berth, but it's still slowing me down, and I need to join up with the captains. I can see from Devers's posture that he didn't like my last comment about Outpost Zulu—O-Z—figuring us for dead.

O-Z is a three-man comm station. It's way up on some koob mountain, sitting on a mesa-like platform carved out by a series of precision orbital strikes. The only way to get there is by drop shuttle. The thought was that the high altitude might help with Kublar's atmospheric magnetic interference. O-Z was supposed to be the hub that kept communication flowing between the *Chiasm*, CF, and the elements in the field.

Naturally, it belly-flopped.

Captain Devers confirms my suspicion over the comm. "They don't think we're dead, *Lieutenant.*" There's a dismissive disdain in his voice that's hard to miss. "Camp Forge wanted this mission finished, remember?"

He's talking to me like I'm an idiot. I hate this guy.

"Let me remind you that I spoke to Colonel LaDonna directly." Devers snorts a half-laugh into his comm. "Command is perfectly aware that Victory Company is still in the field."

"Of course, sir," I say, stopping in my tracks as a gang of koob adolescents blaze past me at a run.

Sergeant Powell chimes in. "It could be that CF hasn't relayed our status to O-Z. Kublar's been hell on medium- and long-range transmissions."

Most of the time in the Legionnaire Corps, Sergeant Powell's input would be appreciated. The Corps sees the value of drawing from the experience and wisdom of its NCOs. These career soldiers are the backbone of our fighting force.

With Devers around, not so much.

"Sergeant, I don't give a space rat's ass about your comm theories."

Devers turns from Sergeant Powell to the koob chieftain. He moves his hands like an interpretive dancer and loudly over-enunciates each word. "Chieftain Kreggak, how soon," Devers points to an imaginary watch on his wrist, even though he's dealing with a species that I expect has never seen them, "until that translator arrives?" He holds his arms out wide like he's asking for a big hug. The universal symbol for arriving, apparently.

The chieftain is the color of brackish pond water—a black that hints at green and brown. He gesticulates, and from my vantage point looks to be speaking.

Evidently, his message is lost on Devers. "Oba," Devers exclaims. "This is getting nowhere fast. Sergeant Powell, go find some pus-peddler who speaks Standard and bring it back here. Now."

"Yes, sir." The sergeant takes off at a jog, moving in my direction as he navigates through the bustling crowd.

I stop him before he runs by. "Hey, Masters is at a stand back there by the sled. Vendor was a koob that spoke passable Standard."

"Thanks, Lieutenant."

"Lieutenant," my L-comm squawks.

"Go ahead, Rook."

"Yeah, uh, the number of koobs over here damn well doubled."

Great.

I turn and look down the road to see if there's anything out of place, like a mob marching down toward Exo and Rook's sled. There's nothing beyond the already bustling marketplace. "Are they armed?"

There's a pause. Rook is double-checking what I know he already determined.

"Nah. Not that I see. But if looks could kill... we'd be dead like *Deluvia*."

Deluvia was a Republic capital ship that spent two cycles deep beyond galaxy's edge. When it returned, the entire ship was empty and all the airlocks were open. Not even bots remained. Holocam footage was wiped clean except for one three-second loop that showed the bridge littered with the dead bodies of the crew.

Not the sort of image I want to conjure up when I think of Victory Company.

"Roger," I say. "I'll see about getting Twenties and Masters to your position. You tell that gunner to keep his kelhorn eyes on those koobs."

"Copy," Rook says.

I realize that I've been standing in place during Rook's report. Busy koobs are passing around me like a river around a boulder. Devers, of course, has noticed as well.

"Chhun! I need you to get your butt—" The chewing-out is cut off by something else apparently more infuriating than my existence. "Oh, what is *this* crap?"

I look through the crowd and see a koob in black robes carrying a tray with cups full of a steaming liquid. He begins serving the cups, first to the chieftain, then to all the others of his kind. When each koob has a cup in his hand, he offers the tray to Devers and Wraith.

"No, we're not drinking that," Devers says.

The koob implores him, moving the tray up and down and urging them to take a cup.

I hustle over, and I'm close enough to hear the wizened croak of the chieftain. "*Kika ke kakay ka.*" He pantomimes taking a drink.

Devers shakes his head and holds up his hand. "Sorry, no. Taking that would be against orders. We're not to accept any gifts from the planetary population."

Wraith is clearly put off. He refers to Devers by his first name. "Silas, what's the point of coming out here if it's just to insult them? Take the drink."

"Damn it, Ford!" The rebuke hisses from Devers's external speaker. I can hear it clearly from my position, meaning everyone else can, too. Devers should have used a private comm channel. But I guess since the koobs don't speak Standard...

"Explain this to me," Wraith continues, unfazed by Devers's outburst. "We both know that there aren't any orders against participating in planetary customs."

Devers throws out his arms, and I wince at the clear disharmony being shown to the people whose loyalty we're trying to secure. "Explain *this*! The agreement was that you would take command of the combat ops and I would handle negotiations. It's not about the gifts, it's about maintaining unity. The helmets stay on. Hurricane, remember?"

With precision timing, helmet-less me, a single raindrop in the hurricane known as Victory Company, shows up. "Reporting as ordered, sir."

Buckets don't usually convey emotion, but I'm pretty certain Devers is glaring at me from behind his.

"*Kika ke kakay. Ka kaky.*" The drink is now offered to me. Koobs are persistent in their hospitality, if nothing else.

"May as well take it, Chhun," Wraith says wryly. "You've spoiled the hurricane."

When Devers doesn't say anything, I take a wooden cup of rust-colored liquid. Yellow granules, maybe some sort of spice, float on the surface and cling to the sides. "Thank you," I say, dipping my head in a fractional bow.

Hopefully a bow isn't an insult.

The chieftain holds his drink high in the air, straight above his head with his arm extended as far as it will reach. The other koobs do the same, so I imitate the pose as well. It's evident that we're waiting on the chieftain—who keeps his arm up for a long while. Long enough that I can feel a twinge in my shoulder muscles. But no arms waver. They all stick straight up like a grove of trees, unmoved by the wind. I become aware of the fact that the bustling koobs all around us have stopped.

They're watching.

Finally, the chieftain says, "*Kalkowah!*" He gulps down his beverage, his purple air sac quivering as he drains the cup. The other koobs are moving in unison, drinking at the same time. When I see that they're not sipping, I tilt my head back and let the liquid pour down my throat. It's warm, and clearly alcoholic. The best way I could describe it is a mix of Pintaari brandy, cinnamon, and fish.

That's actually a surprisingly good combination.

With precision timing, each koob tosses his cup over his shoulder. I follow suit a second later, and my cup clatters just a few moments longer on the cobblestone, like the last person still clapping in an auditorium.

The chieftain smacks his lips and swivels his frog-like eyes to look at me intently. He taps my chest armor, then delicately traces the webbing that holds my vibroknife. "You-ah come for war."

"I, uh..." My stammering is due in equal measure to uncertainty about how to answer and surprise that the chieftain does indeed speak Standard. "No," I manage. "The Republic doesn't come for war. But we're prepared for war. Always."

"Hmmm."

Devers shoulders past me, eclipsing my view of the chieftain. "You speak Standard."

The chieftain peers around Devers and looks at me. "Maybe you-ah find what you prepare for, hmm?" His air sac quivers as he releases a series of clicks. Some of the koobs in his entourage click and croak—in agreement, I suppose.

I step beside Devers. The koob isn't paying any attention to him, just looking to me as if waiting for an answer. Something about his gaze compels me to give a reply. "The Republic isn't here to start a war. But once, in the Savage Wars, a lack of preparation nearly destroyed us. We," I pat the emblem on my chest, "legionnaires, we won't stand idly by when attacked."

"Chhun, shut up." Devers grabs my webbing and pulls me back a step. He addresses the chieftain. "Chieftain, I'm Major Silas Devers. I'm the duly appointed representative of the Republic. In answer to your question, the Republic very much wishes for a mutual sphere of prosperity between the Kublaren and—"

"*Kik-kik-k'etakir.*" The chieftain waves his hand dismissively, silencing Devers. He swivels his eyes toward me again. "Many deaths of *Kublakaren* come from you. Not my tribe have big die. Not my people who attack you. But many deaths, yes. They who live shelter here now, under the protection of *tikrit.* Maybe you come now for Kreg-gak," he thumps his chest as he speaks his name, "and my kin-tribe?"

"Chhun, don't answer him." Devers speaks loudly to the chieftain, as if that will help this koob, who is clearly fluent in Standard, to better understand him. "You need to speak with *me.* I'm in charge here."

The chieftain blinks impassively.

"Chhun, tell him!"

I look down for a moment and say, "Uh, you, uh, need to speak with Captain Devers. I'm not really authorized to—"

"Kreggak only say to this-ah one." Kreggak, the chieftain, raps his knuckles against my armor. He's talking to me, acting as if Devers isn't there. Acting like Devers can't hear him. "You one not hide behind mask. You one drink the *reekau*. To you one, my tribe will speak."

I turn to face Devers. "Captain?"

Devers hisses into his bucket's microphone. "Fine, Ch-hun. Fine. Have it your way. You can relay my messages to the chieftain." He sighs, as if the circumstances of the situation are simply too much for him to deal with. "Tell Chieftain Kreggak that the Republic is here to affirm his support for the lawfully elected Senator Greggorak of the tribe Innik."

I nod and say to Kreggak, "Chieftain, the Republic wishes to know if your tribe still supports Senator Greggorak of the tribe Innik."

"*Lawfully elected* senator," Devers insists.

"The lawfully elected senator of the tribe Innik."

Kreggak lets out a low, throaty mix of a rumble and a croak. "You one... Chh-ahn. This is what *you* want to ask?"

"Yes," I lie.

"Tribe Innik is at peace with my tribe by marriage. My sister-kin, though not my hatch-kin, is coupled with Greggorak. This," the chieftain licks his eye, "is a bond that cannot break but by death. We support the Republic senator by the bond of *driddak*."

Wraith rocks from one foot to the next, his N-4 pointing down. "Sounds like you got your answer, Devers."

The captain turns around. "Not that simple, Ford. I need him to understand that his support should come from a desire to cooperate with the Republic and not from a devotion to local planetary customs. The Republic has so much to offer Kublar..."

I relay the message before Devers has the chance to give me an order. "Chieftain Kreggak, the Republic wants your support. That means backing the senator for the Republic instead of the, uh... *driddak.*"

The chieftain's eyes bulge, and he lets out a regurgitating sort of bellow. "You, Chh-ahn, want my tribe's loyalty above even the *driddak*?"

I get the distinct feeling I may have just insulted the old koob.

"Dammit, Chhun, this is why you shouldn't be within a thousand meters of this meeting."

Never mind that Devers *ordered* me here. I bite my tongue.

"Sorry," I say, more to the chieftain than to Devers. "I didn't mean to suggest..."

"This can be done," one of the koobs from the entourage says, in Standard, because suddenly, they all speak Standard.

The chieftain lazily turns to face the yellow-robed koob with speckled brown and gray skin. The party begins clicking and croaking at one another. Their air sacs fill and empty rapidly, a sign of excitement.

"Looks like Kublarens speak Standard more than we might suspect," observes Wraith.

"No," Devers says, dismissing the comment with a shake of his head. "Anomaly. Repub-Intel says almost zero percent fluency in Standard, planet-wide."

"Well, if that's the case..." Wraith raises his palms. "I'll just ignore that all these Kublarens pretend they can't speak it until it's convenient. Usually I'd say that means they're hiding something, but if Rep-Int says zero percent fluency..."

It takes every last bit of my reserve not to laugh. I never knew Captain Ford to make jokes. I guess becoming an officer grants me some sort of special access.

The koob deliberation comes to an abrupt end. Kreggak steps forward and addresses me directly. "This one can happen. If you leejon-ayers are to fight for this Moona."

"Absolutely." Devers practically interrupts the chieftain in his eagerness to comply. "If it means garnering your tribe's support for the Republic and the senator, absolutely."

I try to mask the bewilderment on my face as I turn to face Devers. "Uh, Captain, don't you think we should find out what he's talking about first?"

"No, Chhun, I don't. There's literally no force on this planet that can stand up to the concentrated firepower at Camp Forge."

I let out a long exhalation. There is nothing I like about where this is going. We were just chewed up in a koob ambush—whether Chieftain Kreggak was involved or not, who knows—and now we're committing to fight *for* the koobs, no questions asked.

Well, as long as the chieftain is talking to me, I'm going to take some liberties.

"Chieftain, we were ambushed on the way here. Our priority right now is taking care of our wounded and returning to Camp Forge for further orders."

Kreggak lets out a long string of clicks. "This was not my tribe, not Moona tribe. This was rival tribe, Annek. You leejon-ayers do much damage. Now fight with us, help destroy Annek tribe in their village. Not under *tikrit* in village. Kill tribe that ambushed you and make much trouble on Kublar to Republic."

I chew on the inside of my lip. "While I appreciate information on who is responsible for the attack on our column, I can't commit to—"

Kreggak bobs his head. "Not hard fight. Annek too hurt. Big die."

"Maybe we can start by having you turn in the Annek who are in Moona Village," I suggest.

"No, nope." Kreggak stoops and squats with each word. "Some of Annek warriors come to Moona Village to seek shelter. Much sacred protection this is. Cannot be broken. But tribal seat is weak. Less than half of two hundreds. If my tribe fight with leejon-ayers, my tribe control Annek. Warriors then fight for me and support Republic senator. Would show Republic friendly for Moona Kublarens killed in fight. Much anger still among youth in my tribe for this."

Devers shoves me to the side, forcing me to take a side-step to maintain my balance. He speaks in an animated, eager tone. "Chieftain Kreggak, this is *definitely* something our unit is capable of, even with reduced numbers. If it means strengthening and solidifying our relationship with your tribe—which was our primary purpose for visiting Moona Village—we'll do it. I already have the full support of Camp Forge if such a situation was presented to me in discussions."

For the first time, Kreggak speaks directly to Captain Devers. "Good thing. Good thing. We leave now?"

"If that's what it will take, yes," Devers says.

"I call Moona war council. Annek not far, this day, night, tomorrow, and morning battle. Together. Moona and leejon-ayers."

"Together," Devers says, sticking out his hand for the chieftain to shake.

Kreggak wraps his three long and slender fingers around Devers's gloved hand, and they're shaking like old Academy friends. I guess we've got some more fighting to do before we get to roll back into CF.

Joy.

11

"Easy with that thing, Masters. Only one of us has a bucket on his head."

The young legionnaire has been swinging his new koob sword—more of an over-sized dagger—in wide arcs as we walk back to our sled. He stops, holding it flat in his hand to examine it for the hundredth time.

"Sorry, Sergeant—*Lieutenant* Chhun. It might be a while before I get the rank right." Masters drops the curved blade to his side, but soon brings it back up, switching it from one hand to another. The weapon is made from some sort of black, volcanic stone, like obsidian but *much* harder. It'll leave a slice in our armor before it chips.

"Just don't want an ear chopped off. And don't worry. Chances are I'll be a sergeant again once we're off this rock."

Masters lets out a chuckle and wraps the dagger in its sheath before tying it to his belt with leather thongs. We walk in silence for a moment. Most of the legionnaires have loaded into their sleds, and the turret gunners aren't chatty. The few koobs making their way up the road toward the village square give us a wide berth.

"How much did you have to pay for it?" I ask.

"Not much, just a little tech."

I stop and turn to face the young legionnaire. "Masters, I don't want any koobs getting their hands on leej tech."

"No, nothing like that—I would never—it was just a few holochits."

"Holochits? Why would they want cheap little holochits?"

Masters shrugs. "I dunno. I don't think the koob had ever seen 'em before. I had to give up four of 'em. They were all of Mendella doing this dance where she shakes her..." He pauses, apparently unsure whether he should continue to describe the gyrations of the nypian singing sensation.

I decide to tease him a little. "Why does a legionnaire need a holochit of Mendella shaking her... talents?"

"A soldier gets lonely at galaxy's edge, Lieutenant."

I shake my head and chuckle. "Well, I guess the koobs get to enjoy Mendella now."

"You think koobs are attracted to nypians? I mean, Mendella is really torrid, but..."

We start walking again.

"My guess," I say, "is that your shopkeeper is going to sell it for the same price as *ten* of those short swords, and the koob who buys it will turn it on and place it in the middle of his dining table whenever company comes over, completely unaware of just how suggestive their holochit is to humans."

"What have I done?" Masters asks in mock terror.

"You're defiling the minds of impressionable koobs, and they don't even know it."

Masters's laugh booms forth from his external speaker. "Oh, hey." He reaches around his hip and pulls out a wicked-looking tomahawk. "I got this for you."

He places the weapon into my hand. It's a good, compact size. A little over thirty centimeters, with a nice blade made from the same stone as his dagger.

"What's this for?" I ask.

Masters looks down. "Earlier." When he realizes I'm not picking up the pieces, he adds, "At the ridge?"

"What?"

"Seriously? You dropped a koob that had me dead in its sights with a PK-9."

I don't remember that at all. Everything was happening so fast, I acted on instinct and training. I know I dusted a few koobs during the charge; if one of them was fixing to blast Masters, all the better. But it's not like I wouldn't have shot the alien anyway. I don't deserve any special credit.

"Hey, Masters, just doing my part. You don't have to—"

"I know." Masters nods. "We'd all do the same thing, I know. Well, except for Point, maybe. But this time it was me who didn't get dusted and it was because of you. Besides, I was getting tired of those holochits, and these are way better than anything I could get on the *Chiasm* for them."

"Thanks, Masters." I tuck the tomahawk into my belt and drag my hand along the side of a combat sled as we pass by it. Exo's sled is next in the line, hidden just behind a bend in the mountain road before us.

A buzzing sound comes from up ahead—scores of alien voices all speaking at once, like another town square bazaar opened up back here.

"That doesn't sound good," I announce to the air. I call up Rook on the L-comm. "Tell me that noise I'm hearing isn't coming from the koobs by your sled."

Rook's voice chirps back. "Momma taught me not to tell a lie, Lieutenant."

"What's the situation?"

"Lotta koobs all barking to each other at once. I don't think they like us."

"Stay cool, but KTF if it comes to it. I'll be there with Masters soon." I can see koobs packed thick along the stairs and in the stoops of the carved stone houses. The combat sled is still hidden by the bend in the road, but I can tell they're all staring right at it.

"I figure we're outnumbered ten to one, but now that I know you *and* Masters are coming, I feel a *lot* better." I can hear the smile behind Rook's voice as he adds, "See you in a few. Bring air support."

A sense of urgency hits Masters and me at the same time, because we both begin jogging. We round the bend and see the sled safe and sound, but the Repub-Army gunner in the turret looks so tense that a sneeze will probably set him shooting. I see Rook and a leej from Specter Squad. I don't see Exo.

I'm treated to what I can only imagine is a rollicking flourish of profanity croaked and clicked my direction. Koobs fill the winding stairways and verandas that lead away from the main road. The reception is so much... *harsher* than what I experienced at the bazaar. And then all at once the reason for this strikes me like a starfighter bolt.

Tikrit.

These are the koobs from the Annek tribe who managed to escape to the safety and protection of Moona Village. These koobs ambushed us. Or at least, they're buddies with the ones who did.

I join Rook, and a sense of dread passes over me as I look into the crowd of disgruntled Kublarens. "Rook," I say, trying to keep my voice calm. "You've kept an eye on the koobs the entire time you've been out here, right?"

"Yeah."

"Did you see any species other than koobs mixed in with the crowd? Like Kimbrin or..." I hesitate to use the word, but my need for clarity outweighs my desire to avoid making Rook and the rest of the leejes jumpy. "... human?"

"No," Rook says, shaking his head. There's a tinge of questioning in his voice, like he doesn't know why I'd ask. "Oh, wait. Are you saying these are the same batch of koobs who ambushed us in the foothills?"

"Pretty sure."

Masters lets out a sort of growl and pops his knuckles. "I thought we got them all."

"Head koob says we didn't."

Rook hoists his repeating blaster a little higher. "What're we waiting for then? Let's dust 'em while they're all in one spot."

"No, don't do that. They're under some sort of koob code of protection. Noncombatants sheltered by the Moona Village's chieftain."

"C'mon, Sarge. KTF." Rook shrugs his shoulders defiantly, like a teenage kid getting shot down by his parents when he asks for the sled keys. "What? We just gonna wait for another koob hatchling to toss a set of charges on a hoversled?"

I press the button on my conduction headset pre-programmed to reach the command frequency. "Doomsday-1 for Vic-1."

Rook takes a step toward me, still pleading his point. I hold up a finger. "Just hang on, Rook."

Wraith's voice comes on the line. "Go ahead, Doomsday-1."

"Captain Ford, I'm here at sled position four. This place is crawling with koobs. Pretty sure they're part of the same tribe who ambushed us."

A pause, then: "Copy. Yeah, Captain Devers and Kreggak talked about them after you left. We can't touch 'em while they're under village protection. But they aren't supposed to touch us either. Still, keep an eye on 'em. KTF."

"KTF," I say. "Acknowledged. We're rolling out momentarily. We'll watch 'em as we go and advise the sled behind us to do the same."

"Yeah, about that, Chhun. Devers and Kreggak just decided they would ride down together as a show of unity and lead the column out of the village. So you're gonna have to keep those koobs entertained a while longer."

I suppress a sigh of frustration. "Copy. Chhun out."

Well, that's just wonderful news. I look up at the crowd of hostile koobs. The one who jawed at Exo while I was on my way up is still there, right in the thick of things, and by the way he's treated, I'm guessing he's important. A steady stream of koobs are coming and going, all croaking and warbling into his ear slits and receiving replies before moving on.

Masters has the stock of his N-4 against his shoulder. Like Rook, he's ready to start shooting. He looks from the sled's gunner to Rook and then me. "Shouldn't the rest of the guys be out of the sled?"

"Nah," Rook says, his black visor reflecting the orange of the sun as it lumbers toward the horizon. "The more of us that were out, the rowdier they got. Plus Exo was pissing them off on purpose. We had to practically pull him inside."

Sounds like Exo.

"Here's the deal, Doomsday," I say, after keying my comm to our squad channel. I don't remove my gaze from the koobs. "We're here until Point—sorry, forget I said that—until Captain Devers rolls by with the chieftain, Kreggak. Shouldn't be long, but until our makeshift Republic Day Parade comes by, we're stuck here with these koobs."

"Request permission to shoot all the koobs, Lieutenant." It's Exo.

I stifle a smile. "Denied, Exo. We can't touch them unless they break the honor code first. Too many of our brothers sacrificed to make this mission a success, so let's not be the ones who undo what's been achieved. The chieftain likes us. Wants us to help him wipe out the koob tribe that ambushed us. Except for these croakers."

I bang my fist on the sled cockpit's side window. The sled has already been turned around, ready to hover back down the mountain once the order is given. The

Repub-Army driver pushes open the triangular clari-steel. "Lieutenant?"

"We're gonna have to sit tight for a while until Captain Devers's element passes us by."

The driver nods an affirmative.

I grab hold of a rung on the side of the sled. "The four of us are going to ride along topside to keep an eye on these koobs. We're not going to have a repeat."

"Yes, sir," the driver says. He seals up the cockpit.

I call out to Rook, Masters, and the leej from Specter Squad. "We're riding topside to keep overwatch. Find a spot and get comfy."

I pull myself up onto the sled and stand on a sideboard. The other three legionnaires clamber up and splay out behind the twin guns like tourists resting on a beach. The koobs are emboldened by this, rightly taking it as a sign that we're about set to leave Moona Village. The epithets and insults are coming our way faster than my ears can keep up with. I don't care. Sticks and stones don't mean much when you wear leej armor, let alone words. But the belligerents are working themselves into a frenzy, their purple air sacs swelling and deflating throughout the crowd like the first bubbles of boiling water. What I wouldn't give to hold the pin that popped them.

The driver of our sled comes over the comm. "Lieutenant Chhun. It sure would be nice to clear these koobs out. They're making everyone jumpy."

"Understood, but we don't shoot unless they present a clear and immediate threat."

"What's that, sir? Having trouble hearing you on the comm."

I cup my hand around the minuscule comm mic. This koob noise is too much. Normally our mics isolate the user's voice and cut off the unwanted sound—but that only works if you have a full helmet rather than just a salvaged mic. "I said we can't shoot them."

"Oh!" the driver exclaims. "No, sir. I had something else in mind. You like music? I've got something—it's practically ancient—that I think will quiet things down."

"If it'll shut them up, hell, even drown them out, be my guest!"

Ampispeakers attached to the sled begin to hiss and pump out the track. It's harsh, fast, played by hand. You can tell. Completely missing are the telltale synth eveners. There's no trace of a tune-orb. It's about as far removed from the vapid Kwiss-pop as one could imagine. The percussion is relentless. The musician is beating on the— what were they called, back then?—*drums* like they owed him money. The chords are harsh, coming from some amplified string instrument in a way that makes you grit your teeth and scowl. This is hard music. The type that, without a single lyric, embodies what it means to be a legionnaire. What it means to fight. To KTF.

"Oh, hell, yeah!" Exo's voice pops up over the comms. "The leej honor band needs to play *this*."

"I doubt they could," the driver replies. "It's so old… no one would know—"

"Maintain comm discipline," I say, channeling Pappy. "Eyes on the koobs."

The singer comes on, delivering the lyrics in Standard, the oldest language in the galaxy. His voice is somehow low and booming, but he's a tenor. It fits perfectly.

Even better, it's working. The rowdy koobs have given up trying to compete with what's blaring from the sled's speakers. They're rubbing their ear ducts. As the song plays on, more and more of them move out of the zone. They're getting as far away from the sound as possible. All of them except the ringleader. He's just looking down from behind a stone balcony with hatred in his eyes.

I stare right back.

Our eyes are locked together when the rumble of a light transit truck pulls my attention away. Most koobs walk or ride beasts of burden, but the wealthier tribes have these white cargo transports that have wheels and treads. Petroleum combustion engines. Savage Wars stuff. One of these squeaks to a halt next our sled. Captain Devers and the chieftain are standing in the flatbed behind the pilot canopy. A column of these transports, filled with koobs holding their slug throwers in the air, is lined up behind the lead element—a confidence-boosting parade. I can tell right away that this wasn't a scheduled stop.

Kreggak is rubbing his ear ducts. He speaks into a comm—*a legionnaire comm!* He shouldn't have that. He should *not* have that.

"Lieutenant Chhun!" Captain Devers's voice screams at me through the open L-comm. "Turn that off, *right now!*"

I can hear the clickety-croaking of Kreggak over the open channel. He's been given access to the legionnaire-only comm channel.

Unbelievable.

Trusting that Wraith will sort this out once we follow this little koob caravan, I nod an affirmative and reach my fist back to bang on the combat sled's cockpit. The music comes to an instant stop, replaced by an even louder silence.

Devers and Kreggak continue on, leaving me to watch the processions of dusty and mud-splattered transports rolling down after them. The koob ringleader on the stone balcony continues to stare blaster bolts into us. Some of his friends re-join him.

Finally, the column of transports passes, and combat sleds from the top of the mountain move down, their gunners on alert, sweeping for targets. Then it's our turn to move. I look up at the rebel koobs as we pass underneath them. The Kublaren sun is glowing in the green sky behind them. The koob ringleader doesn't say a word. He simply holds his hands as if he had a blaster rifle, and motions like he's firing on us. Again and again and again.

CAMPFORGE

12

PLE-1J extended its comm antenna from a port at the back of its head. The bot's optical receptors zoomed and refocused with a mechanical strain. Glowing blue, the optics scanned the empty and windswept horizon for... for what?

For the story, the bot reminded itself.

Why PLE-1J needed reminding was a question it would ponder during its next diagnostic cycle. The story was what was important. The story demanded the bot not linger on the question. As a journalist bot, embedded with Victory Company, PLE-1J was to record for posterity the Republic's work at galaxy's edge.

PLE-1J's body was humanoid, but not full android. A slate gray frame made of a malleable impervisteel alloy kept PLE-1J from looking too human. This was intentional: non-synthetic beings were statistically shown to be more comfortable around bots that were distinctly artificial, robotic. PLE-1J's head was skull-shaped, with circular optics placed in the same location as human eyes. This too was intentional, as bots without this feature were forty percent less likely to elicit emotion from humanoids when interviewing and reporting. A vertical grouping of vocal lights flashed at the bottom of the bot's head to provide a visual cue to supplement its audio output. The research behind the effectiveness of that build was mixed.

Victory Company had hosted PLE-1J through three consecutive tours involving eight planetary campaigns, and it now bore dents, dings, and paint chips that endeared it to the Republic front line soldiers. Even the legionnaires had warmed up to the bot, a Pulitzer Limited Entrenchment model.

They had rechristened it "Pully."

It was the legionnaires Pully searched for along the horizon. This was the direction from which the envoy sent to meet with Chief Kreggak of Moona Village would likely return. A gust of wind showed itself through an oppressive rustling of tall grasses, pushing stalks down as though an invisible freighter were landing. The wind turned into dust cloud as it rolled across the expanse of grass and into the scorched earth surrounding Camp Forge. Most of the fires had burned out within the past three hours.

Pully's optics magnified and strained until it wasn't sure whether its processor would even have the ability to make sense of the blurred and pixelated images. From a compartment on the bot's back, it deployed a TT-10 hovercam. The spherical black and silver bot, no larger than a clenched fist, floated to a stationary position facing Pully. It sent a burst of coded transmission and began to record its host.

Speaking with a male synth-audio voice that researchers found had the broadest appeal to males and females of human, Enduran, Sataar, and other near-human species, Pully began its address.

"This is..." The bot paused. News organizations would superimpose an image of whatever local planetary newscaster they wished to be delivering the report, and would use an autosynth to insert the appropriate name. "... with another special report from the ruins of the joint Republic Army and legionnaire forward operating base, Camp Forge. The contingent of legionnaires comprising the last known survivors of Victory Company, together with support personnel from the R-A 444th Repulsor Division, remain missing. Sent to obtain the support of a local Kublaren tribal chieftain for Senator K'iktor Greggorak, the detachment of nimble Republic Armorworks combat sleds did not return at the scheduled time. Scans of the Kublaren horizon reveal no signs of the contingent, and fears mount that the craft faced a similar fate as did those at Camp Forge."

The hovercam's red light went out. It moved on silent repulsors back into its storage compartment.

Once again whole, Pully reflected.

As fears mount?

The journo-bot considered its choice of expressions. Whose fears? Its own? No. But... who else?

The viewer.

Yes. The viewer. But... Pully's last nine hundred and forty-three transmissions did not reach the *Chiasm*'s relay. Is it *my* fear? Am I afraid?

...

You are programmed to report from combat-stricken war zones without fear.

Without fear for *myself*. But not without fear for others?

...

...

Apparently.

...

...

Curious.

Indeed.

...

The slender antenna on Pully's head lit up with a flowing current of tiny green lights, like sparks taken up by the wind.

Begin Transmission to Relay Station C-1A.

...

...

Transmission Failed.

Begin Transmission to Relay Station C-1B,C,D,E.

...

...

...

...

Transmission Failed.

Begin Transmission to Planetary Archive Station O-Z-1.

...

Transmission Complete.

Another transmission failure. Which meant the *Chiasm* had either moved out of Kublaren orbit, or was destroyed. Given the improbability of the latter, Pully presumed the capital-class destroyer had responded to an emergency situation from a nearby system. Hoethus had seemed primed to explode into chaos the last time Pully was there. Perhaps it had.

The horizon remained empty no matter how long the bot stared into it, and the sounds carried along the wind gave no hint of repulsor engines, no matter how hard Pully's audio-sensors strained.

"I will wait until the first light of tomorrow's cycle," the bot declared to the ruins of Camp Forge. To the dead, waiting for their stories to be told. "If the legionnaires do not return by then, I will initiate a deep-space transmission."

The bot's smooth, holo-newscaster voice sounded... *wrong* in a place of so much death and destruction. Pully lowered its audio output and spoke in a synthetic whisper that felt somehow more respectful. "However, this would require me to shut down for the entirety of the upload. I might miss key events in the story. Protocol demands that an emergency DST include as much information as possible."

Turning on alloy heels, the bot surveyed the carnage of Camp Forge. Bodies were strewn everywhere. Blasters, bullets, and mortars had all done their parts. But most had been annihilated right at the beginning, when the motor pool, full of Republic Armorworks main battle tanks, erupted in a fantastic explosion of munitions and equipment. There had not been much left to be killed once the full Kublaren attack on Camp Forge began.

Pully had recorded the entirety of the battle. The surging waves of Kublarens, the human and Kimbrin attachments of Mid-Core Rebels. The bot had captured for all time the final moments of the surviving legionnaires. They were packed tightly together in a defensive circle, seamlessly firing their blaster rifles, reloading charge packs, and firing again. The holocam had drifted higher and higher in an attempt to see above the mounting pile of Kublaren bodies before, finally, the attackers broke through the line and overran the legionnaires.

A sense of—helplessness?—had come over Pully when that happened. But the bot had continued to narrate the brief melee: the vibroknives slicing through alien flesh, the N-4 rifles swung as clubs, the legionnaire armor finally ripped away by a sea of Kublaren hands.

They were all dead. The Kublarens had made an example of some. Beheadings, mutilations, hanging bodies on the twisted spires of the ruined impervisteel compound. And all the while they chattered and croaked at Pully, wanting their story to be broadcast to the Republic. The bot didn't understand their words—its translator software was damaged by the blast—but their actions were perfectly clear.

When they left, Pully began to record personal interest stories on the dead soldiers. Just the ones the bot's databanks were able to identify. These would be of special interest to their home planets—or home systems, if the deceased were important enough. A House of Reason-appointed officer or the like. Pully did a generic broadcast for those disintegrated or missing in action. The planetary local stations would fill in the blanks.

Pully headed back into the camp. With the fires finally out, there would be many more it could now identify. Many more stories to tell.

The bot waded through the wreckage, seeking the next report.

PART TWO

13

My back is stiff, my right leg is asleep. I hobble out of the combat sled, shaking feeling back into slumbering limbs between every wooden-legged limp. Nights on Kublar are cold. Oppressively cold. I duck my neck down as deep into my armor as it will go. A turtle in combat gear. There's a part of me that wishes I still had my bucket, if only to keep my ears from freezing.

The pre-dawn darkness is like a veil, and I wait for my eyes to adjust before moving too far from the sled. We drove hard from Moona Village, through the end of the day and into the night. When we got within striking distance of the Annek village, Captain Devers finally ordered us—well, more like relayed Kreggak's order—to halt. We probably stopped too close, but the koobs in the valley below us haven't appeared to notice. At least the drivers have gotten a few hours of sleep before the attack.

Sleepy drivers are a liability. Fact.

Koob trucks litter the area. The drivers park with no tactical precision whatsoever. Wherever the driver felt like stopping, he stopped. The Moona koobs sleep just as haphazardly. They're sleeping in the truck cabs and beds where there's space, and where there isn't, they're lying on the ground, wrapped up in their robes, all around the vehicles. Some have even crawled beneath the rigs, sleeping in between wheels and tracks. They'd better be early risers if they don't want their koob spleens crushed out of them. Judging by the way the koobs drive, I'm guessing they aren't the type to check their wheels before they get moving.

Unlike us, and virtually every other fighting force ever, the koobs don't set a watch. I do not exaggerate when I tell you that they are literally *all* sleeping. So the job is left to the ever-vigilant legionnaires. It's probably easy to have sweet dreams when you're surrounded by heavily armed war machines peering through the darkness like sages looking through time. We leejes see all with our perfect night vision. Ready to kill whoever would seek to infiltrate our sanctum before the intruder even knows he's been seen.

There is some moonlight. Not much, but I can see its pale blue rays on the massive stone spires that stand like sentinels on either side of the valley below. The glow makes the spires look vaguely like two towering koob warriors. The koobs down below could use a pair of stone giants. It would take something like that to prevent us from wiping the deck clean of every koob warrior in the valley who helped spring yesterday's ambush.

Driving all this way gave me time to think. I'm thankful for the intel that will allow us to pay the koobs back, but I don't trust the Moona Village koobs who presented us with the opportunity. And neither does Wraith. Devers trusts Kreggak completely, but Captain Ford will have full command once combat operations begin, and we've got a plan to keep eyes on Kreggak and his soldiers while still completing the objective.

"Masters," I whisper into my comm. Into the darkness.

From his overwatch position behind the sled's twins comes his reply. "Lieutenant?"

"I'm moving over to see Captain Ford at the command sled. Watch my back. Make sure not to let any koobs plunge a knife into it."

"Copy."

I move away from the sled only to hear Masters add, "Swords okay?" I make a big show of shaking my head so he can see it.

I find Wraith standing outside the command sled. He holds a pair of field mags up to his helmet's visor. Our buckets have magnification, but to get a really good look at something, you need to use your field mags. Helmets can't do it all.

Wraith lowers his mags as I approach, but doesn't remove his stoic gaze from the valley below. "Couldn't sleep, Lieutenant?" He somehow divines that it's me approaching. "Neither could I."

I take a place at Wraith's side, joining him in his survey of the valley—though without my bucket's night vision, all I see is mottled shades of darkness. The moonlight hits only the tops of the valley walls, casting inky shadows, like pitch on black. I have no idea what's down there.

"Not a wink," I answer, aware of the steaming puffs of breath that escape with each word. "Figured I'd come over and see what our final battle plan is shaping up to be."

Wraith tucks his mags back into his belt compartment. "That depends on where our koobs set up. If they lead the charge, I'm content to send the sleds in and station legionnaires along the walls. Deliver plunging fields of fire."

"That's a big 'if,' Captain."

"Don't I know it."

Footsteps approach, packaged with the soft back and forth of conversation. One speaker is using koob-accented Standard, the other the low external output of a leej helmet.

I turn to Wraith. "Sounds like Devers and the chieftain are coming. We'll have an answer soon enough."

Captain Devers strides into our midst with Kreggak at his side. Two koob bodyguards, specimens of strength compared to the average of their species, flank the Moona chieftain.

Devers looks from me to Wraith, as if inspecting us both. "Chieftain Kreggak says that the attack will commence at sunrise."

I exchange a look with Captain Ford, wondering if he'll take umbrage at Devers's attempt to place command of the operation in the three-fingered hands of a koob. But Wraith simply nods, crosses his arms, and asks, "What will the attack entail?"

Pleased by this, Kreggak swells his air sac. "Moona *Kublakaren* are to use the artillery. *K'kik.* We shoot from truckas. Leejon-ayers drive in when big blasts stop and many big die from tribe Annek. Kill rest of Annek warriors."

Holding out a hand plaintively, Wraith says, "We're more than capable of destroying the enemy. What will Moona's role be during the legionnaire assault?"

Kreggak licks his left eye with his tongue. "Moona stay here. Kill Annek that maybe flee away."

Wraith nods. "Sounds like everything is all figured out." He turns to face me. "Lieutenant Chhun, the sun will be up soon. Get the men ready."

As I turn to carry out the order, Captain Devers speaks up. "So, we'll follow Chieftain Kreggak's battle plan, then?"

Ignoring the question, Wraith asks Devers one of his own. "Will you be participating in the legionnaire assault, Captain?"

This *should* be rhetorical. If you're a legionnaire, you fight regardless of rank. The sole exception is the combat command team, and most of the time even they are in the thick of things. Our combat command, Wraith and Sergeant Powell, would both rather be in the fight. I promise.

"Well, I..." Devers begins. "Yes. Of course. I *could*. It's just, I feel that someone should remain at the top of the valley."

"I agree," says Wraith.

"You do?"

"I do. I need to be in the fight." Wraith points down to the valley. "I can lead better down there, from the front. You should stay up here as a liaison to Kreggak."

"Right," an enthusiastic Devers concurs.

Wraith inclines his head. "To be clear, that's *not* a combat control position."

"No, of course not." Devers is quick in his agreement.

"Good," nods Wraith. "I think we're all set."

The rising sun's first rays shine golden at the top of the two spires framing the valley. I stand with Doomsday Squad. Wraith and Specter Squad are positioned at the far end of the valley, waiting by an anchored sled to use quick-drop ropes to reach the floor. The heavy ropes—impervisteel cables, really—are attached to our own sled as well, and hang down to a short ledge just above the valley's bottom. The rest of the sleds are positioned around the koob trucks, ready to move down the rough road, but just as ready to open up on the koobs of Moona Village if they're thinking of a double-cross.

Captain Devers's voice comes over the comm. "Chieftain Kreggak is prepared to begin the *Kublakaren* artillery barrage."

I notice he uses the koobs' own term—*Kublakaren*.

"Acknowledged," replies Wraith. "Doomsday-1, confirm your squad is ready."

"Confirmed." I don't even need to look back at my men, coiled behind me like a serpent. Waiting for the order to perform a lethal strike.

"Copy. Have visual confirmation from Specter-1, Specter Squad is ready." Wraith's voice is calm, like a doctor explaining some terminal illness. "Captain Devers, inform Kreggak that he is cleared to begin the assault. Vic-1 out."

A pause settles over the comm before Kreggak's voice rumbles across the channel. "We are now to begin."

I clench my jaw at this abuse of the L-comm.

A koob in the truck nearest to me bellows—a deep, croaking noise. The call is taken up throughout the Kublaren line—a primitive comm system—and echoes into the valley.

Just when I start to think that the noise is going to rouse the sleeping koobs below, a barrage of koob artillery booms. Now, this isn't the big stuff shot from the hemispherical guns or down from the destroyers in orbit. When a koob talks about artillery, they mean manually fired mortar charges.

To his credit, Kreggak brought a lot of them. The beds of the koob trucks are continually firing from stacks of rounds supplied by warriors on the ground. It's obvious that the aliens are comfortable with this sort of weaponry, and I wouldn't be surprised to hear that it's the preferred weapon for attacking rival tribes.

The bombs drop onto the village as sunlight drives away the lingering shadows. Compared to Moona, what I'm seeing go up in explosive flames below is practically civilized. There's a mix of permacrete and natural stone buildings, a basic street grid, even a fountain surrounded by a grassy commons. It makes sense. If Annek tribe is better off financially, that would explain how they acquired the tech and surplus they hit us with yesterday. But it's all going to hell for them as the morning's judgment continues.

Most of the koobs aren't leaving their homes. That's the smart strategy. The few who run outside in panic are blown apart as Kreggak's barrage grows in fiery intensity. The assault is relentless, and the valley is soon shrouded in smoke and dust from the collapsing buildings. There may not be a koob left alive for the Legion to deal with.

Fire is followed by fire, explosion after explosion, like some angry cosmic god bringing its hammer down upon an anvil. The legionnaires around me aren't talking. They just watch as buildings crumble and dust clouds mingle with fireballs and black smoke. I would've called a stop to the firing long before now. But it's not my call, and the koobs are in a near frenzy. I don't think they'll quit until there are no more bombs left to drop.

"So… why couldn't these guys just do this without us?" Exo asks over the squad comm. It's the same question I'm thinking. "Because ain't no way the koobs down there survive that."

"Let's wait and see," I answer.

The wait ends up being pretty short. The final trickle of koob mortars ends with a last *whump*. The valley doesn't go silent for even a moment. The instant the last mortar hits, our squad's automatic blasters lay down fire from the valley peaks.

Amazingly, a staccato of machine gun fire barks angrily up at us.

Twenties, standing close by, says, "Holy hell, they're shooting at us. What's the move, Lieutenant? Want me to find a spot to take some shots?"

"We wait on Wraith's command, then we all go down together. Overwatch is being left to the sleds and basics."

I'm not looking forward to quick-roping to the bottom with this sort of projectile fire coming our way. Still, I can't help but be impressed with the Annek tribe's resiliency.

Kreggak rumbles over our headsets. "You leejon-ayers all go down now. This is way of custom and friendship. Moona tribe will wait and stop Annek who flee this way."

Flee up the walls of a valley? That's not passing my think-test.

The chieftain's voice is followed by Wraith's. "All right. Doomsday and Specter Squads to the ropes. Get down fast and clear out that village. Sled Team Silver, remain up top."

A muted croaking comes over the comm, then Captain Devers's voice. "Captain Ford, Kreggak believes all the sleds should join in the assault so that Annek is without time to escape."

"Not happening, Devers. I want a force to remain up here. Tell Kreggak he can drive his trucks down if he wants vehicular support."

More croaking, of a distinctly more aggravated sort.

"Captain Ford," Devers pleads across the open comm. "The chieftain just supplied us with substantial artillery support. To ask him to now lead the vanguard is too much."

With a crisp, measured cadence, Wraith says, "I'm not asking Kreggak to do anything. Legionnaires will lead the way. He can stay or come along. Our sleds aren't moving. Specter Squad, get down those ropes. Lieutenant Chhun, deploy Doomsday Squad!"

"Let's go, Doomsday! Drop and pop!"

My legionnaires grab hold of the cables and zip down to the valley floor three at a time, relying on their grips to keep the fall controlled; synthprene gloves are tough enough to prevent the cable from eating your hand raw, but you feel the friction increase all the way down. The koob machine-gun fire from below is pelting the rocks around the descending legionnaires. Leej armor and quick-ropes are tough enough to withstand a slug thrower, but my concern is over one of my guys getting dinged too many times and losing his grip. Even with armor, they wouldn't walk away from that kind of fall.

"This," bellows Kreggak into the comm, "is insult to Moona!" He spouts off a string of gurgles and croaks.

"Chieftain," a panicky Devers is picked up over an open comm, "this is a misunderstanding. The Republic appreciates the great service you've performed and in no way wishes to diminish our great alliance. Silver Team, this is Vic-2. I want all sleds moving into that valley, now!"

Doc Quigs is the first to push back. "I'm not sending any med-sleds into a combat zone."

I quickly join in. "I've got legionnaires swinging from Silver-4. I'd rather it not move."

Wraith settles the matter with finality. "No sleds will move unless I give the order. And if any of you basics go against that order, I'll have you running a legionnaire gauntlet."

The sleds stay put.

Half my team is in the valley and forming assault groups on the entrenched koob survivors by the time I hear the koob trucks start up.

"Captain Ford!" Devers shouts over the comm. "You're causing a galactic incident. I'm ordering you to apologize to Chieftain Kreggak and get these sleds cleared out!"

"I assume you mean *respectfully suggest* and not *order*. Refused—there's a war on. Vic-1 out."

Sergeant Powell's voice cuts in before Devers has the opportunity to further muck up protocol. "Specter-1 to Doomsday-1, Specter Squad is fully deployed and engaging a preliminary line of hostiles. ETA to center rendezvous... eight minutes."

"Copy," I say. Blazing smokes, Specter Squad is fast. I've got five men, myself included, still waiting to get on the quick-ropes.

The Moona trucks, loaded thick with Kublaren warriors, begin to turn around and drive away.

"They're *leaving!*" There's desperation in Captain Devers's voice. "Do you have any idea what you've done? What the impact of failing to secure Moona—"

Wraith cuts him off. "Maintain comm discipline. Lieutenant, send a pair of leejes to keep an eye on those koobs."

"Twenties! Maldorn!" I call, shooting out my hand to get the legionnaires' attention and bring them away from their place at the quick-ropes. The soldiers leave their ropes and report. "Follow those koobs, but stay out of sight."

The legionnaires move stealthily in pursuit as I grab the last quick-rope and drop into the valley.

14

I can tell even before my feet hit the ground that something has happened. Doomsday Squad is in a defensive position, trading fire with a koob machine gun emplacement. We should have made more progress than this. Something is holding us up.

My boots hit with a thud and I take off running toward the rest of the squad. Bullets snap around my head. Not wanting a new hole between my eyes, I throw myself into a pile of rubble next to a leej who's watching the squad's flank.

"What's the holdup?" I ask in panting breaths.

Masters shouts out an answer. "Guffer fell off the ropes!" Already having a casualty, combined with the adrenaline of the battle, has him all wired up.

I crawl over and see the legionnaire lying on the ground with two others working over him. He looks in bad shape: his right leg is at a ninety-degree angle and his shoulder is clearly separated and caught beneath his body. If he's alive, he's going to need a cycler and confinement to the med-sled.

"You two!" I shout to the legionnaires attending to Guffer. "Do your best to stabilize him until the basics can send down a litter for him."

The rest of the squad look to me for orders. I survey the battlefield as the koob machine gun spews in our general direction. There's a channel between piles of rubble—probably was the center of a narrow alley before the buildings around it collapsed. If we stay low, we might be able to flank the machine gun nest undetected. "Masters, you're with me. We're moving through there to get at the nest. Staying undetected is key, so I want the rest of you to stay in place, watch your angles, and keep them busy with suppressing fire."

Keeping low, I move quickly through the rubble and debris. My nose is clogging with the thick, lingering dust of the collapsed stone buildings. That might not be such a bad thing. Judging by the number of Kublaren appendages I see half buried and blown to pieces, the dust is filtering the fishy scent of alien gore. I bury questions of how many of these dead koobs are Annek warriors and how many are women and hatchlings—not that those are any less deadly.

My heart pounding, I hold up a clenched fist to signal a halt. Masters and I are hidden by the shadow of a six-meter pile of rubble that used to be a two-story stone structure. The steady *brrrp! brrp! brrp!* of the machine gun nest is louder and closer. I judge from the intensity of noise that the koobs are up on the opposite side of the crumbled structure.

"What's the game plan?" Masters whispers over our comm channel. "My HUD shows about five koobs spotted in the nest. All yellow, so they might have spread out..."

I look to the top of the pile of debris hiding us from the enemy gunners. "I'm climbing to the top of this mound. I want you to swing around behind the koobs as a diversion. Stay covered, keep safe. I'll open up on them from above once you grab their attention. Questions?"

"No, Lieutenant."

Masters moves to the end of the debris pile and cautiously crosses a cobblestone intersection as he heads deeper behind the enemy. I look for sturdy hand- and footholds. It takes a while, as the stone fragments tumble down around me. Finally I see an exposed wooden beam and reach up to grab it. It doesn't give as I pull my weight up. I climb the rest of the way as fast as I dare, thankful for the echoes of blaster and machine gun fire that drown out the clattering of loose stone from my ascent.

When I reach the summit, I lie on my belly, trusting in luck that all this rock isn't resting on top of a ground floor that might go crashing down into a basement at any moment.

"Masters," I pant, "I'm all set up. You ready?"

"I can see the nest, but I don't have eyes on any koob targets. I'm gonna toss a fragger inside, so keep low."

"Copy. Go for fragger."

I hug the broken stones beneath me and wait. The machine gun fire abruptly stops, replaced by frantic koob yelling. The fragger explodes, my cue to pop up. I jump to my feet and aim my N-4 down into the nest. The grenade only caught one koob; the rest spill outside and are just now getting up from their cover. I rain down blaster fire, dropping three koobs before one breaks away.

The survivor moves out of my line of fire, running in Masters's general direction. "Squirter coming your way," I announce.

"Copy."

I see a glimpse of the koob just as it reaches an intersection. My rifle is at my shoulder when I see a burst of blaster fire shoot down the avenue and eat up the alien's back.

"Koob down," Masters calls out.

"Gather at the MG nest," I call into our squad channel.

Masters meets me there as I slide down the pile of debris. The nest wasn't pre-planned, just a hollowed mound in the destruction that lent itself to a good firing point.

It's eerily quiet on this side of the village. The only sound reaching us is a firefight between the koobs and Specter Squad way over in the eastern half. I'm guessing the majority of surviving koobs rallied to where the legionnaires made their first push.

"Doomsday, we need to push in until we join up with Specter. Masters and I will move ahead on point, while the rest of you catch up. What's the status on Guffer?"

"Dead, Lieutenant."

I clench my jaw. "Copy."

Masters and I move out of the machine gun nest and into the war-torn streets, stepping over split stones and shattered body parts. We've advanced perhaps a thousand meters when the distant shooting comes to a stop. I key in Wraith.

"Doomsday-1 to Vic-1. Enemy cleared in west village. Moving element to join Specter Squad."

"Copy," answers Wraith. "Enemy cleared in east village. I think that's going to be most of the koob force, but keep your eyes open for snipers and stragglers."

"Will do. Doomsday-1 out."

We patrol in silence, save the crunch of rubble beneath our boots. Masters looks behind us and whispers, "I can see Rook and Exo back there. Main force is catching up."

I nod.

"Lieutenant, I think we got them all. I think—"

A koob comes running from around a corner, dangerously close to Masters. "Leej—" it begins to scream. I double-tap the trigger of my N-4 and send two blaster bolts into its chest. The alien drops face first into the street.

"Oh, shi—" Masters straightens himself, cutting himself off. "T-twice. Lieutenant... that's *twice* you saved me."

His voice is jittery. The kid's shaken up. But I'm too busy watching for more koobs and thinking about the one I just dusted. I'm not an expert on Kublaren physiology or expressions by any stretch, but something about the way that koob looked while it was yelling... was off. I've seen angry koobs. This one seemed... different. I don't see a weapon anywhere close to the body.

"Everything okay?" Exo calls out.

"Yeah," I answer. "Lone koob. I think—"

"Stop firing!" Another figure clambers into view. I spin to meet the surprise and watch as a burst of uncontrolled blaster fire eats into its target. "Stop fi—"

My stomach drops.

Masters holds his smoking blaster rifle in shock for a moment, then drops it clattering onto the ground. He rips off his helmet and throws up his morning rations.

"Friendlies in the combat zone!" I yell over L-comm. "Use extreme fire discipline. Repeat, friendlies in the combat zone!"

I rush over to the woman Masters just killed. She's Republic. Wearing the white jumper of a planetary scientist. I have no idea why she'd be here, but the evidence is right before my eyes.

"Oba." Masters walks up next to me. His face is pale and sickly. "Lieutenant, I—she just... jumped up. I thought she was a koob."

"Vic-1 to Doomsday-1. What's going on over there?"

"Captain Ford," I say into my comm, "I have a confirmed kill here. Human female wearing Republic-issue planetary science gear. We thought she was Kublaren. Thinking she must have been a captive."

"Copy. All squads. Exercise extreme caution. Koobs *will* use hostages as personal shields in a firefight."

Exo and Rook come running forward, leading the rest of the squad.

"What the hell happened here?" Exo says on arrival. "Who dusted the chick?"

Masters, who is sitting on a pile of stones, buries his head deeper into his hands. "I thought she was koob."

"War zone in the middle of a firefight," I say evenly. "It happens. Keep your head straight."

All the helmeted legionnaires swing their blaster rifles toward the area the woman and koob appeared from. My ears catch up later and hear a heavy tromping of footsteps at a run. "Easy," I caution.

A bearded man bursts from around the corner. He's wearing the same uniform as the woman. He looks at us, stunned, as though his mind doesn't comprehend why legionnaires would be in the middle of this. His eyes move to the woman.

"Kalla!" The scientist runs over to the woman's body and drops to his knees. He cradles her in his arms and presses his head close to hers. He's crying. "Kalla... Kalla."

I approach him tentatively, motioning for Rook to come as well. "Sir, I'm Lieutenant Cohen Chhun, Thirty-First Legion, Victory Company. I need you to go with this legionnaire so he can get you to safety."

"Kalla..." the man moans. He looks up at me, tears in his eyes. "My wife. She's dead."

"I know that, sir, and I am sorry. Truly. But this village belongs to a hostile tribe, and we need to keep you out of enemy hands. Are there any more prisoners?"

"Prisoners?" The man's reply is distant, like he heard the word in a dream. He furrows his brow a moment and then begins to stroke the face of his deceased wife.

"Okay, Rook, pick him up and escort him to the drop zone. We've got to clear out whatever's left of this village."

Rook reaches down and takes the man by his arm. "C'mon, here we go."

"No!" The scientist wrenches his arm away and clings to his wife. "I'm not leaving Kalla. I'm not going anywhere!"

"Get your hands off him!"

The voice comes from another human female. Younger than the man and his wife—not much older than the legionnaires around me. She, too, is dressed in the white jumpsuit of a planetary scientist. Was some sort of survey team captured?

She strides fearlessly into our heavily armed midst and stands in front of the weeping man. "Not one of you trigger jockeys puts a hand on him."

This is something we don't have time for.

"Look, miss," I say, doing my best to sound even and diplomatic. "I appreciate your wanting to protect your friend right now, but we're here to help."

She gestures at the village. "Help? You call this *help*? You call shooting Kalla *help*?"

Wraith's voice comes over the comm. "Lieutenant Chhun, what's your ETA?"

"Found another survivor, Captain."

The woman stands up, anger hot in her eyes. "No thanks to you bucket-heads."

Wraith picks up the comment. "Sounds like something is up. I'm bringing Specter over your way. Find out what's going on."

"Copy." I turn to the woman. "I'm Lieutenant Cohen Chhun. The legionnaires with me are part of a diplomatic element seeking to gain support for Republic Senator Greggorak of the tribe Innik. We were attacked by hostile warriors from this village. We're not here to hurt you, Miss…"

The woman stares off into the distance as though she's deep in thought. She shakes her head, causing a dirt-matted ponytail to leave a dry trail of dust. Her anger transforms into what I would call a reserved hostility. "Andien," she says, and I can tell it's only out of a forced sense of shared duty to the Republic that she even gets the name out. "You can call me..." but she doesn't finish the thought. "Which tribe, exactly, controls this village, Lieutenant?" she asks.

I hesitate. "The... Annek tribe. They're in league with the Mid-Core Rebellion. We came here to destroy their base of operations before they could launch further strikes against the Republic. This was their tribal seat."

There's a quiet moment when all that can be heard is the quiet cries of the man over his wife.

Andien erupts.

"Is that what you think? Well, you're *wrong*, and I can't even tell you how many beings are dead because of it!"

"What's she talkin' about, LT?" Exo asks.

"I'll *tell* you what I'm talking about. Yes, this is an Annek village, but it's not a tribal seat. The Annek elders are at least thirty kilometers away. This village is—*was*—a site designated by Senator Greggorak for a small team of Republic scientists to work on a plan to develop Kublar's natural resources. And now they're all dead. Dead!"

A part of me desperately hopes this is just a rebel who's taken possession of some surplus uniforms. But with the way we were able to roll up without being noticed, and Kreggak's behavior when we refused to commit our entire element into this death trap of a valley... I know where this is headed.

"Look," I begin. But I'm at a loss. "I don't... I need to call this in, okay?"

"A fat lot of good that will do."

I don't take the time to reply, walking off and keying in my comm for Captain Ford instead. "Doomsday-1 to Vic-1," I say into the private channel.

"What's up, Lieutenant?"

"Sir, we have a major problem on our hands here. Survivor is claiming to be a Republic scientist working on a project per Senator Greggorak's orders. She's claiming that this is not the Annek tribal seat. I thought we were the only ones the Republic sent to the planet."

"That was my understanding. Let me check with Captain Devers. Wraith out."

I turn back to find Rook kneeling, his head tilted to one side as if listening.

"What's going on?" I ask.

"Shh." Rook places a finger against his helmet, shushing me. "I think I hear someone in the rubble. Trying to dig out."

We all stand stock still before another legionnaire says, "I hear it, too."

Andien turns slowly on her heels, looking at the rubble around her. "This is where most of us were sleeping before the attacks came."

"It's coming from right beneath me," Rook announces.

I set my N-4 down against a pile of tumbled stone and timber. "Okay, I want three guns on the perimeter. Everybody else, dig."

15

The pile of cracked stones and debris I've stacked up beside me is almost as tall as I am, but Exo swears he can still hear someone beneath the ruins, so we keep prying away more pieces of shattered buildings. My fingers feel raw even with the protection of my synthprene gloves. My shoulders ache with each new deadlift and heave. But we're making progress. Specter Squad cleared the village and has joined in the recovery.

I'm worried about Masters, though. He's sitting on a mound of sand-colored bricks, staring off at nothing. The kid hasn't said more than two words to anyone.

Wraith takes a seat next to him. "Tough day."

Masters looks at Wraith, then down at the small piece of rubble in his hands. "Yes, sir."

"Remember your training. These things happen, and it's a shame, but don't let it get in your head." Wraith stands and kicks a brick off the pile. "We're not out of this by any stretch. I need you focused on keeping the men around you alive, and not on the ones it's too late for."

Masters manages to look at the new widower. He still hasn't left his wife's side. I'm not sure a part of his brain didn't crack, to be honest.

"Understood, Captain." Masters stands up as well. "I'll be ready. I just... just needed some time to think."

Wraith nods and walks to me. I straighten my back and feel the vertebrae pop. My arms fall slack, and I'm thankful for the opportunity to rest them. We walk a few meters away, not wanting to be overheard.

"What did Captain Devers say?" I ask. "Did he know there were Republic scientists set up here?"

"Not *here*. He didn't know where the place was. But he knew the Senate sent in a group of scientists to convince the Kublarens to start getting some of the planet's natural resources into the trade lanes even before they're formally brought into the Republic."

"And?"

Wraith sighs. "This was avoidable. But I don't think Devers is worried about anything other than the Moona koobs leaving."

I look back at the surviving female scientist—Andien. She's still pulling away whatever her slender arms can lift. Her hands are bleeding from the effort. "So these Rep scientists. Wrong place, wrong time? Chain of command just forget to look out for them?"

Wraith looks down. "As difficult as it might be to hear, that's what I'm hoping. The alternative doesn't bode well."

There's a flurry of motion at the dig site. Shouts of excitement begin to relay from one helmeted voice to the next. "That's a leg!"

The speed of the dig intensifies as the legionnaires find a new reserve of strength.

"C'mon," Wraith says before sprinting toward the pile. He's already pulling away rocks by the time I'm halfway.

"Quigs." I call the medic, still up top and seeing to the wounded in the converted sleds. "We might have a few wounded to bring up to the med-sleds."

"Copy, Lieutenant." There's a hint of exasperation in his voice that even the comm can't hide. I can't blame him. This op has been a disaster, and as hard as we've fought, I think he's worked twice as hard to keep the wounded alive. I doubt he's slept since we left Camp Forge. "I'll try to make some room. Things are tight, though."

"Understood."

The legionnaires pull what is obviously a lifeless body out of the pile. Another Republic scientist. Andien turns away and begins to cry bitterly. I fight back a sense of helplessness, replaying the events that have brought us to this point.

"I still hear something, though." Exo is insistent. He's still digging. "Nothin's changed, man. I hear 'em."

"Yeah," Wraith agrees, scooping up an armful of splintered timbers. "I hear it too."

I spring up the pile to the work site and join in. We pull everything away until we uncover a solid wood door. It's featureless, any handles or fasteners sheared away in the village's collapse.

Thump. Thump.

Even I can hear that.

As many legionnaires as can fit in the excavation site are working. Gone is the reckless tossing of stones. Each handful is picked up deliberately and delicately handed over to waiting hands, removing it from the site. We're close, and the last thing we want to do is further injure whoever's under us.

More of the wooden door is revealed. We try to lift it up, but it isn't budging. Exo leans down and knocks on it. "Hey, can you hear me?"

Every legionnaire falls silent.

A muffled shout cries, "Help us!"

Again we try to lift the door, but it won't budge.

"How many are trapped beneath?" Exo calls out.

There's no answer.

"Dig around the door," Wraith commands, pointing at the crushed stone along the edges of the door.

Debris is pulled away, legionnaires following orders they didn't need to hear issued. We want whoever is under there out—alive. Chunks of solid stone are unearthed and sent tumbling down the pile, when suddenly the heap we're standing on shifts. We drop an inch, losing our balance. There's a muffled scream from behind the door.

"Hold up!" Exo shouts. "Stop the digging! We can't let it crush 'em."

"Let's think this through, guys," I say.

My comm beeps, indicating a secure channel message. "Go for Doomsday-1."

"Lieutenant, it's Twenties." His voice is subdued, like he's purposefully keeping it down, speaking just above a whisper. "Y'all need to roll out. There's a shit storm brewing."

"Hang tight." I clench my jaw and motion for Wraith. "Captain Ford, I've got the recon team on comm. He says there's trouble."

"Patch me in. What's his call sign?"

I key Wraith in. "Doomsday-4."

Wraith nods. "Doomsday-4, this is Vic-1. Report."

"Copy, Vic-1. We followed the koobs' trucks out through the plains. Found a good spot here on a cliff ledge. They've met up with another force. Big one."

That doesn't sound good at all.

"What are they doing?" Wraith asks.

"Nothing right now. The chieftain, the one who rode with Captain Devers, is talking with what looks to me like another chieftain. But, sir, this looks like a war party if I ever saw one. Every koob out there is armed to the air sac. It doesn't take an intelligence officer to figure out that they're talking about heading back to the valley."

I share a look with Wraith and know we're both thinking the same thing. The Moona koobs set this up. They took advantage of Devers's succeed-at-any-cost attitude and got us to stand by while they destroyed a friendly village. If it weren't for Wraith's refusal to send the sleds down, I have no doubt they would have dropped bombs right on our heads. This must be the backup plan: get a force large enough to try and overpower us in an open fight.

"We need to get out of here and back to Camp Forge," I tell Wraith.

He nods his approval.

"Twenties, hustle back here. Leave a peeper at your position to feed the holo into your HUD. We're gonna want to know when they roll out."

"Copy. You sure you don't want me to take a shot while I've got one? We've got some distance, but I know I can get a kill shot on at least one of the chieftains."

I look to Wraith. He shakes his head.

"Negative," I say. "We need legionnaires more than dead chieftains right now, and I'm not convinced you won't get yourself killed if you take that shot. Get back to the sleds. We won't roll out without you."

"Copy. Doomsday-4 out. See you soon."

The captain and I walk toward the legionnaires still examining the buried door. Wraith points a finger at Rook, then hitches his thumb toward Andien. "Get her to the sleds. We're going to do everything we can to dig out whoever's underneath in the time we have left, but understand that it's short."

"C'mon," Rook says, taking the scientist by her arm.

She struggles, but not much, pulling away from being manhandled more than out of a desire to stay.

"We need to get you to our sleds," Rook explains, holding out his hand in a much more gentlemanly approach. "There isn't a lot of time."

She looks around pensively, her eyes at chest height with the legionnaires around her. She nods, then looks to her grieving colleague. "What about Ontash?"

I step in and speak quietly, though the way he's moaning, I doubt he's aware of anything beyond his own pain. "If we try to pull him away now, he's only going to scream and fight. We need to focus on digging the survivors out before we run out of time. We'll carry him off when we're ready to go, okay?"

This seems to satisfy Andien. She walks with Rook and another leej toward the cliffs.

"Have Doc Quigs check her out when you get up top," I call after them. To the rest of the legionnaires I say, "Let's figure out a way to rescue these survivors."

"How about cutting through the wood?" Exo suggests.

I shake my head. "Cutting torch will cook whoever's on the other side. Something else."

Masters has his koob sword in hand. "Let's do it the old-fashioned way: chip and whittle away the wood until we can punch through."

I nod. The other leejes pull out their vibro-knives and begin the delicate task of carving up the heavy door.

"Vic-1 to Silver-1." Wraith is back on the comm. "I need all sleds ready for evacuation. No big hurry, I'm talking parsecs."

"Copy, Vic-1," comes the command sled's reply.

Parsecs. Not a measurement of time. Legionnaires use the term to mean double-quick. Wraith is subtly telling the drivers to prepare to leave *now* without coming right out and saying it. This is why we don't share our comms with anyone. We've got to assume all L-comm and open transmissions are being listened in on.

"What's this about?" Devers asks. "Why are we leaving?"

"Maintain comm discipline," Wraith says. "We're done down here, so I just don't want to waste time. Village is clear."

"That means combat operations are over," answers Devers. "I assume command in that case. We're not going anywhere. We need to stay put and hope that Chieftain

Kreggak finds it in his character to come back to us, even though we insulted him. Silver Team, stand down."

"Do *not* stand down," countermanded Wraith. "Get those sleds ready to move like your life depends on it."

I don't know how much more obvious things need to be for Devers to catch on.

My comm beeps again, the same secure channel as before. "Go ahead, Twenties."

"Lieutenant!" Twenties in gasping into the comm, and it's clear he and his partner are in a full run. "Peeper shows the koobs moving out. Something made them scramble real quick. You need to get the sleds out of there!"

"Copy. Get back as quick as possible." I turn to the legionnaires hacking at the thick door. "Time to go! Koobs are inbound." I point to the grieving scientist. "Grab him and let's go."

"We can't leave whoever's under here!" Exo says. He begins carving out the wood at a near reckless pace, thick splinters flying everywhere. Masters is working even more frantically, bringing his koob sword down with such force that I'm worried he'll break through and kill the survivors.

But Exo is right. We can't leave whoever's under this pile to suffocate. I remember the tomahawk on my belt, and I use it to help in cutting away. We're like mad men, savagely attacking the door. "Everyone else get to the sleds! We'll break through and catch up."

Wraith stands by for a moment, then repeats my order. "Okay, legionnaires. Let's go."

I hear the bearded man struggle and shout as he's pulled away from his dead wife. It's only the three of us at the excavation site now: Masters, Exo, and me. My arms are so tired that I wonder if I'm doing anything beyond raising my tomahawk in the air and letting gravity bring the blade down into the wood.

We haven't heard any sounds since the earlier cry for help. I'm worried something has collapsed inside.

Finally, a small hole appears.

"We're through!" I shout.

Masters widens the hole with his sword, then peers inside. "Republican Legion!" he calls. "Where are you?" He pauses, then pops his head back up. "I heard a moan, but I can't see anything." He turns on his ultrabeam and shines it into the hole. "Wait! I see movement."

We cut and pry apart pieces of the wood door until we've got a hole big enough to pull someone through.

I can now see three partially buried bodies. I reach down and grab an arm. We pull out the corpse of a Kublaren.

"Too late for her," Exo observes.

We set the dead alien aside and go back into the breach. I grab another arm and follow it to the armpit. It's a woman. "Help me pull her out."

Masters squats down, and together we pull another Republic scientist out of the narrow opening. She's disoriented, her face and hair thick with gray dust.

"Can you walk?" I ask, snapping my fingers to get her attention.

"Help us..." The woman's voice is weak and fragile. It's the same voice that cried out earlier. She seems almost completely out of it. She stands, then cries out in pain, collapsing into Masters's arms.

Wraith's voice comes over the comm. "Lieutenant, get your men out of that valley. Advanced sled says the koobs will be here in minutes."

"There's still one more down there," Exo says, looking from the mound of debris to the sleds on top of the hill.

"Help Masters get her to the sleds," I say. "I'll grab the other one, and if they're alive, I'll carry them."

My men hesitate.

"Go!"

They take off.

The rocks slip around us, and the debris pile shifts. I look back in the opening and can no longer see the third person. I poke my head and shoulders through the door into the cavity. I move brick and stone frantically until my hand wraps around a slender wrist. My first thought is that this is another koob. But when I squeeze the hand, five small fingers wrap around my glove.

Gripping the hand, I start to pull, but it doesn't budge, and a scream of pain makes my ears ring. It's not the scream of a man or a woman—more like a girl.

I crawl in farther and feel the mound of debris tremble from my shifting weight. Groping in the dark, I remember my ultrabeam and switch it on. I see the bloodied face of a child, maybe twelve years old. Perhaps she's some scientist's daughter.

"Lieutenant Chhun." Wraith's voice is still calm, but I know that he wants me on the sleds. "It's time to leave. Right now."

"Almost got her, Captain."

I begin to dig away the stones and lumber around her. She's buried up past her waist. The pile rumbles some more.

I grab her arms and pull. She moves, but not without more agonized screams. I keep pulling, feeling her come loose from the death trap that is this destroyed building. She screams the entire time. But at last she's through the door and I'm cradling her in my arms.

I run down the rubble pile, stopping only to grab my blaster rifle and sling it around my shoulder. The girl doesn't seem to weigh anything. But it's obvious that she's in tremendous pain. She's crying and shouting for pain with every jarring step I take.

"It's okay," I say, trying to soothe her as we sprint toward the sled pickup zone. She cries out, and I repeat the words like a mantra. Like somehow just saying it will make it true. "It's okay. It's okay. It's okay."

I hold her close, whispering the words in her ear. Her screams have become quiet moans. I steal a glance at her face. She's pale, and doesn't seem to have the strength to do anything but remain cradled in my arms. For the first time I see that where her leg ought to be is a twisted stump of flesh with a bone sticking clear. My armor is painted red with her blood.

"It's okay," I lie. "You'll be okay."

I reach the line dangling from a sled waiting for me at the top of the valley's walls. I clip it to my belt and grab hold of it with one arm, holding the girl with the other. She doesn't make any more noises as the sled pulls us up out of the valley.

Up top, I look for Doc Quigs. He's just finished closing up a med-sled. "One more!" I shout. "I've got one more."

Quigs runs over to me. He's staring at the girl. Staring at my armor. Gently he removes the girl from my arms. "She's gone, Lieutenant."

I stand there, covered in this innocent girl's blood. Wondering how it came to be that her life came to an end in my arms on some God-forsaken planet at galaxy's edge.

Doc lays the girl on the ground, then puts a hand on my shoulder. "You did what you could. We need to go."

"Lieutenant!" Exo calls to me from the open ramp of a nearby sled. "Let's go, man! We gotta go!"

I climb on board and close the ramp behind me.

16

My sled is filled almost to capacity. Every seat is taken, and a basic is manning the turret—the same kid we rode with before the ambush. Most of my squad is inside. Exo and Rook are by the back ramp and Masters is next to the partition, sitting next to Andien. The scientist is staring at me—no, not me. She's staring at the still-wet blood staining my armor.

"Did Twenties and Maldorn make it back to the sleds?" I ask.

"Don't know," Rook replies. "Hope so."

"Doomsday-1 to Doomsday-4, what's your status?" I use the same secure channel Twenties called me on, but get no reply.

Exo shifts in his seat. "The drivers relayed a message that no one is allowed to use the L-comm. So unless he's still on the private channel... I mean, if he's running, he ain't gonna have time to key in another frequency."

I nod. We haven't left the site yet, and I don't want to leave any leejes behind. I hail Wraith on our private channel. "Captain Ford, have Doomsday-4 and Doomsday-8 returned from overwatch?"

"Negative," Wraith replies.

"Sir, request permission to remain on site until their arrival." I look at my legionnaires in the sled. They're ready to get out and walk home if that's what it takes to keep from leaving a buddy behind.

"Granted. I already ordered the bulk of the force to return to Camp Forge. Our two sleds will stay back and wait for overwatch as long as possible." The partition screen in our sled lights up with a holofeed from a deployed TT-16 observation bot. "We're tracking their progress now. It looks like it'll be close."

Twenties and Maldorn are running all-out across a rocky terrain littered with scrub. A division of koob trucks is driving hard after them, though I don't think they actually see the legionnaires—no way the koobs wouldn't shoot if they thought someone was out in front of them. The runners disappear into a small forest with a deep, almost blue, canopy of leaves.

The bot approximates the distance to the sled. They should be here in a few minutes. The koob force will be right on top of them, though.

We all wait, eyes fixed on the aerial view of the forest. They should be clear by now. The holocam hovers at the break in the trees where the legionnaires are expected to emerge.

"Why aren't they coming out?" Exo asks.

"Rough terrain, injury—maybe a broken ankle..." Rook says.

Exo gives him a look.

"What? You asked!"

The readouts on the screen now give the Kublaren vehicles an earlier ETA than our legionnaires. The first trucks have entered the forest, which apparently is not as dense as it looks from above. I chew on my lip and stare at the holoscreen, trying to get Twenties and Maldorn out of that forest by the force of my will.

"One more minute and we've gotta go," Wraith announces over my comm.

Gritting my teeth, I stare at the holoscreen.

Two gray armored legionnaires bust out of the undergrowth and run from the tree line. "There they are!"

"They'll never make it," Rook says, swapping out a charge pack on his N-4 all the same. "Those trucks are gonna be on top of them in no time."

As more vehicles enter the forest under the gaze of the TT-16 bot, a fiery light erupts in the midst of the trees accompanied by a tremendous boom. A cloud of black smoke mushrooms from the woods.

So that's what was taking Twenties and Maldorn so long.

"Drop doors!" Wraith orders.

We lower our ramps to see Twenties and Maldorn running all-out toward us, fire and flames behind them. We're about a half kilometer from the trees. Legionnaires take up firing positions from inside the sled, waiting for the trucks.

One of the white vehicles rolls out from among the trees, its wheels burning and its occupants dead or missing. It's rolling forward on sheer momentum. The second truck to come through is a different story. The white vehicle bounces across the terrain, a koob gunner struggling to keep his place in the bed behind a heavy machine gun.

"Contact!" calls out our gunner.

Dat-dat-dat-dat!

Both sleds send rapid fire over the incoming legionnaires' heads and into the koob truck. The vehicle swerves in an attempt to avoid being hit, sending the gunner in the truck bed tumbling over the side. Our gunners lead the target perfectly, though, riddling it with explosive bolts that send it up in flames.

"Two more coming through!"

The sleds' twin guns do their work as Twenties and Maldorn get within a hundred meters.

"Move your butts!" I shout, motioning for them to keep digging and get on the sleds.

"More trucks!"

Five more enemy vehicles crash out of the tree line, shearing saplings at the edge of the blue woods. The gunners each focus on a vehicle, disabling their targets with ease. The remaining three bear down on our fleeing legionnaires. Koob gunners spray inaccurate fire at the soldiers, sending clods of dirt kicking up around them.

"Let's get some suppressing fire and help our gunners out!" I call into the comm.

We form something of a phalanx at the back of our sleds, a tight pack of leejes firing at the windshields of the oncoming trucks. The drivers lose their nerve and veer away, probably looking to avoid fire and loop back in pursuit once they gain on the runners. More trucks emerge from the woods, and the sense that we're about to fight every warrior from Moona Village hits me like a repulsor thrust.

Twenties and Maldorn are close, almost to the waiting sleds, when a koob bullet slams into its target. A loud *crack* rises above the din, and I see an armored sleeve explode and fly into the air as the legionnaire hits the ground hard.

"They got Maldorn!" Masters shouts.

Unaware, Twenties keeps running, leaving his fallen comrade on the field. Wraith leaps from his sled and sprints toward the fallen legionnaire. Seeing this, Twenties stops and turns to follow the captain. They pick up Maldorn and get beneath his arms, helping him run toward the waiting sled.

One of the drivers shouts over the comm. "Let's go, let's go, let's go!"

A new wave of trucks emerges, and we are on the edge of being overrun.

"Keep shooting!" I shout. "We're going out together one way or the other."

Its engine roaring, one koob truck accelerates to the front of the pack. Our trio of runners, hobbled by Maldorn's injury, is directly in the truck's path. We can't get a clear shot.

"Wraith! Behind you!" Calling out the warning is all I can do.

Wraith pulls his pistol and does a half-turn to face the oncoming truck. He takes a moment to aim, then sends three tightly grouped shots at the Kublaren driver. They all seem to hit. The alien slumps onto the steering column, forcing the vehicle into a sharp left turn. The sudden change of direction causes the vehicle to roll toward the fleeing legionnaires.

"Get down!" I hear Wraith call into the comm.

The three soldiers drop onto their stomachs, Maldorn crying out in pain, as the truck bounces and rolls over their heads. It comes to a stop almost directly in front of them. Twenties and Wraith hoist up the wounded leej and continue their trek toward the sleds. Wraith takes care to put a blaster shot into every koob thrown from the vehicle, though I have no idea whether they survived the crash, and perhaps he doesn't either. KTF.

Dat-dat-dat-dat!

The gunners fend off more of the koob vanguard as the three legionnaires climb into the other sled.

"Doors up!" calls a driver. "Let's go!"

I hit the switch and steady myself against the sled's acceleration. The koob trucks shrink away toward the horizon. Those things can't hang with a combat sled when it comes to speed, armor, or firepower. Not that I'm complaining.

Dat-dat-dat-dat!

The twins continue to blaze away until, gradually, the shots dry up like the last lonely drops of a rainstorm.

We drive, reveling in the silence. Our blood was up, and we're content to have it come back down. Relieved to finally be returning to the mind-numbing perimeter patrols and collapsible impervisteel of Camp Forge.

Legionnaires begin to pull off their helmets. I notice Andien watch as the men pull off their grime-stained buckets, seeing for the first time the faces of the men who hurried her away from the wrecked village.

"Everybody all right?" I ask.

"Yeah. What's the word on Maldorn?"

"Broken arm," I answer, relaying a message from Captain Ford.

I tap a legionnaire on the shoulder. Clauderro. He still has his helmet on. "Head up to the guns so the basic can get in from the wind and take a breather."

"Yes, sir."

Clauderro switches positions with the basic, who nods at me before taking a jump seat. His uniform and kerchief are thick with Kublaren dust. The kid pulls down the protective cloth and pushes his goggles up to his forehead. Resting against the headrest, he looks up at the cabin ceiling. Quiet pockets of conversation start up.

I lean in close enough to read the name on the basic's uniform. "Good shooting back there, Specialist Kags."

"Thank you, Lieutenant Chhun." He looks over to Andien, who is holding herself, arms wrapped around her chest. "KTF, right?"

"Absolutely," I answer.

"Yeah, you're gettin' it." Exo has a smile on his face. He punches Kags on the arm. "Come a long way since we rolled out of Camp Forge, huh, Basic?"

Kags doesn't look away. "Guess so." The legionnaires around him smile. The kid is a Republic Army basic, but he's warrior. A brother through combat.

"Tell you boys what, though." Exo stands up and walks past his audience, all sitting in their jump seats. "You want KTF, watch what happens once we report in at Camp Forge."

The legionnaires nod. Once we regroup, the koobs have hell to pay.

Exo continues, "Pappy wakes up from that cycler. Colonel LaDonna finds out about all this. Bet we don't have time to make the latrine bots work before we're speeding back out with the tanks. Bring that whole Moona Village down to the ground."

"Just like that." The comment comes from Andien. There's something hot in her voice, like anger but more controlled. Subdued. A dampened wrath, not yet hot enough to burn. "Bring the whole village down to the ground, repercussions be damned. Considering how that worked out today..."

"Listen, lady," Rook says. "Sorry about what happened to your friends. But those koobs were gonna kill some good guys one way or the other. They'd have ambushed all of us, only Captain Ford and Lieutenant Chhun," he nods at me, "were too sharp to let our unit get caught off guard."

Andien looks to me, trying hard not to glance down at the blood covering my armor. "You'll forgive me for not breaking out into applause. You did, after all, stand by while a village with eighty sentient beings, including a half dozen Republic science officers, was blown into atomized pieces."

Part of me wants to ignore her comment. She's reeling from what happened—from seeing her friends buried alive or dead on the streets. But the way the rest of the leejes on the sled are looking at me makes me feel like I've got to say something. "Miss, I'm sorry for what happened. If we had *any* idea that the village was friendly, things would have ended up differently. We would have cut down the Moona warriors who led us there to kill our fellow citizens. But the koobs who led us to your village were identified as *allies* by Repub Intelligence. They took us to a village that was right in the middle of Indian country, a hostile zone. There was no Republic flag. No banner. Hell, not even a research beacon our comms could have identified. We both know you and your team were operating in a clandestine fashion, and it worked out for all of us about as bad as possible. I'm sorry."

"I'm not the one you need to apologize to." Andien looks away, like she's not interested in talking further. "Ontash is the one whose wife lies dead from a legionnaire blaster bolt. Apologize to him."

I resist the urge to look over at Masters. He doesn't need the added burden of being revealed as the legionnaire who pulled the trigger. Still, from the corner of my eye I see him bury his head in his hands.

The rest of the ride back to Camp Forge is quiet.

17

I'm pulled from a light sleep by the sudden, excited chatter of drivers over the command comm channel.

"... smoke on the horizon..."

"Copy. No beacon at marker 1-dot-actual..."

"... well, try the channel..."

"... —omeone wake up Captain Devers..."

"Silver-3, Silver-3. I'm seeing smoke..."

I shake my head of any lingering sleep and look around. The sled is still quiet, and the legionnaires aren't showing any concern. No one has called anything out over the open comm.

"Uh, hey, guys..." Clauderro calls down from the sled's gun emplacements. "I'm seeing some columns of smoke off in the distance from where Camp Forge should be."

Rook leans forward in his seat. "What's goin' on, Lieutenant?"

"Not sure." I pat Clauderro on the back of his leg. "Clauderro, climb down here and gear up. Specialist Kags, take his place."

"Yes, sir." The basic clambers up into the turret and replaces the legionnaire.

"Buckets on," I order. "Everyone, make sure you're primed and ready."

The cabin fills with clicks and clatters as each soldier double-checks his equipment. I hail Wraith on our private channel.

"Go for Wraith."

"Getting reports of smoke from CF," I say.

"Yeah," Wraith answers. "I got up on the turret to use my mags. Doesn't look good. We'll speed in—ETA three minutes. Meet me outside, but keep your leejes in the sleds. Door guards only. My speeder is scouting ahead to make sure the area is clear."

"Copy." I'd like to ask more, go over strategy... something. But unlike Wraith, I don't have a bucket, and anything I say will be heard by the rest of the cabin. And based on how Wraith sounded, I suspect we've not only lost the *Chiasm*, we've also lost Camp Forge. I'm not sure I want the unfiltered truth coming out just yet. At least not until I've got some idea of a plan.

"Okay, listen up, legionnaires." I sling my N-4 over my shoulder and move to the sled doors. "We're two minutes to CF. Early indications are that there was some kind of attack..."

I'm cut off by a chorus of involuntary curses and hissing sighs.

"... some kind of attack," I repeat, getting control of the cabin. "Advance scouts should report soon, but be ready for anything."

"Sir, do we know if—"

Hearing an incoming chime from Wraith, I hold up my index finger, cutting the legionnaire off. "One second, leej. Go for Chhun."

"Okay, it's like this," Wraith says. "Site is clear, no hostiles. But everything is gone. I mean everything. One hundred percent KIA. I'm looking at them now. Speed in and order your squad to remain at the doors. I want to be able to move off in seconds if need be. Once you arrive, meet me outside and we'll put together a plan."

"Copy. Chhun out." I swallow. This is about the worst news possible.

"What's going on?" Andien asks from her seat. She's picking at her fingernails.

"We're in control of the situation," I answer.

That's technically true. We control the battlefield. It's just a burning wreck of destroyed Republic equipment and dead soldiers. I give myself three seconds to be sure my voice is composed and then face the men.

"Okay, leejes. I heard from our advance sled. There was an attack, and it was bad."

"Like... how bad?" Masters asks.

"Total team kill."

There's a stunned silence in the sled.

Exo shakes his head. "No way. *No way!*"

"That's what I'm hearing. When we stop and drop, I'm going out *alone* to meet with Captain Ford. Rook, Clauderro, you're guarding the door. Everyone else stays inside. Captain Ford wants us ready to speed out the moment the order is given."

Our combat sled slows and stops. I drop the ramp and exit.

I'm immediately greeted by the smell of burning. Fuel cells, munitions, impervisteel, flesh—you name it. The sheer devastation of the fort is almost enough to make me stop in my tracks. Dead legionnaires and basics are strewn all over. Few of them are still in one piece. Some are victims of what must have been a massive blast, judging by the crater where the tank bays once stood. The impervisteel buildings of the camp are twisted and disfigured, and not one of the structures still stands.

Wraith is waiting for me, N-4 at the ready. I run out to greet him as the sled turret gunners maintain a vigil, scanning for another attack.

"Any clues about how this happened?" I ask.

"No. But this is a total loss. We need to think about where to go next, what our best option is for staying alive until someone notices the *Chiasm* has stopped reporting. Could be a while. You haven't seen the west end of the camp."

"What'd you see?"

"Looked like a last stand. Lots of dead leejes, most of 'em bunched up together. Most of 'em mutilated. A whole lot of koob blood, but no koob bodies. They had time to remove the dead. Our ambush, this, the *Chiasm*—this was all planned. Coordinated. And from those Kimbrin and human corpses back on the ridge, we both know who had a hand in helping plan it."

I see Captain Devers approaching from his sled. He stops in his tracks, staring in awe at the destruction. "What... what happened?"

"That's what we need to figure out," Wraith calls out. "Get over here, because I don't want us to stick around any longer than is necessary."

"But who did this?" Devers insists, still taking bewildered baby steps in our direction. "Who could have...?"

"Captain Devers, focus." Wraith gives me a look. "You said you were in contact with Camp Forge and the *Chiasm*. Judging by these fires, CF was hit not long after you closed comms with Colonel LaDonna. I need you to think to the exact time of your last transmission."

"I..."

"Captain Devers, this is critical. Did you speak with the *Chiasm*?"

"I..."

The comm chimes, and Doc Quigs speaks over the command channel. "Captain Devers, I've got a lot of legionnaires and basics in a bad way. Is there any medical salvage? Because I'll be frank, some of these soldiers are going to die if they don't get more than skinpacks soon."

"I... I..."

All the questions seem to hit Devers at once, and he's frozen with indecision.

"Captain Devers... the *Chiasm*?"

"I need supplies, now!"

"Sir... we need to speed out of here."

Devers takes a half step away from us, pauses, and says, "You... you two have this covered, I think. I'm going to return to my sled and make sure..." He jogs a couple of steps. "Make sure..." He doesn't bother finishing the sentence. He just runs off.

He's about halfway between his waiting sled and the two of us when I see a gray blur streaking toward him. Exo makes an open field tackle and drives Devers hard into the ground.

"You point sonofabitch!"

Devers is on his back, trying to scramble away from Exo, who leaps on top of him, driving an armored forearm into the captain's bucket. "You see all this? This is on *you*, Point! I'm gonna kill you!"

Exo rains down blows on Devers's head and neck, but the leej armor takes almost all of the impact. Frustrated by this, Exo slips around the struggling captain and pushes his knees into Devers's chest. Fending off Devers's attempts to slap his arms away, Exo pulls at the captain's bucket, removing it with such violence that I worry for a second that he broke Devers's neck.

Raising a fist high in the air, Exo utters a curse and drills Devers square in the face. The punch causes an audible *crunch,* and blood pours from Devers's nose. Exo rears up and brings his fist crashing down on the side of Devers's jaw. The force is enough to cause Exo to nearly fall over.

I realize that no one, myself included, is making a move to stop what's happening. Legionnaires and basics have all left their sleds and are standing as spectators. There's a part of me that's content for this to just play out to its conclusion. Even Wraith, so quick to take action, is standing by, unmoving.

Exo rises to his feet and removes his own helmet while Devers writhes on the ground, utterly defenseless.

"Stinking point!" A well-placed kick is driven into Devers's ribs right where the armor opens up to allow for a fuller range of motion in the arms.

Captain Devers rolls onto his stomach with the impact, gasping for air. His mouth is wide open, like a koob. Blood and saliva spill onto the fractured permacrete deck of Camp Forge. One of his eyes is swelled completely shut, and the other is blood red. He looks like a prizefighter in a fight that should have been called three rounds ago.

Exo kicks him again. "You talked to CF? You didn't talk to no one!" Another kick. "Nah! You just got my buddies killed! And for what?"

I realize that I'm running toward the fight and that Wraith is keeping pace. "Exo, that's enough!"

Exo looks up at me, his eyes wet and half-crazed. "He deserves to *die*, Lieutenant."

Devers lets out a groan and crawls on the ground, clawing his way toward Wraith and me. "H-help... meeee..."

Exo kicks him again. "You deserve to die, Point!"

In a flash, Exo draws his vibroknife and rolls Devers onto his back. Seeing the blade, Devers gets a burst of adrenaline and is able to throw up his arms before Exo drops down on top of him, trying to plunge the knife into the officer.

"Exo!" I scream, sprinting toward the melee. I see the other legionnaires break and move to stop what's coming.

Devers pushes at Exo's chin with his right hand while his left hand grasps Exo's right wrist, struggling to keep the knife at bay. But the captain doesn't have that legionnaire strength the rest of us have. The knife is driven toward his heart as if in slow motion, as every muscle fiber in the captain's body is overcome.

Seeing that he can't keep the knife away, Devers cries out, "No! No... no!"

The tip of the knife penetrates the armor as Exo turns his head left and then right in an attempt to get Devers's palm off of his chin. Nearly all of Exo's weight is being pressed into the knife, and it slowly bites through the armor, coming ever nearer to ripping into the flesh beneath.

I'm within five steps of the skirmish, and I don't think I'll make it in time.

But Wraith is faster than I am. He leaps and spears Exo, driving the legionnaire off of Captain Devers. In a moment, the attacker is surrounded by legionnaires.

No one handles him roughly. No one hits him, and he doesn't try fighting us. He just stares at Devers, who's lying flat on his back, exhausted and helpless. There's a pool of blood around his head, but it's from his broken nose. The knife didn't make it through.

No one goes to Devers until Quigs comes out of a medsled. "What's going on out..." He stops mid-sentence and runs to the captain to start treating his wounds. "What happened?"

"Don't worry about it," I say.

"Subconjunctival hemorrhage," Quigs mumbles to himself. He pulls out a clotting agent from his belt and begins to sprinkle it on Devers's face. "Well, I *am* worried about it, Lieutenant. I don't have the supplies I need to keep half the men in the sleds alive for another week, and I damn sure don't need more wounded coming without the enemy's help."

Rook walks up to Quigs, his rapid-fire squad automatic blaster hoisted over his shoulder. He looks down at Devers's bruised and bloodied face. "You ask me, Exo did you a favor, Doc. Captain Devers can't get the rest of us dusted no more now that he's out of the fight."

I look to the sleds, where the surviving scientists and Repub-Army basics are watching. That they're without hope is obvious from the forlorn looks on their faces. A flush of guilt and shame washes over me. If legionnaires can't keep from almost killing each other in this situation, what prospect is there for them?

Captain Ford must feel the same way, because he takes this opportunity to address the living in this place of the dead. "This is the last time something like this happens. Does everyone understand that?"

The gathered legionnaires nod. Exo is calm, sitting on the ground with Twenties kneeling by his side.

"Let me give everything I know to you straight. Camp Forge is a total team kill. I don't know exactly why or how, but you can see the evidence in front of you. That's not the worst of it. During our ambush, Lieutenant Chhun witnessed the *Chiasm* explode in orbit. Now, I asked him to keep that under wraps until I could confirm it, and this," Wraith waves his hand at the ruins of Camp Forge, "coupled with our complete inability to get any comm traffic to or from them, is confirmation enough. Lieutenant Chhun is no liar.

"That leaves us stranded on a hostile world with no friends. And I mean none. Senator Greggorak was at Camp Forge when we left, and I'm willing to bet we'll find his corpse under all this impervisteel if it wasn't incinerated in the blast. Our priority is to salvage what we can, speed off to a hidden and defensible location, and hunker down until another destroyer arrives in orbit. Questions?"

Wraith is answered with silence. What he's laid out is the only move we have left.

But then a voice sounds in the distance. It's familiar. Like... a newscaster.

18

"Anybody else hear that?" I strain my ears, but they've been plagued by a low ringing. No matter what I stuff into them, nothing has been as effective as my helmet.

"Yeah," Wraith answers. "I hear it too."

The voice carries over the dead, like a ghost talking in a graveyard. "... hours since the surprise attack. However, the contingent of legionnaires has returned to the devastation. The sight of the carnage has resulted in tense exchanges and, in some instances, even open hostility. We'll continue to update our audience as further developments arise. Back to you..."

I look up and see a TT-10 bot hovering overhead, its red light flashing as it records me and my leejes. At once it dawns on me what we're all hearing. The journalist bot must have made it through the battle intact.

"It's Pully," I announce, moving toward the bot's voice.

"I'm coming with you." Wraith motions for Sergeant Powell and points at Exo. "I want that leej kept away from Captain Devers at all times."

Exo stands up. He holds out his N-4 for the sergeant.

"No," Wraith says. "I need shooters. You give me your word you won't turn your weapons on Captain Devers or any other person here, and you've got my trust. Can I trust you?"

After clenching his jaw tightly, Exo relaxes his face and nods. "You can trust me, Captain Ford."

"He can keep his weapon," Wraith tells Powell. "I need two leejes to come with Lieutenant Chhun and me. The rest of you, reset and be ready to speed out if I give the order."

Twenties and Masters run up and join us. We climb over a twisted mound of impervisteel that used to be the mess hall, if I've got my bearings correct. As we reach the crest of the debris pile, we see Pully just ahead, surrounded by more dead legionnaires. There are a few dead koobs as well, but I can tell by the way they've been chopped up and dismembered that these weren't friends of the tribes that attacked us.

The hover bot whizzes by us. It returns to its compartment on Pully's back as we scamper down to the bot.

Pully looks up, his blue visual receptors glowing. "Lieutenant Ford, Sergeant Chhun, Specialists Masters and Denino. I am..." He pauses in what seems to be a feigned consideration. "... *relieved* that you have returned safely."

"Thanks," Wraith says. "Pappy made Chhun brevet lieutenant and me brevet captain. Now, I need for you to—"

"Congratulations."

Wraith pauses. "Thanks. I need you to tell me exactly what happened."

The bot nods. "Yes, this story is of galaxy-wide importance, I agree. I have amassed over twenty standard hours of footage, including three hours of unedited combat holos. I also have footage from the period before your contingent left for negotiations at Moona Village, though sub-cipher cross-checks do not reveal anything of note. A more thorough check will need to be made upon returning to the *Chiasm*. I will require authorization to plug into the supercomputer's mainframe and ask the native intelligence for access to—"

"Pully," Wraith interrupts, "we don't have time for full analysis. We have to get moving. There's a hostile force that knows we were headed in this direction, and we've got no idea how close the attackers of Camp Forge are right now."

"The attackers left in a southerly direction at approximately 15:08, local time, on the day of the attack."

Wraith shakes his head. "Unless you can tell me how long they drove after leaving your field of vision..."

"I cannot. Are you available for an interview, Captain Ford?"

The bot wants to be helpful, but he also wants to follow his directive of recording as much information on the story as possible. I step in to try and streamline the process.

"Pully, we aren't staying long, and you can have full access to everyone you need once we speed out. But we need to know what happened. Have you already recorded a summary news brief that you could play for us?"

"Of course. It was among my first transmissions."

"Play it," Wraith orders.

"Right away. Would you prefer the report rendered by a human male or female?"

"Girl," Masters interjects before anyone else has a chance to answer. "Play the girl. If we're all gonna die out here, I'd like to see one more pretty face before I'm dusted. Should've held on to those Mendella holochits after all."

The glow of Pully's eyes intensifies, and dual beams of holographic light shoot downward, creating the image of a youthful, attractive female news anchor—the type you'd see behind the desk on the top network of any planet or space station in the galaxy. Of course, she isn't real, just an advanced rendering pulled from the bot's processing and imaging caches. The anchorwoman sits with a static smile across her face as a countdown appears next to her chest. When it reaches zero, she puts a hand up to her ear and looks down at her desk, studious and concerned.

"We are just receiving breaking news here at..." There's a pause where the local station identifier would be supplied; Pully's told me all about how this works during our time on tour together. "A Republic outpost on the planet Kublar has been attacked by a joint force of native Kublarens in opposition to the peacefully elected Senator Gregorrak, along with human and Kimbrin terrorists identifying themselves as part of the Mid-Core Rebellion. We understand the battle ended mere hours ago and that our embedded journalist"—there's another pause to fill in whatever local computer model has been reporting—"survived the attack and is reporting from the scene. The images that follow are graphic, and holoviewer discretion is strongly advised."

The holo cuts to a man in his mid-fifties, still handsome and fit. "Thank you..."

"Ah, why can't he be a woman, too?" Masters says.

"Stow it, leej."

The reporter continues. "I'm at Camp Forge, the scene of a violent and brutal conflict. It started this afternoon just after one p.m. local time, when a massive explosion took place in the garage where the Republic forces stored their main battle tanks. This blast killed a number of troops and was followed by an invasion of vehicles that arrived from the flat expanse behind me that leads into Kublar's Lendrah province. The attackers were Kublarens, Kimbrin, and humans arriving by truckload. Republic legionnaires immediately rallied to launch a counter-assault."

The footage switches to a group of ragged leejes rushing to form a perimeter, creating a firing line. The dead and dying lay strewn around them.

"A fierce firefight raged, but the sheer volume of enemy combatants allowed them to overrun the base. While the legionnaires kept the terrorists from breaching the west end of the base, the insurgents quickly took control of the northeast section, where Senator Gregorrak was visiting the company commander, Colonel Delt LaDonna. There are no signs of the senator or LaDonna at this time."

Scenes of the battle, the dead, and Gregorrak from the weeks prior, are interspersed throughout the narrative, deftly edited together by the journalist bot.

"The fight continued until the weight of the MCR and Kublaren force converged on the legionnaire holdouts. The battle played out for nearly two more hours before the legionnaires were finally overrun. No survivors remain on site, and the insurgents took no prisoners. There remains on Kublar one joint force of legionnaires and Republic Army on a diplomatic mission. They have not yet returned. Hails to the *Chiasm*, a capital-class destroyer overseeing this sector of galaxy's edge, have not been able to penetrate the Kublaren atmosphere. More details as they become available."

The holofeed switches back to the anchorwoman, but the playback is stopped before she can deliver her reply. A heaviness sits in the air until Pully speaks.

"That is the entirety of the summary briefing. I transmitted it as soon as it was complete, but all uploads to the *Chiasm* have failed."

I nod. "The *Chiasm* isn't there anymore. It blew up about the same time the base did."

Pully inclines his head. "That is unfortunate, but does provide a plausible explanation."

"Any idea if LaDonna or the senator made it out alive? Maybe as hostages?" Wraith asks.

"We could form a rescue mission," Twenties suggests.

"I believe Colonel LaDonna was killed in the blast, based on my examination of bodily remains." The bot points at an exposed beam high overhead, bent over so that it resembles a massive fishing pole. "The head of Senator Gregorrak is mounted up there. I did a full news report on its discovery. Would you like to see it?"

We all look up at the grim spectacle.

"Who's the koob swinging by a rope next to him?" I ask.

Pully's optics grind as he looks where I'm pointing. "I believe that was one of the senator's wives, Ma'asog, of the tribe Moona."

I take one more look at the body dangling in the wind. What was it that Chieftain Kreggak said? Something about supporting the senator by some customary bond—*drid-*

dak. I'm thinking whoever attacked the base severed that bond, and the moment the Moona chieftain was free to act without its restraints, he was setting himself up to kill some Republicans.

Wraith picks up a tattered piece of fabric that was lying at our feet. It looks like a scrap of the Victory Company flag. Maybe all that remains. "Okay," he says, "here's what comes next. Pully, you're coming with us."

"This is agreeable," answers the bot. "The story of how the remaining legionnaires survive will ultimately prove of greater interest to the galaxy than my cataloging obituaries for the deceased. Now that the appointed officers are finished."

Pully doesn't mean to cause offense, so I don't take any. He's right, though. Those appointed as officers by the House of Reason or Senate, sons of the rich and famous, are the ones the galaxy will care about. Not the nameless and faceless leejes who volunteered for academy training out of a desire to be the best the Republic had to offer. That's just a fact.

"Silver-3," Wraith says, "divert a peeper from perimeter duty and have it circle the compound for anything living or salvageable. I don't think we'll find anything, but I want to check before we speed out." He keys the side of his helmet. "Sergeant Powell, I want you to get the sleds loaded up."

We walk back to the staging area, our pace slowed somewhat as the bot attempts to navigate through the debris. It does well enough, though. Better than most humanoids would, just not as good as a leej.

I notice that Twenties is rubbing his face. "Something bothering your eye?"

"Yeah," Twenties answers, trying to blink away whatever's bothering him. His eye is allergic red, maybe from all the touching. "I must've gotten something in it while we were chased back to the sleds. Can't seem to get it out."

"Have Doc Quigs look at it when we get back."

"Yes, sir."

The staging area is free of most personnel. Only Quigs, a few leejes pulling sentry duty, and the Rep-Army basic point who defended Devers are still outside the sleds. Through the open doors of one of the sleds, I see Andien sitting across from the scientist who lost his wife. She's trying to talk with him, but he appears catatonic, just staring into the void.

"Lieutenant Selmer," Wraith says to the point officer, "are the sleds ready to move?"

"Yes." Selmer's tone is icy.

"Then get in your vic and await my orders to move out."

"All *due* respect, Captain Ford, but my fellow R-A drivers and crew are a little disturbed by the way you handled the unprovoked attack by one of your legionnaires on Major Devers."

"*Captain* Devers," I correct. This guy sucks.

"So you say," Selmer replies with a fractional nod. "Protocol requires that—"

Wraith cuts him off. "I know what protocol states. Arrest, investigations, statements accusing or defending the actions for conduct unbecoming an officer or foul play or intentions with the enemy. But guess what? We're out and stranded. What you see behind you? That's our fate if we stay here and play advocate general for a fight between two leejes. I'll worry about whether the altercation was just once a rescue comes—*if* a rescue comes. Now get back to your vic and be ready to speed out."

Somewhat tersely, Selmer says, "Yes, sir," and moves to his combat sled.

"Hey, Doc," I call to Quigs. "Can you check out Twenties's eye?"

Quigs removes a light pen from his pouch and clicks it on with his thumb. He shines it into the legionnaire's puffy and swollen eye. "Does it feel hot?"

"A little," Twenties answers. "Mostly itches. Kind of a painful itch, though."

Clicking the light pen off, Quigs says, "That's because it's infected. Probably got something in there from when we lanced the blisters during the ambush. You need a skin-pack." He turns to Captain Ford and me. "And I don't have any more left. Every wound from here on out needs healing the old-fashioned way."

"I've got a TT-16 overhead looking for salvage," Wraith says.

"Here's hoping." Quigs lowers the volume on his bucket. "Because I've got nothing left. I mean *nothing*. Pappy is going to come out of his coma before the cycler finishes if I don't get some additional pain numbers and narcos. I don't need to tell you the kind of pain he'll find himself in."

"We'll find what we can and take what we can," Wraith assures him. "What we need more than that is a way to notify the nearest Republic destroyer of our situation."

"Can't you do a deep space transmission?" I ask Pully.

"I have already done so." The bot's smooth voice fills the staging area. It's surreal. "But with our placement in galaxy's edge, it will be weeks before the signal reaches a network holo receiver."

"Why?" I ask.

Andien jogs over to our discussion. A legionnaire calls for her to stay in the sleds, but I wave him off.

"You know something about this?" I ask her.

"Maybe," Andien replies. "I'm familiar with the real space and subspace communication relays. I degreed in technical communications before going back to school to study edge-space geology." She turns to Pully. "Your deep space transmission is sent in the direction of the nearest holo receiver owned by your network, right?"

"That is correct."

Andien nods rapidly, as though the bot's confirmation launched her thoughts. "That won't do us any good unless you think we can survive for a month out here."

Wraith shakes his head.

"The message has to reach the commercial station, go through processing, and then needs to be forwarded to an appropriate Republic station." Andien frowns and takes a few paces. "That could add more time before the right person gets it and a relief ship is sent. But, if the bot's broadcast can be transmitted directly from a military comm burster, it's sure to find a closer holo receiver. A deep space supply platform, if not a destroyer."

"Only problem with that," Wraith says, "is that Camp Forge's burster is destroyed, along with everything else."

"They wouldn't have gotten Outpost Zulu," I say. "No way the koobs can access it without air support, and we haven't seen any evidence of that."

"Does O-Z have an array capable of reaching deep space?" Wraith asks. "I thought it was just a comm booster for the planet and any orbiting ships."

"It wouldn't, no," Andien answers, "but that's okay. This bot has a very compact and powerful transmitter. If we can get it to the outpost, I'm sure I can wire it into the comm station and reach deep space using the proper military frequency."

Wraith nods. "That's our plan, then."

"Captain Ford, this is Silver-3. Observation bot is showing something that looks like intact medical crates at the camp's north end."

"More good news," I say.

Quigs practically jumps at the report. "Permission to assemble a salvage team."

"Granted," Wraith says.

A burst of static hits all of our comms at the same time. The L-comm open channel conveys Chieftain Kreggak's dry and craggy voice. "Leejon-ayers. This... *kk'k* ... Chieftain Kreggak of Moona tribe. New chieftain of Annek tribe. Chieftain of all tribe. My sister-kin is gone. My allies and I come now for you now. Big die. *K'kk'k*. Big die for you soon."

"Silver-3!" Wraith calls over the L-comm, I guess no longer caring if the koobs hear him. "Do any peepers show an incoming force?"

"Uh, nothing close by. Wait. Yeah, I see a dust cloud."

Masters swears beneath his breath.

"I'm seeing outlines of the same vehicles that pursued us earlier. Looks like they've caught up already. Projecting an ETA of ten to fifteen minutes."

"Everybody back to the sleds!" Wraith orders.

"What about the supplies?" Quigs asks.

"Sorry, Doc."

Quigs sighs but returns to his sled with a nod. Andien and the remaining legionnaires also load up.

"Silver-3," Wraith says, "recall all the observation bots except one. Keep it overhead and try to get as much intel on what this force is composed of until they shoot it down."

"Copy."

"So we're speeding for Outpost Zulu?" I ask.

"God help us

19

It didn't take long to reach Outpost Zulu by sled. Maybe a two-hour trip. But the time spent in transit felt oppressive. The reality of what happened to Camp Forge was a part of that, but not a huge one. I sort of expected it, to be honest. This whole time—really, from the time I saw the *Chiasm* explode—I knew that Camp Forge was gone, too. Call it a soldier's intuition.

Bad as that was, what bothered me more was the feed that came in from the TT-16 observation bot we left behind. Wraith had the footage showing on every sled screen—said he wanted everyone to see what we're up against. That there was no room for error. That this was survival time.

There were just so many of them. I was looking out at a sea of koobs, their white trucks the foam in the waves. And it wasn't just koobs. Mixed in were uniformed fighters from the Mid-Core Rebellion. Human and Kimbrin alike. Not near as many of them as the koobs. But it was enough to confirm that the loss of our destroyer and base, the ambush that killed half our sled force, was calculated. I had no idea how long in advance it was planned, but I knew that the other leejes and me had a front row seat.

Guess we were just lucky.

Of course, this wasn't even supposed to be a possibility. Kublar was tense—the Republic wouldn't have sent us down if it wasn't—but this was supposed to be a local skirmish, warlords gearing up to resist the progressive march of the Republic, not the staging ground for a major galactic insurgency. Every intelligence brief had said the same thing: the MCR didn't have the resources or numbers to go up against a company of legionnaires. They were terrorists, content to bomb a planetary police station or ambush a small Republic world's local militia away from the Core—and then fill the holofeeds with their crap about the decline of the Republic and the need for revolution. Watering the tree of liberty with blood.

But it's never really about liberty with these types. It's about power. They get it outside of the established order and then want more of it. And let's be honest: it's always violence, or the threat of violence, that acquires and sustains power.

Well, these mukk'kas were going to find out why the Republic had stood the test of time from the Exploration to the Savage Wars.

Assuming I could make this climb.

Which, standing at the base of the nearly sheer mountain that O-Z is nestled into, doesn't look much like a sure thing. I'm staring straight up a long way, and all I can see is the needle tip of the comm dish, projecting to a destroyer that probably made a new crater somewhere on the planet's surface. And other than some synth-rope, we've got zero mountaineering gear.

"Climb team ready?" I ask.

My two volunteers step forward. Rook checks the knots used to hook up Pully. The two of us are team-climbing with the bot attached to our webbing. It probably weighs close to two hundred pounds, so I'm gonna need Rook's servo-enhanced forearms to help with the load. Almost all of our gear is stowed inside a sled. We're going up with nothing more than hydration, N-4s, rope, and our armor.

The other volunteer is Kags. Turns out, he grew up in the mountain passes of Kenne. Climbing is second nature to him. His going up is mission critical. We've tied Andien to him, trusting that if she slips, he'll have the ability to hoist her to safety. So, three soldiers carrying two VIPs. If we don't make it up top, well, we've got nowhere else to go.

At least this mountain is defensible. Our backs are pressed up against solid stone, and there are plenty of crags and positions for our snipers to work from. Lots of overhangs to help with mortars. We'll give the koobs and MCR a good fight when they show up. That's in maybe six hours, given the speed of their vehicles. More if it takes them a while to figure out where we went.

"I'm ready, Lieutenant." Kags rubs his hands and shakes his arms and legs loose.

"Okay, let's mount up." I motion to a waiting hover sled, and we climb to the top of it. The plan is to use it like an elevator. Have it hover as high as it can and get a head start on the climb. "Go for climb."

The sled's engines whine, and we slowly rise from the ground. The noise increases and the hull begins to vibrate as we move up the side of the mountain.

"Oh!" The sled pitches forward, and Andien loses her footing and grabs on to my arm. The driver quickly compensates, but it's clear that we're at the zenith of what the sled can do while still keeping level.

"I think that's about as high as we can go," the driver announces over the comm, confirming my suspicion. "Any higher and I'm worried we'll dump you over the side."

I look down. We're about twenty feet off the ground. Just enough to hurt if we fall off. Still, it's twenty feet we didn't have to climb, and I don't see any sense in pushing things to get up another few feet. "Let's step off here."

We reach out to find hand and toeholds. It's still a long way up.

I pull myself onto the mesa with panting breaths. Rook's enhanced strength allows him to hang on tightly and bear Pully's full weight. There's nothing I want more than to just sit here beneath the thin sun and recover. But Rook can't hold on forever, and I don't have the wind to call for help. Thankfully Kags shakes the sleep from his eyes and comes running over. He leaves Andien snoozing in the shadow of a boulder. Can't blame 'em—they reached the top a good forty minutes before me.

A rock spire juts out near the edge of the cliff like a jagged thumb. I push against it to test its stability. It feels solid, so I tie my line around it. Kags arrives, and together we work to pull my partner up to the top.

Rook stretches out his arms and grabs as much of the artificial mesa as he can. Kags and I run to the edge and pull him the rest of the way by his webbing.

"Almost done," I say, near breathless. The three of us pull on the rope until the bot joins us just outside Outpost Zulu.

Rook and I collapse onto the ground as Pully attempts to remove the ropes tied to his frame. "That was certainly an interesting experience," the bot says. "I hope my questions were not a distraction."

"We didn't fall," Rook deadpans.

"It was fine, Pully. Helped pass the time." I look over at the rock shading Andien. Just over her head is the cylindrical impervisteel structure housing the listening station. Not much more than an observation room with a combination bunk-galley and a whole lot of circuitry. I was given the three-credit tour once while stationed in the inner core. It feels cramped with two techs working inside, and Zulu has three.

I plant my hand to push myself off the ground and feel a twinge in my forearm. It's like there's no strength from elbows to fingertips. I want to rest, to curl up and go to sleep. But there's an army of koobs and insurgents playing search and destroy with us, and we need to get another destroyer here. Yesterday.

"Specialist Kags," I say, my breathing finally even, "go wake up the scientist. We need to start that transmission."

Rook uses the rock spire to pull himself up. "I can't get anyone down below on the comm."

"I would not register surprise at this," Pully answers. "The combination of kividiary rock formations along with the Kublaren atmosphere all but eliminate comm-to-comm reliability at this altitude."

I nod in agreement. "Let's get you inside O-Z, Pully."

Kags returns with a sleepy-eyed Andien, her hair puffing out where it rested on her arm. "We're ready, Lieutenant."

We follow a trail that leads to the outpost facility. I'm on point, with Rook the last man. A blue-and-black-feathered bird squawks at us from its nest midway up a comm tower, but other than that, the only sound is the whipping of an icy wind. It strikes me that no one is talking, even the bot. No one is making idle conversation with the civilian or cracking jokes, even though this outpost is probably the safest place left for us on the planet. If the others are feeling like I'm feeling, they've given up on any pretense of security. Hell is breaking loose sooner or later, and we seem prepped for sooner.

The comm station is a circular building built from impervisteel. A massive dish points skyward, and the area surrounding the structure is littered with signal-boosting comm towers. One side of the outpost is built right up to the edge of the mesa, allowing those inside to get an expansive view of the land, and on the other side, at the end of our path, is the access door.

It's shut tight. The emergency doors—two massive slabs of armor plating that slide over the primary entrance like a blast door—are in place.

"Looks like the techs are a bit spooked," Rook says, looking up at the observation cam above us.

"Can you blame them?" Andien asks. She glances up at the bird as it beats its wings in flight, leaving the nest. "This feels like a walking nightmare. Virtually every colleague I've had for the past six weeks is dead, and I don't know whether to hope I make it out or pray for a quick and painless death."

Kags rests a gloved hand on Andien's shoulder. "We'll make it out alive."

She shrugs it off. "Forgive me for not getting my hopes up."

"If it is any comfort," Pully says with his antenna extended, "I have been recording and logging your interactions, and I will certainly broadcast a holocast that paints you in the fondest light for your friends and family to view should you become deceased."

We all stop what we're doing and stare at the bot. I exchange a look with Andien and say, "Thanks."

She shakes her head, tossing her hair as she does so, and looks up at the holocam. "So, are they going to open the doors, or...?"

Rook cups his hands around his bucket's external speaker. He looks like a yodeler serenading the mountainside. "Hey! Techs! Let us in!"

Pully inclines his head and focuses his blue optics. "That does not appear to be working."

"Ya think?" Rook counters.

"I can override," I say, opening a panel near the blast doors.

A keypad lights up with a soft green glow, prompting me to enter authorization credentials. Normally I would just air-connect with my bucket's transceiver—I'm really starting to miss that helmet—but instead I key in the command codes Wraith provided me.

The console beeps twice and the blast doors slide open, revealing a standard security door with *Outpost Zulu* painted beneath the starry Republic liberty emblem. I was worried I'd forgotten the code, to be honest. It's nice to see it work.

"Now for the next one."

I punch in a standard access code common to all legionnaires. There's no rank limiter assigned to enter an outpost, and the common code is a lot shorter than my lieutenant passkey.

The console beeps three times and flashes red. Invalid entry.

I enter the code again. *Beep-beep-beep.*

"Code not working?" Andien asks, looking over my shoulder.

"Techs must've increased the access threshold. I was just using a standard legionnaire identifier. I'll enter my officer pass."

Rook slaps the side of his rifle. "Let 'em know who they're dealing with! This isn't some enlisted leej, this is *the* Lieutenant Chhun!"

I smile, feeling more at ease hearing the jokes coming again.

Beep-beep-beep.

"That's not right..."

I key in the passkey again.

Beep-beep-beep.

With deliberate slowness, I punch in the code, careful not to hit the wrong key.

Beep-beep-beep.

I slam both fists against the door and shake my head in frustration. "I can't get in."

"Curious that it worked on the security doors, but not the primary entrance," Pully says.

"Can I give it a try?" Andien steps toward the keypad. "I have a clearance code that's supposed to work like a skeleton key."

I step aside and hold out my hand. "Be my guest."

Pully seems intrigued. "Tell me, Miss... Is Andien a first name or surname?"

"First name. Andien Broxin, Republic Corps of Science and Engineering."

"I see." Pully stands frozen for a moment, a sign that he's processing data. "I do not find your name listed among the *Chiasm*'s personnel manifest."

Andien smiles as she types in her keycode. "That's because we didn't arrive with the *Chiasm*. We came a standard month prior to get a head start on the surveying needed to get Kublar ready for resource development. We dropped from the super-destroyer *Mercutio*. My hope is that it's still close enough to the system for the transmission to reach it."

The other soldiers and I share a look. The *Mercutio* is the big dog in this part of galaxy's edge. It's three times the size of the sixteen-hundred-meter *Chiasm* and serves as the flagship of the sector admiral. Not exactly the sort of spacecraft you'd expect to drop off a science team.

With an acceptance chime, the door whooshes open. We step inside the temperature-controlled outpost, and the chill of the mountain air is instantly replaced by a cushion of warmth. The outpost has the familiarity of a Republic military installation; the glow of the overhead lights and the mirrored black shine of the floors make me feel at home. There's no sign of the tech crew yet, but we're only just in.

Rook is the last one inside. He pushes a button to close the door and asks, "So how come your code doesn't work, LT, but hers does?"

"That's a fair question," I admit.

Andien meets my eye. "Just lucky, really. I was given an override code in case I needed to bypass any Republic equipment locks. Everything we were working with was military, you understand. Your code, Lieutenant, worked on the shield doors, and it should have worked on the main door. But I'd wager that the crew inside raised the clearance rank to something higher. Maybe a major or colonel—who knows? They can do that in an emergency, but they'd have to come outside to do the same to the shield doors."

I want to ask her how she knows all that. And why she came here aboard the *Mercutio* instead of on some bulky research space-hopper. But that's all luxury. Information I don't really need to know and don't have time to ask.

"Something tells me the techs aren't interested in leaving this place," Kags says, holding his blaster rifle out in front of him. "No welcoming party."

"Think of this as the lobby," I say, pointing to the area in front of us. "That center door leads to the observation room, the hallway to the bunks and a galley."

Pully swivels his head neatly, scanning the area. "Is it possible the tech crew left their post? AWOL stories are generally of interest to Republic military network stations, particularly in a combat environment."

Rook shakes his head. "Where would they even go? I mean, we'd have found them if they jumped."

Pully considers this. "Ghost stories are of interest across virtually all demographics."

We stop and stare at the bot.

"That was a joke," Pully says.

I straighten myself to my full height and let out a hiss of air. "Kags, check the bunks. Maybe the techs are sleeping."

"On it, sir." The basic moves down the hall while the rest of us move to the door that leads to the main observation room.

I stack up on the left side of the door, by the keypad, while Rook moves to the right. The bot and scientist linger directly in front of the door. I motion for them to move. "Pully, line up behind Rook. Andien, behind me. Each of you hug the wall and don't come inside until we give an all clear."

"Is this not," Pully says, "a Republic installation?"

"Doesn't pay to play," answers Rook.

"I take your point," the bot concedes.

Looking across to Rook, I say, "Let's knock before entering. They're probably jumpy." I pound my fist against the door. "Republic legionnaires!"

There's no reply. Rook catches my eye and shakes his head. He isn't picking up any sounds through his bucket's audio enhancers.

I pound again and wait. Still nothing.

Kags comes back down the hall and joins the stack, putting himself against the wall between Andien and me. "Empty, Lieutenant. Three beds. One was a mess, the other two were made with fleet precision. The rest of the room didn't look like they were expecting an officer inspection any time soon."

"Thanks, Kags. Sounds like at least one quit on rules and regs. Pappy can deal with that when he wakes up."

Rook looks around the halls. "You think they all went for a walk?"

I chew my lip. "It's a three-man crew. At least one of them should still be stationed. Let's open the door."

I press the recessed entry button beneath the keypad, and an automated chime comes over the station's comms. "Security key required for entry."

I key in my lieutenant passkey, then stop and hover my finger over the final digit. I nod at Rook, who nods back, and I press the button.

The door retracts upward with a whoosh. The hum of holotransmitters and dataservers comes forth from the newly opened room, but there are no sounds of life.

20

"Republic legionnaires," I announce. "Is anyone in there? Are you hurt?"

When no one answers, I make to roll into the doorway and clear the room, but Rook holds out his hand to stop me. "I've got a bucket on. I'll go first. What if you bumped your head on a low beam or something?"

He turns into the doorway and quickly moves inside. I spin out and follow. We enter at the point of a corner— Rook goes straight, one wall on his left, and I follow the wall on the right, trusting that we'll see whatever might be in the middle. Usually there would be a few more leejes behind us to clear center, but Kags is the only one with any combat training, and this sort of close-quarters room-clearing isn't something he's familiar with. Besides, I don't particularly want to risk getting shot in the back by an overeager basic.

We move past desks and blinking comm stations, our view occasionally interrupted by semi-transparent grid screens showing the location of all known friendly and hostile elements on the planet. We'll converge at the large observation window that overlooks the cliff. If you follow seamball, think of Rook going up the third bag line while I head toward first bag.

"Clear." Rook reaches a series of three steps that run the back end of the room. He climbs them, arriving at the concave wall with a horizontal viewing window running the length of it.

I'm just a few short paces from saying the same when I see a pair of shiny Republic Army boots pointing at the overhead lights. My brain processes the sight of two dead Republic techs in an instant, and then I see who killed them. "Get down!"

A pair of ear-splitting twin booms sound as the third tech fires some sort of slice-rigged blaster pistol at Rook. The weapon looks to be an unstable fusion of three Republic-issue blasters wired into one. The massive blaster bolt brightens the room and slams into Rook, sending him flying into the wall. A second later, the unstable gun explodes in the tech's hand. I hurl myself away from the blast instinctively.

As I lie on the ground, blinking away the white flash burned into my eyes, I hear the distant shouts of Kags as he runs into the room. My vision comes along quickly. I'm staring at the tightly woven carpet fibers of the comm station's floor. It still smells new. I push myself up, and a moment later Kags is at my side. He's looking from Rook to the tech, waiting for me to give an order. Both men are still alive, but in bad shape. The tech's arm was blown apart, and fragments of bone and blaster are embedded in his face, neck, and chest. He won't last long.

"Watch the tech," I order Kags. "Try to stabilize him. But be careful."

Kags reaches him in seconds as I stumble toward Rook.

"What the hell, man?" Kags shouts at the tech.

"He was coming for me!" the tech croaks in a raspy voice. He doesn't even seemed fazed by his wounds. "They're all coming for me! I saw it! I kept seeing it! Every-one's dead! The holos wouldn't stop coming to me show-ing everybody! I saw them! Saw what the koobs did. They were sending the holos to me because they want to kill me, too! Kill *me*! No! Noooo!"

"Lieutenant," Kags calls over to me, "this tech's lost his mind. And from the look of all these med-tabs on the ground, he's hopped up on Zulu's entire supply of med-stims."

"Just keep an eye on him. Don't let him do any more damage."

I drop down at Rook's side. He's lying flat on his back, taking tortured breaths that come out of his helmet speak-ers in ragged bursts. I prop his head up with my knee and gently pull off his bucket.

"I'm sorry, Sarge—*Lieutenant*—I'm sorry." Rook sput-ters a cough and paints his lips red with blood.

"Hey, no. You did great, Rook." I look down at him. There's a fractured hole where the blast hit his armor, and blood is seeping out. Not as much as I expected to see, though.

Andien runs into the room. "Can I help?"

"Maybe," I say, watching her as she moves toward us. "You have any medical training?"

"Just basic aid in case of field accidents."

"That's better than nothing." I look past her for the bot. "Pully! There should be a medkit in the galley. Bring it in here!"

"Of course, Lieutenant Chhun." The bot moves down the hall, but not before detaching his hovercam, which floats in and starts recording the carnage.

"Not a good time, Pully!"

"Sorry," the bot calls from the hallway. The hoverbot scoots away to reunite with him.

"Tech's dead," Kags calls.

"See if you can help Pully," I order.

Andien looks over Rook. The leej isn't talking, and I can tell it's taking him every bit of strength he has not to cry out in pain at the slightest touch to his abdomen. He winces and sucks in his breath as Andien pries away a loose fragment of armor.

"Sorry," she says.

Rook nods, a pained smile on his face. "What's—*ah*—what's the..." He grimaces and shuts his eyes before spitting out the last word. "... prognosis?"

"Better than it could have been, but not good." Andien motions her head toward the center of the room. "Can I speak to you a moment, Lieutenant?"

"You good, Rook?" I ask.

"Pretty sure you being by my side isn't slowing down the rate I'm dying."

I smile in spite of myself. "Yeah, I guess not. Don't get ahead of yourself, though, okay?"

I join Andien at the center of the room. She's looking down at the tech corpses. They haven't been dead long. Maybe a few hours.

"What's up?" I ask.

"Your friend doesn't have much time. The intensity of the blaster bolt seems to have cauterized his wound. He's only bleeding from where the shattered armor punctured his flesh. That can be fixed up by a medic and some skin-packs. But I'm sure he has internal injuries. Bad ones. I have no way of telling, of course, but suffice it to say he needs a cycler or a med-drop as soon as possible."

"I doubt there's a cycler up here." I look to the doorway for Pully and Kags to return. "And he's in no condition to climb down."

"Even if there were a cycler," Andien says, looking back at Rook, "neither of us knows the proper dosage of seda-tive. We'd likely kill him through guesswork or cause his system to fail from the pain of the cycler bot doing its work on a conscious patient."

I nod, feeling grim. "So where does that leave us?"

"When the bot comes back, I need to start the trans-mission right away. The sooner it reaches a ship—*any* Re-public ship—the faster help can arrive."

Kags and Pully appear in the doorway, carrying what looks to be a drop crate full of medical supplies.

"Republic overstock," Kags observes.

"I'm not complaining." The soldiers below us could desperately use these. "Here's the plan. Pully, work with Andien to begin the transmission. Kags, grab some blan-kets and do what you can to keep Rook comfortable."

"What about you?" Andien asks.

"I'm going to strap myself to this crate and climb back down. Doc Quigs can use it. I'll leave a few skinpacks to try and help Rook ward off any infection."

"Lieutenant," Pully says, looking me up and down. "This crate is very heavy for a human. What if you fall?"

"Either way, it gets down. Drop crates will hold together, even if I don't. Everything clear?"

The team acknowledges their understanding and gets to work. Andien pulls over a conduit and plugs it into Pully's back, while Kags moves to the bunks. I bend over and pick up the crate. The bot wasn't lying—it's heavy.

I turn to take one last look at Rook. "Keep fighting, leej."

"KTF, sir."

"Ooah."

The climb back down is nerve-racking. I've got a fifty-pound crate of medical supplies attached to my chest webbing and I'm hanging from a line of synth-rope. Aside from the fact that going down is tougher than coming up, having the thing banging against the rocks and continually pulling me off balance has me thinking I'll join the rest of the legionnaires the fast, hard way. But I hang on, and soon I'm only twenty meters from the ground.

There aren't any sleds rising up to meet me. In fact, everyone below seems busy to the point that I'm not sure they even know I'm up here. I debate cutting the rope, but decide against it. Mercifully, the crate eases onto the ground as I descend, making my final ten meters a comparative breeze.

A legionnaire rushes past me, a gunnysack of charge packs over his shoulder. I hold out a hand and call to him between heavy breaths. "Slow down, Leej. What's going on?"

The trooper stops, but with reluctance. He was likely ordered to go from Point A to Point B quickly. "Koobs are coming in force. Captain Ford has us setting up a defensive line."

He makes to take off again. "One more thing," I call. "I brought back some med supplies. Where did Sergeant Quigs set up?"

"He has the wounded set up in a cave. Captain Ford wants the med-sleds reconverted to allow for combat ops if possible."

"Can you lead me to the caves?"

The leej grabs one of the med crate's handles and helps me carry the load. "This way, sir."

It doesn't take long to reach the cave opening. Once inside, I see that there isn't much room. Just a narrow tunnel that leads to a cavern, maybe a hundred and fifty square meters. One of the first people I walk by is Captain Devers. He's standing under his own power, leaning against a wall close enough to the outside that it doesn't need any portable lighting. The captain looks away the moment he sees me, but I get a long enough glimpse to see that his face is a wreck. There are deep cuts on the bridge of his nose and beneath each cheek. One eye is swollen completely shut, and the other is red and weeping, with a black bruise circling it. His lower lip is split nearly in two. Yeah, he could use the skinpacks I'm carrying.

Quigs is standing over Pappy, examining a datapad. He joins me in the center of the cave as I set down the med crate. "Is that what I think it is?"

"Yeah." I rub the back of my head. "Brought it down from O-Z. Thing nearly pulled me off the mountainside a few times."

Quigs drops to a knee to open the crate, then sorts through it beneath the artificial light suspended from the cavern ceiling. "How did it go?"

"Transmission is underway, but at a price. One of the techs got into the stim stores. Got paranoid from the journo-bot's transmissions. Killed his crew, probably killed Rook, too."

Quigs stands up. "Rook was shot?"

"Yeah. Tech made some kind of a high-powered super-blaster by splicing together a few service pistols. Hand cannon. Blew a hole in Rook's armor, burned him up pretty good. Blew the tech's arm apart. He died before I left."

"I can't get up there to help him..."

I nod. "Yeah, I know. Just have to hope he holds on until relief comes."

"Well," Quigs says, closing the crate's lid, "let's hope it comes soon. This will help—there's some antibiotics and skinpacks—but it's not enough. No stims, obviously. No demidural, so I can't extend Pappy's coma or give anything to help with pain."

I look over at the major. He looks at peace. Next to him is the scientist whose wife was killed. He's just sitting still, catatonic.

"What's the plan with Pappy then? If he comes to with a cycler still moving through him…"

Quigs nods. "Bad, yeah. I traced the cycler's movement and issued the shutdown sequence about an hour ago. I figured if he went into cardiac arrest or showed signs of trauma, I could prime it again and let it finish the job, painful as it would be. But he seems okay. I'm hopeful the cycler repaired most of the major damage already, and what was left can be healed by Pappy's body."

"Good. And Devers?"

"Other than looking like he was trampled by a taurax, he'll be okay."

I turn to take my leave, but Quigs holds up a hand. "Wait." He reopens the case and pulls out a slim cylinder. "Take this to Twenties. Tell him to drink the entirety of the contents. Should clear up his infection within twelve hours."

I shake the cylinder at Quigs in a salute. "Thanks, Doc."

21

I make my way past legionnaires and Repub-Army basics hurriedly digging trenches. The excavated soil, dry and rocky, is scooped up by waiting soldiers and formed into berms. Sled drivers have positioned their vehicles behind these, and gunners are already in place, scanning the horizon for any sign of the koob-MCR force. I'm sure we're expecting a lot of incoming fire, and the berms will protect the repulsors' engines beneath the sleds, keeping the vehicles mobile in the event we have to make a last-ditch attempt to break out.

Hopefully it doesn't come to that. Our position is defensible. Our line has a clear field of fire for miles, plus the protection of sheer mountain walls at our back and sides. We're dug in deep, and it'll take a day of hellfire before anyone can even get close enough to pull us out. It's going to be all about attrition of resources. Insurgent bodies against Republic ammunition. Whichever side runs out first, loses.

A group of basics are grunting as they stack up aero-precision missiles behind a high berm. One of them nearly drops one on its head. The legionnaire overseeing the group's efforts rushes in to help grab the missile before it has the chance to clatter into a munitions pile. "Nice catch," I say as I walk by. "It'd be a shame if we blew ourselves up and deprived the koobs the opportunity."

"That you, Lieutenant?"

I look up to the sled and see Exo standing in the gunner's hatch. He's in one of the med-sleds, so there are no twin blaster cannons. "Have you set up as a mobile anti-vehicle gunner?"

Exo nods. "That's about right. Lock and pop until all the koob trucks go boom. Hey, how'd it go up top? We got help coming?"

"Time will tell. They were initiating the transmission when I left to bring some med supplies back to Doc Quigs."

"Oh yeah?" Exo taps out a beat on the top of the sled. "How's Point looking?"

I look back in the direction of the cave. "Like he went three rounds in the cage with O'Connor Malice and didn't bother putting his hands up."

"Good," Exo says. "He deserves worse. Where's Rook?"

I frown, regret and worry quickly washing over me. "Took a blaster bolt to the stomach by some half-crazed tech on Outpost Zulu. He was alive when I came down, but it's not looking good."

"Oba." Exo looks to the sky and rolls his neck. "That's just great." He reaches down for his rocket launcher, hoists it onto the sled's hull, and begins fiddling with the targeting assembly.

The basics continue to work. A silence grows until I understand that Exo is done talking. He needs time to deal with what happened to his friend. "I gotta go. Where's Captain Ford?"

Exo points farther down the line. "Over there. He set up a command overwatch on a protected ledge."

"Thanks." I move on, leaving Exo to do whatever it is he does with his emotions. I know that, ultimately, it'll be the koobs who'll bear the brunt of it.

Wraith isn't far from Exo. A five-minute walk and a brief climb, and I pull myself onto the flat slab of overhanging stone where he's perched. It's a perfect setup. Boulders dot the edge of it like castle parapets. The mountain itself serves as a sort of roof, with only the very end of the ledge exposed to the elements. "Nice place you have here, Captain."

"Thanks," Wraith says, turning from a datapad Sergeant Powell was showing him. "But I'll be setting up elsewhere. This space will be better used by a sniper."

"Twenties?" I ask.

Wraith nods. "He's on his way, along with his spotter. How did the op go?"

I brief him on what happened from climb up to climb down. He folds his arms and rocks on his heels. "That's too bad. For Rook, sure, but for us, too. We need every legionnaire we can get. I'm halfway hoping Pappy comes to with enough strength to grab an N-4 and join the fight."

I set my jaw. "The scientist—Andien—she says her dropship was the *Mercutio*."

Wraith taps his foot on the ground. "I wouldn't have thought Admiral Ubesk would be in this part of galaxy's edge. And I don't see why the *Mercutio* would be the ship to drop that field team—or why there seems to be a comm expert on a team designed to get the ball rolling on ore and mineral extraction."

"The *Chiasm*, Camp Forge, now this." I drop my arms to my sides in exasperation. "I've given up trying to make sense of what's going on. I'm just trying to get everyone back home."

"Yeah," Wraith concedes, "that needs to be our focus. And as long as a Republic warship gets to us before our ammunition and rations run out, I think we can do it." He points at the line. "I've got legionnaires dug into trenches, plus all sleds with twins ready to lay concentrated fire on an advancing enemy. We'll build a wall of bodies before any force moving on foot has a chance to reach us."

"How do we make sure they move on foot instead of in their trucks?"

Wraith holds out an open palm. "Sergeant Powell, can I see that datapad again?"

"Yes, sir." The sergeant walks the pad over. Wraith holds it in my view and scrolls through a series of graphs and text strings.

"One thing we should have enough of is AP missiles." Wraith taps the screen, bringing up a schematic of the anti-vehicle ordnance and launcher. "The loadmasters at Camp Forge gave us more than we needed and stuffed 'em in one sled. Sergeant Powell and I calibrated the range of the koobs' mortars based on some holofootage I recorded during the barrage. Our heavies will be able to engage with AP missiles a full three hundred meters before they can answer with any kind of effective fire. It's not much, but it should be enough to keep them from getting comfortable. That, combined with focused sniper fire, should make the koobs have to choose between trying to starve us out—which works to our advantage if help is coming— or go all out in an attempt to overrun us. We both know how much that will cost them."

"How do we handle communication?" I ask, looking up from the datapad. "Without a wide L-comm, it'll be difficult to get orders across the line without the koobs listening in."

"Still thinking that one over. The L-comm master channel can only be changed via narrow-beam recalibration by a destroyer. I guess Republic engineering didn't anticipate a company being isolated without capital ship support, and we don't have time to wait for R&D to come up with a hardware patch. Suggestions?"

I put my hands behind my back. "Each comm has the ability to set up, store, and encrypt two secure channels. I'd suggest we daisy chain beginning from you. Your orders go to Sergeant Powell and me, and then we send down the line of command until it reaches the end."

Wraith considers this for a moment. "Good. Let's go with that. I'm setting up at the center of the line. You may as well stay in this sector and oversee the AP fire. You stay linked to me and then pick out your other line. Have them link to Sergeant Powell. He'll be set up farther down."

"Yes, sir."

Twenties and Maldorn scrape up the rock onto the ledge. They both look banged up. Twenties's eye is a flaming, pus-lined ball of pink, and Maldorn's arm is in a sling, with a splint replacing the sleeve of battle armor that was destroyed. Maldorn is struggling to make the short climb one-handed, so I reach down and pull him up.

"Specialists Denino and Maldorn reporting for duty, sir." Twenties gives Wraith a sharp salute.

Saluting back, Wraith says, "That eye looks pretty bad. You sure you're okay to shoot?"

"I've got another eye, sir."

"Actually..." I pull out the vial of antibiotic and hand it to Twenties. "Doc Quigs wanted me to give you this. I brought it down from O-Z. It should clear up that eye in a few hours."

Twenties takes the vial and gives an appreciative nod.

"Don't suppose you brought back any bone-binders?" Maldorn asks.

"No, sorry. Your arm will have to heal the old-fashioned way until we can get you off-planet."

"Permission to set up, sir?" Twenties begins to unwrap his N-18.

Wraith steps out of the way, sweeping his arm toward the forward portion of the ledge. "Be my guest. Lieutenant Chhun, let me know when you're in position. I don't anticipate the koobs arriving before nightfall, but it could be any time after dark. Set up some sleep rotations along your section of the line."

Twenties is already on his stomach, the now-empty vial placed neatly to one side. He extends his rifle's bipod and looks into the scope. "Let's make sure we're ranged in for when the koobs come."

Maldorn drops to a knee and looks through his spotter's macro. "What's the high end you're looking for?"

Keying the preprogrammed adjustments on his scope, Twenties says, "I don't want to waste blaster charges, so let's not try for a new record with the N-18. How about three thousand meters?"

Maldorn sweeps his macro over the field, then stops and holds his finger over the spot-share button. "I see a group of three rocks at about that distance, a few degrees west of your position. Sending now." He presses the button, sending the info to the scope; Twenties will now be able to see the direction he needs to adjust his weapon inside the scope itself. With this spot-share technology, a comfortable spotter/sniper legionnaire team can wreak havoc on enemy forces, dropping targets from extreme distances almost as fast as they can pull a trigger.

Twenties slowly moves the rifle. "I see it. Lieutenant, will you call out my test fire?"

Usually this would go out over the L-comm, but orders were to shut the frequency off, so I yell down to the soldiers below, "Range fire!"

"Range fire!"

"... Range fire!"

The warning carries down the line. Twenties waits until the calls die down, then fires at something so far away I can't even see it.

"First try," observes the spotter. "Nice shot."

"Thanks."

"Good shooting as always, Twenties." I key in my comm to open a secure channel with him. "I want you to send me reports of whatever you see. I'm also going to have

Sergeant Powell link up with you. If I give you any company-wide orders, you relay them to him."

"Understood, sir."

I walk beneath the stars, just finishing up my inspection of the line. It's another freezing night, and I've been moving as quickly as possible in an attempt to get my limbs warmed up. But now I stop and crane my neck upward to stare into the brilliant Kublaren night sky. There's nothing out here. No flashing holo ads, no buzz of lights. Instead of the constant din of noise you find on most populated worlds and city centers, there's just... silence. I can hear soldiers roll over in their sleep. It's striking how spending time where it's still and clear and wild impacts you. I'd put nights like these—minus the gathering army marching our way—right up at the top of the list of what's best about serving in the Republic military machine. You can barely find places like this in the Mid-Core, and with a few rare exceptions, the Core worlds only offer an escape from metropolises for those with enough credits to afford it. But if you become a legionnaire, you get to see pristine beauty without having to make a single transaction.

Though you might pay by a blaster bolt through the head.

I stare at the stars a moment longer, wondering which one will be the point from which our relief comes. Wondering if this is the last time I'll get to take in a majestic view like I'm enjoying now.

"Comin' in," I whisper before dropping down into my trench. I pull out my mags and sweep the horizon. Still no sign of koobs.

Masters pushes himself up to a sitting position, his back against the trench wall, and adjusts his blanket.

I turn to look down at him. "Your watch doesn't start for another fifteen. You can go back to sleep."

The legionnaire pours water from his canteen and drops a caff-tab into the cup. The water darkens and bubbles, heating in an instant to two hundred degrees. "No thanks, Lieutenant. If I go back to sleep now, I'll just be even more tired when I really do have to wake up."

He offers me the cup. I take it and let the steam warm up the tip of my nose.

He prepares a cup of kaff for himself. "Any sign of the koobs?"

"Not so far," I say, setting down my field mags so I can hold my warm cup between both hands. "The ETA we calculated for them passed a few hours ago."

"Maybe they got lost."

I laugh, sending ripples through the black kaff. "It *is* pretty dark out."

My comm chimes with an incoming message. "Hang on," I say to Masters. I turn on my headset. "Go for Chhun."

Twenties's voice comes to me in a whisper. "Pretty sure I see movement through the scope. Didn't want to wake up Maldorn if I don't have to. Will you take a look?"

I pick up my mags and search beyond our lines.

"Are they here?" Masters whispers.

"Maybe," I answer in a hushed tone. "Okay, Twenties, where am I looking?"

"Focus in on the lone peak. North-northwest."

The mags sweep across the barren landscape until a lone mountain comes into view, pointed like a wizard's hat. "I'm oriented."

"Continue west another thirty degrees."

I do as Twenties says, and I'm looking at a series of boulders—not exactly the sort of terrain an armada of trucks would drive through. I watch in silence, involuntarily holding my breath, waiting for something to happen. There are no vehicles... no anything.

"There!" Twenties calls calmly over the comm. "Did you see that?"

I did. Or at least, I think I did. I focus my mags in. We're not exactly alone on Kublar—there are a number of nocturnal predators and prey. Twenties *could* have seen a jaghound loping along a game trail, or one of the many rodent-like insectoids scurrying for shelter from some unseen threat. I purse my lips, ready to set my mags down, when from behind one of the boulders I see a humanoid form peek out.

"Yeah. I see it. Looks humanoid."

The figure slowly reveals more of its body, until it's clear of the boulder. It's walking in a crouch, carrying something in its arms. A blaster rifle. Soon more humanoids emerge, imitating the lead creature's stealthy motions.

I save the field position in my mags. "Twenties, hold fire. I'm going to call this in to Captain Ford."

I key my comm to Wraith's direct channel.

"Go for Vic-1. You see something, Lieutenant Chhun?"

"Yes, sir." I tell my mags to transmit the image and position through the secure channel. "Just sent you a still and the spot. Twenties has them on overwatch."

"That's them, all right."

I nudge Masters with the toe of my boot. He's already primed, his rifle ready and the blanket stowed. "Start waking everyone up," I say. "Keep them quiet."

Masters hops out of the trench and moves slowly, shaking basics and leejes awake.

Wraith's voice comes back over the comm. "Let's get everyone primed."

"Already on it." I'm looking through my mags, following the enemy movement. More silent commandos are shuffling toward us, though they're still well out of blaster fire. Twenties is probably the only leej who could dust them at this distance.

"Good. I'll transmit the location to all the leej HUDs. Good thing Kreggak wasn't given a bucket, just an L-comm."

"Tiny blessings," I say dryly. "Should I have Twenties identify targets and take some of them out?"

There's a pause before Wraith answers. "Not yet. As good as Twenties is, he won't dust more than a dozen before they retreat behind those rocks. Let's see if they get close enough for the sleds and blaster rifles to eat them up. I'd like to take as many as possible in round one."

I nod, though Wraith isn't there to see it. "Understood, sir. I'll have the men ready to fire on your command."

"On *your* command," corrects Wraith. "You're going to have a better position. The line will wait for your section to open up, and then we'll join."

"Yes, sir."

"Vic-1, out. KTF."

Masters hops down into the trench, causing me to jump back and reach for my pistol. "Oba, Masters. Don't do that."

The kid rubs the back of his helmet. "Sorry, sir. I got the word out. Everyone's up, waiting for orders. What do you want me—" He stops suddenly, listening.

I look at him. "What's up?"

"Orders just came in. Text string since there's no L-comms. We've got the spots on our HUD, and we're to hold fire until you give the order. How will the men know when you give the order?"

"They'll hear you start shooting." I key Twenties on my comm.

"Go for Twenties," comes the quiet voice of my sniper.

"Okay, Captain Ford wants us to take the first shots once they're close enough that we can do some damage with the sleds and rifles."

"Yes, sir," whispers Twenties in reply. "Maldorn was just reading it to me from his HUD. Are you watching them right now?"

"Not yet." I pull up my mags. "What's up?"

"See how there are two waves spread out and coming our way?"

Through the night vision, I see a fanned-out force creeping steadily closer. A second wave moves behind them, keeping its distance. "Yeah, I see it."

"Well, it looks to me like that second group is humping mortars. They're grouped in threes, two of 'em carrying something, the third with what looks like a rucksack on. Probably the bombs."

"They're gonna try to soften us up before that first wave attempts an overrun."

"That's my guess," Twenties says. "I can start picking 'em off. Maldorn says the other snipers in the unit each have a mortar crew painted on the HUD. We can dust 'em right now..."

A deep breath escapes my lungs. "Keep your focus on them. But don't dust them yet. I want those other koobs in closer before we let them know that we see them. Wait until the last possible second."

"Yes, sir."

I watch as the first wave gathers closer. They begin to slow down and look back through the darkness in the direction of their counterparts. I tear my eyes away to look up and down the line. The turrets are manned, and every soldier present has his weapon aimed and ready to fire. I'm sure if my bucket was on, I'd see which legionnaire was painting which koob so that as many targets as possible go down with the first trigger pulls.

I go back to the mags, my elbows resting on the edge of the trench. Masters stands next to me, following his own target through his N-4's holographic sight. "Masters," I whisper, "I want you to open up the moment Twenties shoots."

"Copy."

The three-koob mortar crews stop moving. Each group begins setting up their base plate, unrolling their cache of bombs, and fixing their firing tube's bipod. But the front line continues to inch closer, rifles held at the low ready. I'm chewing the inside of my mouth so furiously that I can taste blood.

The mortar team I'm watching—the one Twenties spotted for me—finishes setting up. One of them grabs a mortar round and holds it above the tube. Its air sac inflates, and a sharp, piercing croak fills the night air. The advancing koobs halt, and the alien I'm watching grabs hold of the tube with its free hand to load the mortar.

An explosion of gore plays out on my field mags as the koob's head explodes. The round tumbles harmlessly to the ground. I hear the *krak-bdew* from Twenties a microsecond later.

"Open up!" I scream.

Masters is shooting before I've finished my sentence, and then every legionnaire is firing his N-4. The snipers are multiplying this overwhelming force with their N-18s, picking apart confused mortar teams still desperately trying to get a round launched toward us. Then the sled gunners catch up.

Dat-dat-dat-dat!

The dark veil of night is lifted as brilliant light from the blaster bolts illuminates the battlefield. My mags immediately adjust for the light source, protecting my eyes from being dazzled.

The first wave of koobs, the entire advance line, is taken completely by surprise. Within sixty standard seconds they're cut down and out of the fight. Maybe one hundred fighters, and most of them never even had the chance to shoot back.

KTF.

It's a different story with the mortar crews. The snipers picked them apart and sent them running, but not before they had the chance to get a few rounds off.

"Incoming!"

We brace ourselves against our dugout walls, then return to the surface upon hearing the rounds land. Koob calibrations were off, and the mortars impacted *behind* the line of the dead koob wave. Maybe they were just panicky. It would be hard not to be when everyone in front of you dies in the span of a minute and the buddies to your left and right are exploding before they can even hear the blaster round that hits them.

Broken and routed, the last of the koob mortar crews turn and run. Our snipers drop them with pinpoint accuracy, rounds tearing through their backs. At last, only one remains, still a long way from the protection of the rocks. The calls for a ceasefire travel along our line, as he's out of most of our ranges. So we watch.

The koob stops, turns, and sees the trail of righteous judgment behind it. He stands there, as if stupefied—then falls over sideways after an N-18 round blows off his left arm at the shoulder.

"Holy strokes," Masters says, vapor rising from the barrel of his rifle. "Those koobs just got wrecked. *Man*, it's gonna stink tomorrow. I hope the wind blows the other way."

My headset chimes, and Wraith's voice comes online. "Lieutenant Chhun, nice work. Tell the men to reactivate the L-comms."

"Copy." I relay the order to Masters, then climb out of my trench. Fast-walking along the line I shout, "Turn on your L-comms!"

"Turn on your L-comms!"

"... Turn on your L-comms!"

The order is sent down the line, traveling faster by word of mouth than my two feet could hope to move.

"Excellent work, men," Wraith says over the L-comm. "The entire enemy probe is destroyed. Chieftain Kreggak, I assume you're listening in. Your Kublarens aren't coming back. Consider this a courtesy call so you don't stay up too late waiting for them. I suggest you refrain from any further attacks, unless you're looking to rule over a tribe of graves."

The chieftain growls out an answer. "*K-k-k...* We will see, leejon-ayer. Maybe you big die?"

"Maybe," Wraith concedes, his voice calm and even. "But you won't see it. My snipers have visual scans of you and all your accompanying elders. Our battle tech will find you out of a sea of ten thousand koobs. Their orders are to blow your heads off the moment they spot you."

Kreggak must've had Wraith set to external message, because a hubbub of koob croaking erupts in the background. I think our captain touched a nerve.

A new voice comes over the comm. Human. "What is your designation, legionnaire?"

"LS-33," Wraith replies. "I take it you're with the MCR?"

"I am," the voice confirms. "General Vantage Poll."

"The Republic does not acknowledge military rank among insurgents. That said, you will be given the most lenient terms deemed reasonable by me should you surrender your force now."

"And what terms might those be?"

"The Kublarens will disarm and return to their villages. All non-Kublaren species not claiming the rank of officer will disarm and surrender. They will be tried as insurgents by a court of the House of Reason. All self-proclaimed MCR officers will be executed by legionnaire firing squad. Should you refuse, your entire force will be destroyed."

Poll laughs into the comm. "Legionnaire, I think you overestimate your strength. It is *I* who should offer terms of surrender, not that the MCR has any such intentions. We have, after all, destroyed your planetary base as well as your capital ship. You are in no position to dictate terms to the Mid-Core Rebellion."

Wraith is unfazed. "I need an answer now, or the offer will be retracted."

"I'm afraid I must decline. I am, however, willing to—"

"Acknowledged," Wraith interrupts. "Legionnaires, prepare to destroy the insurgents and their koob allies at the first opportunity. KTF."

"Ooah!" shout the men over the comms.

"Legionnaires," says Wraith, "terminate L-comm."

22

A group of leather-winged lizards are fighting over a piece of koob. The battlefield is full of these mean little scavengers. They hiss and bare rows of tiny, sharp teeth while they jockey for feeding positions. No matter where you go in the galaxy, you see the same type. Different species, different animals, but the same type. When it comes to flying carrion-eaters, I prefer the feathered sort. Just feels like home, I guess.

Masters watches an enhanced view of the wildlife before bringing his field mags down to his waist. "Well, that's disgusting."

I'm sitting in the shadows of our foxhole, dreading the time when the sun positions itself directly over my head. It's already too hot without my bucket there to help regulate the temperature. I drain the last bits of a unit of water. "At least the wind is blowing out. Not that it would bother *you*. *I'm* the one who would have to smell it."

Masters shrugs and goes back to his nature documentary. I stand up and dust off my gloves. "I'm gonna walk the line. Watch for living koobs, too. Not just the dead ones."

As I move down the line, legionnaires clean their rifles while basics do their best to stay cool in their uniforms. I'm making my way toward Exo's sled when my comm chimes. "Lieutenant Chhun, can you hear me?"

"Andien? Miss Broxin?" I'm surprised to hear her voice. Does she have a status update on Rook? Is relief coming?

"Yes!" she exclaims. "I figured out a way to recalibrate the L-comm frequency from the outpost, but I wanted to make sure it worked before I adjusted all your comms. You can't communicate with anyone else until they get on the same frequency—this overrides any preset encryptions. Didn't want the entire company unable to communicate by comm..."

I frown. But a gust of wind brings some slight relief from the heat, enough to curb my annoyance. I go for mild sarcasm. "So you just risked cutting *me* off. Thanks."

"I'm sorry." There's an impatience in her voice that cuts away at the sincerity of her apology. "You're the only legionnaire whose name I recognized from the database. But now I can start patching in the others, so long as there's someone who can give me an exclude list. Specialist Kags has a good handle on who's there from the regular army, but not the Legion."

This is promising, but it will need to be done quickly. I don't want half our force to be cut off from the chain of command if the attack comes mid-transfer. "Can you switch us back if something goes down?"

"I can."

I look out for any sign of an advancing enemy. They didn't come at daybreak, when we most expected them. Maybe Wraith's warnings were heeded after all. "Recalibrate Captain Ford. He may be listed as a lieutenant."

"Updating now..."

As soon as Wraith is looped in, I get him up to speed on what Andien is doing.

"Good work," Wraith says to Andien. "Did you hear anything back after sending the transmission?"

"No, but I don't expect we would. We got the message out by amplifying the bot's deep-space communicators, but Outpost Zulu isn't capable of receiving a deep-space comm relay without a capital ship in orbit."

"Understood." If Wraith's disappointed, his voice doesn't betray it. "And you're sure that Kublaren-controlled L-comm won't receive this update?"

Andien sounds certain. "No. Not as long as I don't push the recalibration to whoever's device they own. I have a database listing all the legionnaires from Victory Company, but I don't know who's... well, I don't know who's with you. If you have someone who can give me a list of men needing the update..."

Wraith assigns the task to his senior NCO. "Sergeant Powell can tell you who else to add."

"I'll get right on it. Oh, and Lieutenant Chhun? Your squadmate is still holding on, in case you were wondering."

I feel a sudden flush of shame. When Andien first came over the comm, I meant to ask her. Maybe it's unfounded, but I'm bothered that she was the one who brought up Rook's condition instead of me. "Glad to hear it."

"I'm going to inspect the left flank's AP setup," Wraith says. "Let me know when the comm system is up, and I'll inform the men."

Another billow of wind pushes past me, sending small pebbles skipping and causing the dust to swirl. I still need to check on Exo. Need to be sure he and everyone else are prepared for an attack that could come at any time. The TT-16 observation bots show that the koob force is still out there, holding its position about eight kilometers away, but it won't take long for the trucks to make that distance. We'll need to be prepared to hit them the moment they're in range.

I find Exo leaning in the turret of his operating sled, arms crossed and facing the general direction of the enemy position.

"Hey, Exo."

"Hey, Lieutenant."

More wind kicks up, causing some of the dust to brush across my face. I squeeze my eyes shut and wait for it to pass. I blink away the silt from my eyelids and reach for a pair of polarized goggles from my kit. If this wind keeps up, I'll need them. "Just checking in. What's your status?"

"Uh…" Exo looks around, double-checking that everything is as it should be before giving me an answer. "Good to go, LT. Got my launcher down here to keep the dust out, got enough missiles to take down a destroyer, and my crew all know where the casualty collection point is. All I need now are some koobs to kill. Maybe a beer. Did you bring any of those down from O-Z?"

"Sorry, forgot to check."

Exo leans his head back. "That's the problem with you, Lieutenant. Priorities get all out of order."

I smile and put on the goggles in anticipation of another cloud of dust I see pushing toward us. "We figured out a workaround to the L-comms. We should have private squad and company links before much longer."

"Kind of enjoyed the silence, sir."

I nod out at the horizon before turning to head back to Masters. "Wouldn't last."

By the time I reach my foxhole, the wind has become a sustained howl, almost a gale. My armor clinks from the tiny pebbles and grains of koob-dust peppering it. I pull my shemagh over my mouth and nose to keep from choking. I drop into our dugout and pat Masters on the back.

"This sucks, sir!" he yells above the gusts.

"I don't like it, either," I reply, ducking below ground to talk with him. "But we need to get back up there."

Masters drops his head. "I knew you'd say that."

"Think tactically. If we were assaulting an enemy position that had a range advantage..."

Pulling himself to a standing position, Masters finishes my sentence. "This is when we'd hit 'em." He looks into the ever-thickening storm of dust. "I can barely see the ground twenty meters in front of me."

"That's twenty meters more time to react than we'd have just sitting around." I shake out the dust that's settled into my ear, then adjust my scarf in an attempt to keep any more from getting in.

The all-comm chime sounds over my headset.

"Victory Company, this is Vic-1. Someone up at Outpost Zulu was able to re-secure the L-comms, so we're back in business. I want you all on high alert until this dust storm dies down. *Expect* an attack. Also, some good news: Pappy regained consciousness, and it looks like he'll pull through. You can visit with him whenever our rescue ship arrives. Vic-1, out."

I squint behind my goggles at the maelstrom. Exo's voice comes over the comm. "You guys think this storm is bad, wait until Pappy finds out what the point was up to."

"Maintain comm discipline," I chide, cutting off snickers from the other legionnaires.

"Yes, sir," Exo agrees. "I was just testing the Doomsday Squad channel. It works, everyone."

There's more laughter, then the men settle into a quiet vigil. The dust storm swells into a rolling mass of tan, arid topsoil that boils up to the silver cloud sky. The noise is intense, my ears filled with the howling of the wind and the pounding of dirt and pebbles. I'm not sure that even with a bucket on I'd be able to hear anything other than the storm. From within the roiling wall that sweeps across the field, my eyes continually spot shapes that prove to be phantoms. Like a child seeing animals in the clouds, I keep thinking a koob truck or MCR tank is moving my way.

The wind changes directions and blows stiffly at our backs. The storm pushes away from us, the sudden crosswind halting its intensity. Most of the open field lying beyond our line is still hidden from us, but our visibility is improved. We can see reliably to one hundred meters, with the promise of more if the clean wind continues to push down from the cliffs and over our backs.

My comm pops alive with Twenties's voice. "Hey. I see something. Looks like lights inside the storm."

Squinting, I see the same thing. I announce it over the L-comm. "Doomsday-1 to Victory Company. We're seeing what looks to be lights moving our direction through the storm."

"Copy," Wraith answers. "Leejes, be ready."

I stare at the pair of dual lights bouncing toward us. They grow in intensity, and then a white koob truck bursts out of the dust storm as if emerging from behind a curtain. The vehicle is loaded heavy with koobs, all of them wrapped in their linen garments so that only their eyes are exposed.

"Here we go!" Exo screams, the *whoosh* of his aero-precision missile capping his battle cry like an exclamation point. The ordnance tracks the koob vehicle even as it attempts evasive maneuvers, drilling top-down into the truck and sending it—and its payload of koob soldiers—up in flames.

More vehicles break out of the dust storm, and more AP missiles go after them. It soon becomes clear to the koobs that the drivers aren't going to be able to avoid getting cooked, so they begin to jump from the moving vehicles preemptively. Other insurgents, running toward us on foot, are met with a storm of Republic counterfire—and as the koob trucks emerge suddenly from the storm behind them, the drivers find themselves in the middle of chaos, running over their own foot soldiers.

This has all the makings of a koob disaster, which is just fine with me.

"Don't let up!" Wraith orders.

We pour more fire into them, halting their advance. The drivers of the trucks fishtail their rigs sideways and jump out. We pepper those on foot as they take cover behind flaming wrecks. The koobs form a line behind their trucks, sending ineffective blaster and slug-thrower fire in our general direction.

I key up the squad comm. "Exo, save the missiles unless you see a truck trying to break past that line. It looks like the vics out this way are all personnel transport."

"Copy, boss. My N-4 was feeling neglected anyway."

I catch my first glimpse of humans and yellow-skinned, spike-covered Kimbrin from the MCR. They arrive on the field through repulsor transports. They don't appear to be military-grade or equipped with gun emplacements, but a few leej heavies hammer them with AP missiles. The rebels finally wise up and start disembarking before their vehicles break the wall of dust that shields the main force from our weapons.

"Outpost Zulu," I call into the L-comm, "see if you can pick up and decrypt any other comm signals out there. MCR is using something we can spook."

"Um..." Andien says. Her uncertainty at being roped into battle intelligence is evident in her voice. "Okay, I'll try. Yeah. I think I can do that."

"Once you decrypt," a rough and raspy voice says over the comm, "patch the feed to me, and I'll sort what's important to Captain Ford and Lieutenant Chhun. You're doing a hell of a job, legionnaires. Keep it up. KTF."

Holy strokes, that's Pappy's voice.

The moment he goes off comm, the men—who already were giving the joint force of koobs and MCR more than they could handle—step up their game. Insurgent after insurgent is dusted as they run for the cover of the abandoned trucks. I don't care how many of them there are, once this storm lets up—and it's already noticeably dying down—the only thing that will stop us from dusting them all is if we run out of charge packs.

More insurgents run through the dwindling dust storm and struggle to reach the front line survivors. The sled guns rage out their steady *dat-dat-dat-dat-dat-dat*, rising above the noise of blaster rifle fire. The koobs and their co-conspirators fall in heaps. They tumble head over heels, are struck square, and drop. They spin and twist and dive and fall. Some crawl, bellies against the ground, digging their three-fingered hands into the soil in an attempt to reach sanctuary before they're struck dead by blaster fire from multiple angles.

Beside me, Masters is shooting with a controlled fury, selecting his targets, killing, and finding the next koob. I leave him to it and set off along our line, calling our opportunities and repositioning firing teams to keep the aliens at bay. To fulfill Wraith's warning that death is all that awaits those who come for us.

I'm beneath Maldorn and Twenties's position when I hear an incoming buzzing, followed by an explosion in the area between us and the enemy. It's followed by four more rapid *crumps*.

"Koob mortars!" someone calls out over the comm.

I duck down instinctively, memories of the barrage on the village coming immediately to mind. I'd really prefer we not have to take that volume of incoming fire.

Another mortar whizzes through the sky, but instead of detonating near us, it falls short, landing next to one of the burning koob trucks and sending an insurgent flying. Are they blind-firing through the storm? If so, they're welcome to keep it up.

The next round of mortars remains ineffectual, but they're closer to our line than the previous ones. Not good.

Pappy's voice comes over the comm. "I know enough Kimbrin to understand that there's a spotter on this side of the storm, helping the firing crew walk their shots forward. Have your snipers find and eliminate."

"Copy," I answer. "Maldorn! Someone—probably Kimbrin—is helping the mortar teams home in their fire. Spot 'em and take 'em out."

"On it, sir."

I pull up my field mags and join the search. I see a Kimbrin crouched next to a destroyed repulsor transport who looks to be speaking into a handheld comm. I paint him with my mags. "I think this is our guy."

"Yeah," Twenties says, his voice not betraying the adrenaline rush I hear from the rest of the squad. "I see him. He's pretty well covered by that transport, though. I don't have a clear shot. Anyone else see this space rat?"

"Yeah," Exo answers. "I see him. Definitely out of N-4 range."

I move toward Exo's position. "Let's find a way, guys."

I arrive just in time to hear the *whoosh* of Exo's AP rocket. I jerk my head to watch its trajectory, thinking for a moment that more vehicles are attempting to drive hard in our direction. Instead, I see the rocket free-fire toward the Kimbrin spotter. Exo used his weapon like a heavy-duty sniper rifle, and his aim is perfect.

"Forward spotter eliminated," I report over the comm. "Looks like the storm is dying down, too."

The wind reduces to a breeze, and the wall of dust sprinkles back to the earth. Visibility gradually improves, allowing those with buckets to switch to infrared and begin dusting targets farther into the cloud. I watch through my field mags as the mortar crews, their positions no longer hidden, are picked off by our snipers.

With the storm's passing, we can finally see the mass of MCR and koobs on the battlefield. They waver under fire and begin to withdraw, diving behind rocks and scurrying off behind distant hills. If we had capital ship support, now is the time we'd call down tri-fighters to pound them into vapor. If we had a secure forward operating base, like Camp Forge, we could paint their hiding spots and coordinate an orbital strike... with the capital ship we don't have. Instead, we watch them go, and prepare for another attack.

My comm beeps. It's Twenties. "Lieutenant Chhun, you want me to pick 'em off until they're out of range?"

"How are you on charge packs?"

"Green. But I'll be black before much longer, sir."

I wrinkle my nose, like I somehow don't like the smell of what he's telling me. Unlike the sleds, which have self-contained recharging cores for their weaponry, our blasters need charge magazines to work. Once we've depleted what we've got, that's it. Our blaster rifles become little more than expensive clubs. "Better hold off."

My comm chimes again.

"Go for Chhun."

"Lieutenant, it's me," Masters says. "Checked with the guys. Most of 'em are green for blaster charges, but a few are almost black. I'm gonna see if I can redistribute some charge packs. You got any extras on you?"

I look down at my munitions satchel. I have about eight charge packs left. It's an unusual feeling to give these up—I'm already fighting against the instinct to stand and bang away during the fight—but my role is to coordinate Doomsday Squad for optimum battle efficiency. "I can give you six."

"Be right there, sir."

Again my comm chimes. The lull in the fight has every-one scrambling to tie up loose ends. "Go for Chhun."

"Lieutenant Chhun," Wraith says in his cool battlefield voice. "Specialist Kags made the climb down the mountain while we were slinging blaster fire at the koobs. He want-ed to get in the fight, so I sent him your way."

"Copy."

The incessant chime of my comm sounds yet again. "Go for Chhun," I say, careful to hide the annoyance in my voice. I haven't been able to take more than two steps without getting a call, and it's starting to piss me off.

"Got something here." Twenties's voice is almost trem-bling; he's either terrified or excited. "HUD has a positive ID on the head koob from the village. He's talking to some humans, squatting behind cover. Not well enough behind cover, though. It's a long one, but I have a shot."

"Mark the target and take the shot," I order.

I struggle to pull my field mags from their protective case, eager to get my eyes on Twenties's target. Following the reticule, I find myself looking at a distant outcropping of rock, shaded by a copse of defoliated trees. But that's all I see. From my vantage point, no one is anywhere nearby. I hear the shot and see what has to be little pieces of koob fly up over the rock.

"Target eliminated," Twenties announces over the comm.

"Nice shot, Twenties," I say, again amazed at the legionnaire's ability to hit, well, *anything*. No matter how difficult.

"Victory Company, this is Pappy. I'm monitoring the observation bots. Confirm identity of target just hit."

I announce what happened over the L-comm. "LS-81 has a confirmed kill on Kreggak, the koob chieftain from Moona Village. ID was made by HUD facial recognition at range."

"Outstanding work." Pappy's voice scratches out praise. "I'm watching the koobs, and they look to be bugging out. Tribal structure requires the election of a new chieftain—but I think they've just had enough of getting their asses kicked."

A cheer goes up from the line. And, indeed, I can see koob combatants attempting to leave the battlefield over a distant ridge. My mags catch a glimpse of a human attempting to turn the koobs back, but the koobs aren't having it. I figure this is an MCR insurgent leader, at the very least. I paint him with my mags, and just as I'm about to call him in for Twenties to try another long-range shot, I see him point frantically skyward. The koobs stop in their tracks, look up, and begin filing back toward the front.

We're in trouble. I search out the heavens, squinting from the glare of the sun. I see it a second before the call comes in from Andien.

"An Ohio-class space cruiser arrived from hyperspace!"

Ohio class. These are ancient, massive, near-derelict, deep-space cruisers, incapable of orbital bombardment but able to take a beating in ship-to-ship combat. Capable of carrying a full wing of starfighters.

Needless to say, it's not Republic.

23

Sergeant Powell is barking orders over the comm, filling the void of depleted NCOs by making sure every leej in both squads is ready for what comes next. "You heard Captain Ford! Wounded to the CCP! Everyone else, get in your foxhole. Heavies—*shoot them down*!"

I look up as a wave descends toward us. Initially no bigger than a shining star, the incoming fighter wing gradually takes shape, revealing the sleek snub noses and dual blaster cannons of K-13 Preyhunters. These are older starfighters, but still effective.

My mind is spinning with thoughts. I'm relieved that it's K-13s—ships without bombs—coming our way. I need to make sure heads are down for what will surely be a blaster-strafing run. But how long did it take the MCR to piece together a functional Ohio-class cruiser? How long were they planning today?

Running toward an open foxhole, as legionnaires stream past with deliberate hurry, I catch a glimpse of Exo. He's got his AP missile launcher ready and is shouting for the incoming starfighters to "Bring it!"

With a *whoosh,* Exo's missile streaks up toward the lead fighter. Seconds later, three more follow it from the other heavy leejes with functional aero-precision missile launchers. The lead Preyhunter pitches into a downward roll and breaks formation, seeking to dodge the incoming fire. But Exo locked on before firing, and the missile quickly compensates, catching up and erupting into a massive fireball that incinerates the starfighter.

"One!" Exo shouts. He deftly reloads and locks on for a second shot. This one hits its target straight on, but more Preyhunters shoot through the flaming debris and wreckage, continuing their attack run.

"Two!"

Whoosh!

Another explosion.

"Three!"

The fighters are close, and there's no way Exo and the other heavy leejes can wipe them all out before they're on us. The lead starfighter opens fire at the north end of our line, targeting the sleds.

Zet-zet! Zet-zet! Zet-zet!

The blaster fire tears along our line, chewing up rocks and dirt before tearing into a combat sled, blowing holes in the hull. As a second Preyhunter swoops down, one of its wingmen explodes behind it.

"Four!"

The starfighters' blaster cannons begin ravaging the ground. I dive away from the strafed path and shout, "Exo! Get out of that sled!"

Whoosh!—comes Exo's reply. He gets off a final rocket before leaping off the sled and sprinting toward me. The sled erupts behind him. We grit our teeth as the rest of the starfighters, now unchallenged, rip into our line.

When the Preyhunters climb once more, to no doubt circle around for another pass, our line is left with the screams of the wounded and chaotic shouts to regroup.

"Missiles!" Exo calls out.

I look to his cache and find the basic who'd been supplying the ordnance dead, nearly cooked by the blaster cannon fire. "Let's go get 'em!" I say, and the two of us run over to grab as many AP missiles as our arms can carry.

Exo jumps into a foxhole and motions for me to lower the missiles to him.

"The whole cache will explode if they score a hit on the next pass," I warn.

Moving his fingers rapidly as a request that I hurry, Exo says, "They score a direct hit on this hole and I'm dead either way."

As I start handing down the rockets, Specialist Kags shows up, dirt smeared across his face, an N-4 slung in front of him. He crashes down on his knees next to me, sucking in gasps of air. "Give me a hand, Kags," I say, handing Exo another missile. The Preyhunters are lining up for another attack run.

"Yes, sir, but sir—" Kags points a finger toward the line. "They're coming for us!"

I look over and see koobs and Kimbrin sprinting across the kill zone, moving en masse toward our lines. We're going to be overrun if we don't get some firepower on them—and with some of the sleds down, that's going to be tough. "Get Exo his missiles," I order, then key my L-comm. "The koobs are coming this way. Repulse their charge!"

The last missile delivered, Kags and I find our own fox-hole and take up firing positions.

"I only have three charge packs, sir," Kags says, his voice betraying desperation.

"One more than me," I say, swapping out my partially depleted pack for a new one. "So don't waste 'em."

Our snipers begin dropping targets, and the *krak-bdew* of the N-18s is augmented by N-4s as we pour fire into the thick wave of oncoming insurgents. I hear the rhythmic hammering of our remaining sleds. The charge begins to falter as the traumatized insurgents see their comrades brutalized by these powerful blaster cannons at close range.

The *whoosh* of AP missiles tells me that the Preyhunters are coming in for another pass. Kags and I duck our heads to avoid the onslaught, hoping we didn't jump into an unlucky foxhole. I hear the deadly incoming starfighter blaster fire, Preyhunters blowing up in the air, men screaming, and the rattle of insurgent blasters and slug throwers growing ever closer.

But the sleds have all quieted down. I hazard a look. Dead gunners are slumped in their turrets.

"Preyhunters are disengaging!" Exo informs the company. "Koobs and MCR must be too close for another pass."

The insurgents are almost upon us. Kimbrin howls and human screams intermingle with wheezing battle croaks as the koobs' air sacs swell in anticipation of making contact with our line. If I still had my bucket, it would be screaming at me to control my breathing, steady my heart rate. I'm gripping the stock of my N-4 so tightly that I wonder if they'll find my fingers' imprints there when they pry the weapon from my dead hand.

Dead hand. I'm going to die. This is it. We positioned ourselves for maximum survival and maximum damage, like our brothers at Camp Forge before us. Now it's our turn to be swallowed whole by the raging charge of the insurgents.

Kags is sweating, his eyes wide. I gather myself, pat him on the back and say, "KTF."

He nods. "Yes, sir."

"This is everything, Victory Company." Wraith's voice, impossibly, is smooth and in control. Like he expected this. Like it was all part of some plan. "These kelhorns are going to pay such a high price that the very thought of more legionnaires coming to pick up revenge will keep them from ever sleeping soundly again. KTF."

We unleash a veritable hell of blaster fire. I'm killing insurgents with every squeeze of my trigger. Exo is shooting unguided rockets into the fray, blowing patches of insurgents apart from the blast. But still they keep coming.

"Changing packs!" Kags calls out. I heat up my firing as he swaps out his blaster pack before popping back up to rejoin the fight.

My own blaster dry fires—I've spent my last magazine. "Kags! Kags! Any more?"

"Using my last one, Lieutenant!"

I pull out my blaster pistol and take carefully aimed shots at the rampant horde. When they find us, they'll say we gave our all.

Something scurries behind us, and I swing my blaster pistol around. It's aimed directly between Captain Devers's swollen eyes. He's carrying four charge packs in his arms.

"Found these," he says, handing them to me. "Here."

A fusillade of enemy fire snaps and buzzes overhead. Devers hugs the dirt while Kags and I swap in fresh charge packs. We open up on the enemy, but it's like trying to stop waves by throwing stones at them. Suddenly I hear a beautiful noise.

Dat-dat-dat! Dat-dat-dat-dat-dat!

I look for the origin of the sound and find—God bless him—Pappy lying across a sled, firing its twin blaster cannons at close range. Each blast tears through multiple insurgents.

"Don't let up!" I call out to Doomsday Squad.

We fire again and again into the enemy. A bullet strikes Captain Devers near his collar bone. Blood squirts from his neck with every pump of his heart. Kags moves to stanch the bleeding as Exo and I continue firing. I want Masters to be here, if he's still alive. And Twenties. Maldorn. And Rook. I want us to die together.

Soon, my charge packs are again depleted.

I drop my N-4 and pull loose the tomahawk Masters bought for me. I hold it at the ready as a fleet-footed koob rushes toward me, a gleaming long knife in his hand. The insurgent attempts to plunge his weapon into me, but I sidestep and bring the tomahawk down on the back of his neck, sending up a spurt of the phosphorescent yellow blood. This one was an outlier, well ahead of his comrades. But they'll all be on top of us before long.

For reasons beyond my comprehension, I look up to the sky. A Republic super-destroyer appears in orbit, fresh from hyperspace.

"The *Mercutio*! The *Mercutio*!" Andien screams over the L-comm.

"Keep fighting!" Pappy orders.

I watch, mesmerized, as our tri-fighters engage a growing swarm of Preyhunters spilling from the MCR Ohio cruiser. The two mammoth ships rip into each other with heavy laser batteries. Dropships fall toward us, the glow of atmospheric entry making their white hulls glow red. These are engaged by MCR starfighters, and many are shot from the sky as they plummet down to relieve us.

Exo drops back to my position. We're out of our holes and fighting behind the cover of ruined sleds and wrecked Preyhunters. My tomahawk finds the forehead of an MCR human. Everything moves slowly, quietly. Legionnaires to my left and right spew out lethal fire. The insurgents roll toward us.

Death.

Soon.

Darkness.

Time accelerates to normal speed as a Republic drop-ship lands hard between us and the insurgents. Wings up, the dropship opens its side ramps. Inside, a legionnaire mans a heavy repeating blaster. He hurls fire at the koobs so fast that one shot is indistinguishable from the next. *Deeeeeeeeeeeeeeeeeeeee!*

A Republic Navy captain jumps from the sled. "Captain Devers! I'm looking for Captain Silas Devers!"

"Over here!" Kags shouts.

The captain runs to our position. He looks at Devers's battered face and bandaged neck. "Oba... Get him on the dropship. All of you. It's too hot, and we're getting out."

Exo, Kags, and I carry Devers to the waiting dropship. We place him on board, then jump on ourselves. The doors immediately begin to close as the ship rises back into the air. I stare out to my left and see more leejes and basics entering other dropships. But some of my men are cut off, still fighting.

"Hey!" I scream to the captain. "I still have men down there."

"Too hot!" the captain yells back, shaking his head.

I see Pappy's body, lying prone on the sled he manned, a pool of blood flowing over the side of the vehicle.

"No!" I protest, leaping to my feet. "Take the point and put me back on the ground!"

"That's not happening," the captain answers, his voice firm.

Exo pulls me back into the jump seat. "C'mon, sir."

"Don't tell me that's not happening!" I grab the captain by his arm. "We've held off an entire army with half a company!"

The captain wrests his uniform free of my grip. "Stand down, Sergeant!"

Exo physically restrains me. "Sir, c'mon!"

Kags helps Exo place me in a jump seat. The moment I sit down, I feel all my strength leave me. I feel utterly and completely expended. A medic looks over Kags's work, applying skinpacks to an unconscious and pale Captain Devers.

Something like pity comes across the naval captain's face. "Look, legionnaire, I understand."

I want to tell him that he doesn't. That he couldn't. But the words die at the bottom of my lungs.

We climb higher into the atmosphere. An intense, deep *zersh* sounds somewhere outside the dropship, causing the spacecraft to rock. The *Mercutio* has begun an orbital bombardment of the battlefield.

The captain reaches out to an overhead bulkhead to keep his balance. "I understand how difficult this is, but dropping legionnaires would only get more Republic soldiers killed. We have a heretofore-unheard-of army of insurgents massed at one location. The admiral couldn't let the opportunity to destroy this force in one blow pass by. As a legionnaire, I know you understand that."

Exo sits between Kags and I as the ship is buffeted by the turbulence caused by powerful orbital laser blasts from the super-destroyer. Exo tosses his bucket to the floor and stares up at the dropship's ceiling.

Kags leans out from his seat, looking past Exo to me. "KTF, right, sir?"

I pull my thoughts away from my men. From Wraith, and his men, and the burning hope that they found their way to their own dropships. Staring at the deck between my boots, I nod. "Yeah. KTF."

EPILOGUE
Awards and Ceremony

The skies are always blue, the winds fair, and the streets are paved with gold on Rep-1, capital of the Galactic Republic. This month the House and Senate named the planet "Utopion" in honor of this ideal—and because some Republic-approved poet laureate typed a screed against all the perceived injustices the lad could imagine. Last month it was called Tolera. It would change again next month. Most folks just called the place "the capital" or "Rep-1."

Exo was done with the Legion. He'd walked away from the ceremony and the parade ground in his legionnaire dress blues and silver knowing he was done with everything. All he was looking for now was a strong drink. A lot of strong drinks. And then he was out. Done with the Republic… and the Legion. Done with heroes who weren't heroes, and the real heroes who were real dead.

He wandered to the private government shuttle stations, away from the glitz and glamour that marked the center of the galaxy and the ruling elite. He would find some dark place that served his particular brand of poison, and he would just…

… he would just fade away.

He found a place and slithered into its forgiving darkness. Didn't even bother to read the name on the holo-sign.

The ceremony honoring the point was over. It still burned seeing that puke standing up there like he'd done something. Getting all the glory. Acting like he'd done anything other than make sure everyone got good and killed.

Almost everyone.

At least Devers's shiner hadn't fully healed. Exo smiled at that small victory.

He drank the first one to Pappy. It went down hard. Its burn felt like some just punishment that had finally caught up with him.

Outside, beyond the darkness of the bar, the sun wasn't yet overhead. It was still late morning. That's when the Republic liked to hand out their shiny medals. Then give everyone the day off.

What was it all for?

You got into the Legion "for adventure, and glory," Exo murmured as he ordered another from the hulking bartender.

"What?" asked a voice from the darkness of the sprawling yet nearly empty cantina.

Exo normally wouldn't bother to answer anyone about anything when he was in this kind of mood. But today, watching the phonies get to go on living while the real heroes got quietly forgotten, cached on some memory bubble no one might look at for a thousand years, well... today he was surly enough to repeat himself.

Just to see.

Just to see if he could pick a fight and get tossed in a brig somewhere long enough to clear his head and get his mind right. Then he'd be back in formation and ready to kill, kill, kill, for the Republic.

"Adventure and glory," he spat, the words a challenge.

The bartender raised his eyes, gave a half-hearted jowly smile, and moved on.

Exo realized he was talking to himself. A voice deep inside had asked, "Really?" As in, "Is that what you joined the Legion for, young leej?"

Exo smiled bitterly. He tossed back a little more poison, hating himself for being that guy. The guy who's doing it for all the wrong reasons.

"Legion ain't about fortune and glory, kid," creaked an old man's voice.

Exo looked around, searching for who it was that wanted an elbow smash to the face. Along the dark cantina's ancient bar, where a thousand drinks had been served to a thousand drunks headed out into the deep dark never to return, an old man sat in the shadows. He stared up at a screen showing skiff racing. The spindly old figure nursed a small drink.

Though his eyes remained on the screens, it was clear to Exo that the man's mind was far away. An old fool killing time among memories of what was and what might have been.

Then the old man turned toward Exo and smiled.

Exo shook his head. Just some old wreck talking trash because he knew no one would do anything about it.

"Didn't say fortune and glory." Exo waved the guy off. "*Adventure.* Adventure and glory," he mumbled. He swallowed what remained in the glass before him.

"Same thing," whined the old man distantly.

The guy was right, Exo thought. He had it all wrong. The Legion was always about getting over your malfunctions and toughing it out. How many times had DI Mard pounded that into his thick skull back in basic? "Know thyself, maggot... and stay alive." That and, "Check yo'self before you wreck yo'self."

Except Exo didn't really know *what* the Legion was all about now. Not here. Not after what had happened on Kublar.

He'd lost his way. And he knew it.

Lost the meaning of it all.

Gotten everything wrong.

"So what's got your weapon all jammed up, Leej?"

Exo shook his head. He didn't need some barroom rummy psy-empath.

"Ah," continued the old man. "Lemme guess here... Ah. Those fine people you call your superiors have probably gone and done something completely stupid. Like getting your buddies killed. And then, to top it off, they've doubled down and given themselves some award, or a shiny medal... while you got a big old fat nothin'. So your buddies probably got killed in the process, and you think that's all sooooo unfair." He took a sip of his drink and smacked his lips together lustily, as though warming up for something bigger. "Now you wanna go ahead and quit the Legion."

Exo said nothing, choosing instead to stew in his own simmering bitterness.

"Go ahead and try to make it out there on your own like some hired blaster. Maybe even get yourself a ship and try smugglin'. Get that fortune and forget the glory... because, well, it don't pay."

"*Adventure*," Exo corrected again.

"Oh, yeah, sorry kid, fortune and adventure. You're just dying to find that out there somewhere right up next to the galaxy's edge. Where your blaster can make a name, and only the quick, as opposed to the dead, get that great big old award, the only one that really counts—gettin' to live another day."

The bartender passed through, checked Exo's drink, and got the next ready with little fanfare. Not even bothering to ask if Exo wanted another. He knew a binge when he saw one.

"Is that about right?" continued the old man when the bartender had played his part and moved on.

Still, Exo said nothing. He sat considering his next round of poison.

"Well, Leej," whined the old man as he picked up his drink once more. "You got time for one last story before you go?"

Nothing.

"It's a good one. Real heroes. Real adventure."

The old man waited, as though hovering over some fine steak, waiting for permission to continue. When Exo didn't bite, he took another drink and shrugged in an "Oh well, your loss" sort of gesture. He returned to the screen above the bar, and its ghostly blue light turned his creased and wrinkled features to stone.

The return to silence and the red murder raging inside Exo's head was almost too much. He barely waved his hand. Rotating it in the air. The Legion signal for *continue*.

"This was way before you were born," began the old man after a moment. "Place was called Khan Saak. Don't hurt your head—you've never heard of it. It's way out there in the big deep dark. Ain't nothin' there now, I just about promise you that. Nothing except some leej graves. Mighty fine boys. Men. All of 'em. Though... if you woulda asked me at the time, I might've had a different opinion, but... ah, well, I was young. And dumb. Then. Like you are now.

"And believe me, if you think the Republic has changed, gotten worse like it's all going downhill fast nowadays, well, it was horrible then too. You just had to look around in all the wrong places.

"The good old days... weren't. Simple as that.

"So, where was I? Oh yeah—Skaurvold's piss pot. See, this Skaurvold was a regular pirate prince. He'd been making trouble out in that sector for a long time. Knocked off a few ultrafreighters, took some hostages, he was, as they like to say... going places.

"Until one day he pissed off the wrong people, and they sent us in to fix his little red wagon. Real good. You know the drill. Go in, break their stuff, kill their leaders. Except... well, honestly, kid, we got in way over our heads real quick-like. All the Repub intel was crap. Lemme ask you: is it still crap?"

Exo nodded.

"Figured. Well, old Skaurvold had found himself a little treasure out there on the rim of the galaxy, the edge.

Y'know, where stuff gets real weird sometimes—of course you know, you just came in from Kublar. Well anyway, he found a whole new race. No first contact records or nothin'. Maybe there was once. Maybe the Repub went in and found out why no one had ever come back from that system survey. Once we showed up, we coulda told 'em exactly why. Because whoever discovered that system ran smack dab into the perfect killing machine."

Silence washed over the bar. Down the way, the bartender seemed to be working at something.

"They tell you that in the Legion, don't they? Tell you you're the pinnacle of the art of killing other life forms. The perfect killing machine. Well... nuh-uhhhhh!" The old man let out a wheezy gust of what breath remained in him. "We met those monsters in no-holds-barred, toe-to-toe, man-to-man combat right at Skaurvold's palace. And you wanna know the funniest thing about the whole mess? If some old diplomat no one ever heard of hadn't tried to blow up the House of Reason, we might never have known about these things until it was far too late to do anything about them.

"See, whoever that old geezer was, and that's funny because I'm an old geezer now, he tried to assassinate the council. Said they'd lost touch with the people. Ha! Ain't that the truth? I bet the guy wasn't half bad. Anyway, they killed him. And he had this daughter, a real fox, and they sent her to be executed at Demaron V. Well, good old Skaurvold hijacked the ship she was on, an Omicron-class starliner—can you believe I remember what kind of ship she was on after all these years?—and made off with her.

"Boy, I'd give anything to be that young and stupid again.

"So this Skaurvold takes her back to his palace on his little nothing world, and he makes her a slave in his harem. But see, Repub wants to kill her real bad-like. So they send us in to rescue her so they can kill her. Crazy, huh?"

The old man stopped, wiped some spit from his lips, and took a sip of his drink. After this he coughed.

"You know who we were?"

Exo said nothing.

"Ever hear of the 101st Screaming Raptors? Some used to call it Rex's Dogsoldiers?"

Yeah, Exo had heard of one of the most decorated leej units ever. Everyone had. Except they all got wiped out at Andaar.

"And how about General Rex?" the old man continued, staring intently at Exo. "You ever hear of him?"

Exo hadn't.

"Why, General Rex was a basified hero. Back when heroes were real heroes, mind you. Savage Wars. Rebellion at Tychon. The Gomarii Actions. The Spinward War. All the big ones. And he was our general."

The old man straightened a bit in his seat. As though the mere mention of this fabled general had reawakened some long-lost pride that allowed him to carry himself with dignity and bearing worthy of the young man he'd once been.

"So... we go in hot. Assault corvettes laying down prep fire. Three of 'em. Big sky battle over the palace. Skaurvold's got all kinds of pirate freighters and attack fighters from just about every surplus local navy in the galaxy. We lose two corvettes to a planetary ion gun no one told anyone about, but we manage to get our ship planet-side. Except she ain't goin' nowhere now, since the old bucket was shot to pieces and burning by the time we started digging in.

"Well, then we get into a big old fight. I tell ya, I never seen the likes of it. And that's when we met the perfect killing machines. The Cybar, they were called. Biomechanical AI lifeforms almost as old as the Ancients. You know what that is? Well, if you don't, I'll tell you. They were living machines that could think. Not like stupid servitor bots—these could really think and reason. And what they thought a whole lot about was killing.

"So… you gotta imagine a spider crossed with a velociraptor. Kinda like a tyrannasquid but… human-sized. Like us. And to boot—just for giggles, ya know, cause we're already up to our eyeballs in pirates with guns—these freaky monsters don't feel pain. And they also don't go down all that easy. In fact, almost not at all. They come in at you hard and fast, and you could be putting blasts on target and your marksmanship doesn't seem to do anything to them. Them Cybars was tough.

"But somehow this Skaurvold had gotten them under his control. Later we'd find out he was breeding an army of them out in some old ancient ruins up in these high jungle mountains beyond the palace. In other words, he was looking to next-level his game from pirate to downright warlord. Who knows what after that? Seems like any old local thug can run for the Senate these days.

"So we go in blasters blazing on the palace for this 'rescue' mission to get some fox the Repub wants to kill themselves. Again, parse that out, young leej. What have we lost so far... close to five hundred leejes and three corvettes and crew? Just to kill one pretty little fox? Somethin' don't seem right, but I never did find out what.

"And maybe that's the thing. Maybe none of it don't never make no sense no matter how many times you try to fix the jam. Maybe war ain't s'posed to make sense. And if it did, then maybe smart people wouldn't do it. I know they wouldn't try to be a legionnaire. You got to have no sense to try and pull that off."

The old man cleared his throat once more.

"I can think of a dozen better ways to die. But back then we was all real excited to get ourselves killed. Y'know... leej tattoos and ooah. What's the old saying? 'Heartbreakers and... and... and lemme see...'"

"Lifetakers," said Exo.

"Yaassssss!" cheered the old man. "Heartbreakers and *lifetakers*! That was us. We got pirates with trick blaster rigs and even mean old mercs shooting at us as we advance on the palace. In fact, we're takin' real heavy, and I mean heavy, casualties from all directions. I mean fire. Fire from all directions. Casualties everywhere. But you know how it is—Sarge says keep moving forward. You have a good sergeant, leej?"

"The best," Exo answered, staring into the empty bottom of his glass. "Made brevet lieutenant. And then they took it away from him."

The old man nodded. "That sounds about right. So you keep on movin' forward. I was a sergeant, so I had to say it. LT told me. Cap'n told him. General Rex probably told the cap'n... so you know the drill... move forward no matter what.

"Well, once we reach the palace—and that, as they say, was something in and of itself—we see that it was old. *Real* old. Real old ruins the Ancients left behind long ago, and this Skaurvold had turned them into his personal pleasure palace. And you know how those old Ancient ruins is when you get to crawlin' around inside 'em. All weird angles and passages that don't make no sense. Those weird runes. Crazy-cray."

The old man's face was ghostly white and gray. Exo knew that death had made its appointment with this old leej. It was coming for him despite his attempts to get killed by the galaxy. The old man knew it, too. It was known. Not that day. Maybe not the next. But soon. The appointment had been made for this dodgy old leej despite his best attempts to delay the inevitable.

Exo vowed not to get old.

Not to die.

As if.

The old man leaned forward into the pale light above the bar like some master storyteller on the shows and said, "We lost half a company in them ruins. Half a company. Of legionnaires. And that was just to start."

Silence covered the bar. Far down the way, near the exit out onto the street, the door opened, and white light washed across the bar. Outside, the world was alight and bright and the opposite of all that was hidden here in the shadows. The door slammed, and darkness returned again.

"That's when the old pirate slipped the leash on most of his Cybar. Sent 'em right on us," whispered the hoary old man.

Pause.

"They came out of the walls like real live monsters, or so it seemed. In a moment we was getting chopped to shreds. See, they'd come in at ya, you doing that sustained firing thing they teach you back in basic. Doing your almighty best to put them down. But they don't care about center mass. Their systems just rerouted power and kept coming at you while some sort of internal repair function started rebuilding the damage right before your eyes. They come in with two to three solid hits from the old N-16 dead on target. Pirates and mercs, they'd be dead with shots like that. The Cybar still come straight at you. And those things acted like they were mad. How do ya stop that kind of real life crazy-cray?"

The old man searched the ether before his eyes as though he might find the answer to that particular question all these years later right here in this bar. But he didn't, and he continued on.

"That ain't half the worst of it. See, then they start to cut into ya once they got you all pinned down with these flexible metal tentacles. And believe it or not they'd download... something... some kind of virus, right into your brain. They'd re-wire you right on the spot into some kind of living death. I ain't kidding here. Within a few minutes you're a walking host for another one of 'em as it starts to cannibalize your biologic for its mechanical. Yeah... I know... it don't make no sense. It didn't then either, and I saw it right with my own eyes. Did I mention my buddies' eyes have rolled back in their heads and they're using their blaster rifles on their fellow leejes?"

Exo stared at the old man in silence, wondering if everything he said was true. Or just crazy.

The old man must have sensed this, as he moved in for the kill. "They don't tell you this story, do they? In basic. None of the old DIs tell ya because only a few of us made it out of there alive. I'm one. And no, we didn't get no medals or fancy award ceremonies. We got told to shut up because the Repub don't like failure. 'Specially when they tryin' to kill someone. So I know all about where you're at right now, young leej. Been there. Done that. Got the scars."

The old man stared at Exo for a long moment. As though he were still a heartbreaker, and a lifetaker. As though he was daring the young leej rippling with muscles to call him a liar. Or even crazy.

"We made it," said the old leej. "We made it to the girl. Into the inner sanctum of Skaurvold's fortress. Blasting our way and watching corners. Tactical. Shoot, move, and communicate. You know all that stuff. Made it in there, and don't she look like a real live slave girl princess from one of them films. Silk bikini and she's putting a knife right in old Skaurvold's big belly. Fat bastard is dancing around with a double-barreled blaster, tryna pull it out hisself. He was a Cyclorean, so you know they're real big to begin with. But there's just five of us left, and the general. And we ain't doing so hot.

"We're about fifteen stories up the side of Skaurvold's palace and we got all these monsters howling on the far side of the harem door. Screaming like a banshee's nightmare. Don't know why they did that. But they sounded like they were in some kind of eternal torment. And mixed in with them is all the dead leejes that were our buddies just two hours ago.

"General Rex, he's wearing that old Mark I armor. A real operator from the big book of old-school bad dudes. He just says, 'Time to go,' like we can just waltz on out should it please us and such. Never mind all the demons tryna get to us."

The old man laughed, but it was really a gargling cough.

"'Sir,' says I, because I was just a sergeant then and my LT was too awestruck to say anything to the greatest hero the Legion ever managed to squeeze out, I says, 'Sir, we're fifteen stories up. How we gettin' out of here, exactly?'"

The old man leaned in closer. As though he was giving an aside to some witty cocktail party anecdote.

"Mind you, this ain't a polite conversation like you and I are having right in this here bar. This is us in an improvised firing position inside a princess slave girl's fantasy harem with these weird, shrieking Cybars coming at us like screaming smart-bullets and the pirates taking shots at us at every possible opportunity.

"There was just us. No leej fire support. No Repub close air or strategic on station. No medics. No supply convoy or heavy armor. It was me, Lieutenant Hilbert, Corporal Tacas, and two privates. Ahamalee and Ren. In system we had a carrier task group—the *Orion*—on standby, but none of the group ships could get close to that ion gun."

"I had a CO named Hilbert," Exo offered. "Damn fine legionnaire."

The old man nodded. "Good name. Where was we? Oh, right. 'Sir,' I says to the general, 'how we gettin' outta here? Exactly-like.' 'Cause remember I told you we was fifteen stories up. His reply is, 'Five clicks back to the LZ. That's how, Sergeant,' he says to me.

"So at that point I'm like every NCO you ever met. Officers sure are dumb, but I ain't gonna get no court-marital. So I guess I'll jes' get killed and all doin' what he says I gotta do.

"'Mother, this is Little Boy Blue.' That's what he said. General's on tac support calling in an orbital strike. He says, 'Mother, this is Little Boy Blue... I say broken arrow.' Uh-oh. Broken arrow! Now, I don't know what you guys use for codes these days, but that was one no leej ever wanted to hear. Ever. You guys still use it?"

Exo nodded.

"So you know what it means then?"

Exo nodded again.

"Good. 'Cause this is where things gets real woban-ki hairball. I'm screaming at the general, and I'll be real honest here, I'm calling him every name because he's just killed us faster than any of them freaky Cybar, and gettin' court-martialed would be a privilege compared to what was about to happen next. At the time I was sorta thinking, even though I was mad, that it wasn't such a bad idea.

Better than being turned into a host zombie by those alien robots. But no leej ever wants to die, amirite?

"Hells yeah I'm right!" roared the old man suddenly. He took a gusty drink even though his liver-spotted hand trembled as he held the glass up to his quivering lips.

"Tac Com comes back with the strike authorization. This means the battleship running alongside the carrier *Orion* is aligning its main gun for a strike that will hit within in meters of the target. To be more specific—that means *us*. For all intents and purposes... we dead.

"I remember when I heard the support operator tell us to seek cover—'Orbital Strike inbound'—that it was probably the last thing I was ever gonna hear. Except they're way out in space. It's gonna take a bit for that big old beam to hit us.

"'To me, legionnaires,' says the general. He's got the girl over one shoulder and he's dropping Cybars danger close with his sidearm.

"One of them Cybars grabs a hold of Ren, its tentacles all over him as it goes in to take a bite with its hydraulic jaws. Lieutenant Hilbert breaks away from our formation to go after him even though the weapon is about to hit us.

"The LT screams, 'Not today, you piece of worthless junk!' and he's unloading full-auto point-blank. You know the old N-16s with the full-auto blast feature was real wonky. Hell, even we known they was dangerous. You couldn't control the muzzle. He pulls Ren away from the flailing corpse of the dying monster and starts draggin' Ren, who's screaming like he's just had the worst nightmare of all time, across this polished marble blue floor that seems like some map of a whole other galaxy. But you see weird stuff like that in ancient ruins all the time. Stuff that makes your head hurt to think about, so you don't. And there's all the bodies.

"Then one of them Cybars gets one of its tentacles around the LT's throat. Opens it up with blood and everything right before my eyes. And I'm shootin' at all the other Cybars tryna rush our position."

The old man suddenly stopped. His eyes glazed over for a second as though some strange idea had just occurred to him.

"Did I mention the general's gonna activate a personal force repulsor field? Yeah... I mighta mentioned that earlier. That's real important to this story. That's why the LT went out to drag Ren back in close. 'Cause there was a radius. And now that thing's got ahold of him and it's cuttin' his throat. All 'cause he went out for a dumb-as-a-bag-of-spanners private. But that's a leej for ya.

"Even with an orbital strike about to rain down on us and turn everything to little bitty pieces, the general thumbs a switch on this big old relic he's usin'—a slug thrower from the Savage Wars was my guess. He thumbs it off full-auto to single shot. Cool as a Vanu courtesan dripping with jade lotus blossom, he puts a bullet right in the main processor of the Cybar that's cuttin' the LT's throat. LT stumbles forward, dying 'cause his throat's been cut deep, but I slap a med-seal over him, thinking he might live, and set it for full spectrum pain relief and thermaheal. That's when the strike hits us."

The old man smiled like he's about to deliver the punch line to a joke.

"You ever been inside a fifteen-story fortress when it got hit from an orbital strike by one of them big old Republican battleship main guns? Huh? You ever have that happen to you, Leej?"

The old man almost died laughing. Then he started coughing and hacking like he really was about to keel over.

"Didn't think so. Well... the world made no sense after the bright light and searing heat of the strike. Suddenly everything's going all hit-by-a-wave-of-deadly-energy. And that's when the building collapsed in on itself. Millions of tons of rock went sliding down past us like a waterfall of debris mixed with brief glimpses of nightmare visions of dying killer biobots shrieking and screeching and being crushed and carried away while we're inside this force-field bubble that will give out at any second. You know how *that* is. There was smoke and dust and debris everywhere. And then we were falling. Falling with everything else. And everyone, except probably the general, was screaming, leej or not. Because that's what death is like. You gonna scream even though you told yourself you never would.

"When we came to, it was still raining debris and clouds of dust down on what was left of the general's force field. Which was collapsing. The two suns of that planet, which had been close and burning directly overhead, now looked like distant red dwarfs at midnight."

The old man paused and took another sip of his drink. He licked his dry lips and continued.

"Bad. Sure. That was bad. Except those Cybars don't care about almost being killed inside a falling building. They're coming at us across the piles of debris. Suddenly we're in a firefight once again with dust and smoke everywhere. Optics and HUDs offline due to the EMP effects of the strike. So it's all iron sights until the software reboots.

"I try to grab the LT, but he shrugs me off and tells me to cover the general. Except he croaks now like a frog 'cause his throat got cut. We lay down as much covering fire as we can, takin' 'em out as the Cybar come at us across all this ruined end-of-tomorrow wasteland that was once Ancients' ruins. We egress out of the AO and manage to get back to the road that leads out of Skaurvold's pleasure palace. Which is now just a big old crater. We reach a raised thoroughfare that led out to the starport. Which was of course, five clicks back. All transport has been destroyed by the strike, so we got to go on foot. And because we got no electronics, we got no commo. Rescue can't pull us off the battlefield. We got to make it to the LZ through this swampy jungle.

"Except now the Cybar don't want to let us go. All the pirates is good and dead, but the Cybar on the other hand are coming at us in waves. And the waves are getting bigger and bigger as more and more of them gather and repair. At times they get danger close. And we get beat to shreds by the time we make it to the outer gate that led out to the starport above the jungle. The whole city behind is a smoking crater. Big old pirate raiders have been ripped to pieces and tossed out into the landscape like toys.

"In other words... we ain't making it back to the LZ. There's nothing but burning jungle between us and the rendezvous. Jungle's on fire from the strike."

The old man picked up his drink and considered it a moment as though waging some internal argument. Then he set it down gently with some moment of finality.

"That was when LT tells the general to go on. He tells him we'll try to hold the Cybar back long enough to let him and the girl get a head start. Did I mention she was a real looker? Then he asks the general something. LT says, 'Sir, don't let them kill her.' He said that because she'd been right with us through the whole thing. Picked up an N-16 and started firing point-blank into those monsters. She'd've made a real good leej. So I guess we just couldn't let the Repub kill her off."

The old man at the bar nodded to himself. Just stared at something Exo couldn't see and nodded to himself. Then he cleared his throat.

"General said he would send someone to pull us out if he made it back to the LZ. He'd keep a dropship on station. But you know how promises are. And besides... we knew we weren't gonna make it. But we buy 'em enough time so *they* might.

"And we did," said the old man quietly. "We held the line. Ahamalee got it first. Those monsters just dragged him out of his position near the ruined gatehouse. Went down like a man. Didn't scream or nothin'. Just waited till they were all over him and then he detonated his demo rig. Must've taken about twenty of them all at once. Didn't matter much, because more of them just came on at us all over again.

"Me and the LT and Ren fell back inside some kind of old temple structure and formed up around a bottleneck in a side passage. Until nightfall we held them there. Then Ren's rifle malfunctioned, and about ten seconds later they got him. *He* screamed. Screamed a lot, in fact."

The old man turned to look at Exo. His eyes were haunted by what he saw inside his memories.

"There's some nights here, when the bars are all closed and I can't sleep, that I'd like to forget that scream. Forget what he was begging for. Who he was asking for at the end. I'd like to forget that, and to tell you the truth, I hope that's what death's all about. Not nothin'... but forgettin' the bad like it never was."

For a long moment there's nothing but silence in the bar. Beyond its walls, galactic civilization hurries on, heedless of the heroism and tragedy needed to maintain its thin veneer. But here in the shadowy cool bar... the memories are hauled out and examined once more. Debts paid are remembered.

The old man holds the glass to lips and takes a slow, small sip. He mumbles some words Exo doesn't catch. They're too low and too silent to be heard in the quiet of the bar.

The cantina is still in its perpetual night. But the clock on the wall reads afternoon Utopion local.

The old man swallows hard and rattles the few cubes in his glass.

"Another?" asks Exo hopefully.

The old man says nothing, just smiles sadly at the young leej. Sad for all the dead. Where have they gone, and, when will we ever learn, as they say.

"Almost time to go home," whispers the old man. "My little granddaughter's coming to stay with us tonight. I only ever just have the one here. It's my last treat. And I know... I ain't got much longer left this side of the galaxy. But thank you all the same. Your drills would be proud of you, Leej. You didn't forget an old brother. And you were kind enough to sit and listen about times long gone. When we were young, and brave."

"How did you get out of there?" prompts Exo after a long, quiet moment.

"LT carried me," states the old man simply. "During our escape out of the ruins, one of them got me in the leg pretty bad. It was half-hanging off. We tournicreted it. But I wasn't using it anymore. Not ever again, really. I says to the LT, 'We gonna die here, sir.'

"He says, 'No way, no how, Sergeant.' Except he can only talk in that whisper cause that thing half-sawed through his throat. He carried me through some sewers we found and out into the jungle. Full dark by the time we got out, but the whole jungle is still on fire. Them things is howling in the jungle like nightmares. But I told you that.

"LT was a real hero, Leej. Carried me out there and into the jungle, and I'm thinking, what the hell for? We'll just die out here in a few.

"'Let's just set off our demo rigs, LT,' I says to him. But he says we're gonna make it. 'Just hang in there, Sergeant. You don't mind... it don't matter.'

"We laughed because I'd lost my rifle when I spring-bayonetted a Cybar who got up close and personal. It was a real knife and gun show inside that temple. Then LT's rifle malfunctioned and exploded a second after he tossed it away. He only had his sidearm.

"We were laughing because we weren't gonna make it on our own. And we knew it. But that didn't matter no how. Not to us. Not at that moment. We didn't care about awards or ceremonies. Or medals. At the end... we were just two leejes who managed to be dumb enough not die up 'til then... and it was good to have someone to die with. No leej should ever die alone out there. Galaxy likes it that way, though. Gets you all alone and makes you feel small. And then it kills you dead like you were never nothin' to nobody. That's the way the galaxy is. You'll die all alone out there. 'Cept leejes stick together when everyone runs.

"The jungle was filled with them things," the old man whispered "It was a real nightmare. But General was true to his word. Search Air Rescue tac shuttle comes in all mounts blazing and clears off the LZ. We try to make it through the swamp we're crawling through, and the blasts from the shuttle's turbines are pushing us back. Door gunners are firing away in every direction, and by the flashing light of their heavy blasters I can see we're surrounded by not just hundreds, but *thousands* of Cybars closing in on us.

"'Don't give up, Pappy!' I'm screaming over the turbines. And out in the dark beyond the perimeter I see something bigger than everything else comin' straight for us. Like the monster of all monsters. Galaxy's a weird place. Sometimes it'll throw some bizarre stuff straight at ya and ask ya how you like them tarpples."

Pappy? Exo opened his mouth to give voice to the question in his mind, but closed it when he saw the old man's look. He was building to an end, reliving triumph through honor. Exo didn't interrupt.

"'Leejes don't give up,' roars the LT. 'Never,' he croaks, and I see blood come from around the bandage on his throat. But we made it onto that shuttle, and we got out of there. Just barely. Things were holding on to the damn shuttle when we went to full throttle."

The old man picked up his glass, forgetting it was empty. He rattled the cubes, set the glass on the bar, and stood awkwardly. He fished an unseen cane from beneath the bar and hobbled over to Exo.

"I don't know what the Legion is about any more than anyone else, kid. But maybe... maybe it's not about dying alone out there. If it hadn't been for Lieutenant Hilbert— we called him Pappy because he looked like an old man, gray hair at nineteen, you know the type. If it hadn't been for Pappy, I'd've never made it home. Wouldn't have met my Zandra. No kids. No granddaughter coming over tonight to let me play Candyship with her. This leg never worked right again. They put me out of the Legion—and I loved the Legion. You never saw such a damn fine NCO, I can assure you that."

Exo begged to differ, but he kept his thoughts to himself.

"They never gave us commendations, nor medals neither. They just wanted to cover it all up because it was really just a hit mission on that beautiful girl. Whatever happened to her... I'll never know. I suspect General Rex did right. He was that kind of man.

"But Pappy didn't let me die alone out there in the big dark. He was a real hero. Heroes like him may not ever get any medals, but he's a hero all the same. My Zandra would tell him that if she ever met him. She'd tell him... thank you. 'Cause her sergeant made it back, mostly in one piece—though I suspect she wouldn't care how many pieces didn't come back.

"Me too. I'd tell him that. I'd tell him he was a real hero, never mind no cheap piece of metal they stick on your dress uniform."

The old man patted Exo once on the shoulder. "Well. You take care, boy. I got to go home now."

He continued on down the length of the bar. The door opened out into the last of the Utopion daylight, and the legionnaire was gone.

Read on for a special note from the authors.

MORE
GALAXY'S
EDGE

**GALACTIC
OUTLAWS
is available
now**

GALAXY'S
EDGE
GALACTIC OUTLAWS

ANSPACH · COLE

AUTHOR'S NOTE

How's it going? We hope you're enjoying *Galaxy's Edge: Season One* so far. This first book is one we wanted to write for a long time. It combines the idea of the galaxy-spanning wars we loved to think about in *Star Wars* with the modern warrior ethic exemplified by friends and family, like SSG Christopher C. Kagawa (Kags was named for him). These warriors who fought in Iraq and Afghanistan, as portrayed in books like *House to House* and *Ambush Alley*, are the inspiration for the Legion, and we've got nothing but love and respect for them.

With *Legionnaire*, we've led off with gritty military science fiction, because that's life in the Legion. (Unless you're a point.) But as you might have inferred from the epilogue, the world of *Galaxy's Edge* is a whole lot bigger than Kublar. We'll be going beyond the men of Victory Company to fight epic space battles, launch desperate rescue missions, take down double-crossing spies, and of course stave off threats to the very future of humanity itself.

But don't worry. Chhun, Ford, and the rest will never stray too far from the heart of the action.

So what's coming next? That depends on how you like your stories. In order to present certain reveals in a satisfying way, we deliberately told the next part of the *Galaxy's*

Edge story... out of order. Just a bit. Specifically, the second book in the series, *Galactic Outlaws*, jumps ahead in time, introducing new characters and following the General Rex of the epilogue as he's swept up in a path that will lead him directly to Victory Company. The second book also has a different feel to it—a bit more lighthearted and less battle-heavy. Our readers and listeners have grown to love the way we chose to let this story unfold.

But—if you're the sort who prefers to read things in chronological order, or if you just want to stay by Chhun's side, you should feel free to go straight to book three, *Kill Team,* to find out what happens next to Chhun, Ford, Exo, Twenties, and the other survivors of Victory Company immediately after *Legionnaire.* You can then go back and read *Galactic Outlaws* with a better understanding of who its characters are... and what they're *really* up to.

And you'll be glad to know we kept things strictly chronological starting in book four.

As you've probably guessed, Season One suggests a Season Two—which we're working on now! But don't let the word "season" fool you. Season One is a complete, self-contained story, with a satisfying ending that brings everything together. No loose ends, no cliffhangers. Season Two will be an entirely new and independent story.

In addition to Season Two, we're also working on other *Galaxy's Edge* stories, including stories of the bounty hunter Tyrus Rechs, intense military battles in the Order of the Centurion series, and an upcoming series about the ancient Savage Wars. If you want to know when those books release, please sign up at inthelegion.com. We'll give you a free, exclusive short story called "Tin Man," you'll get free concept art, and you'll only ever receive emails that relate to *Galaxy's Edge.*

Until next time, stay frosty... and KTF!

—Jason Anspach & Nick Cole

PS. Amazon won't tell you when future books come out, but there are several ways you can stay informed.

1. Enlist in our fan-run Facebook group, the <u>Galaxy's Edge Fan Club</u>, and say hello. It's a great place to hang out with other KTF-lovin' legionnaires who like to talk about sci-fi and are up for a good laugh.
2. Follow us directly on Amazon. This one is easy. Just go to the store page for this book on Amazon and click the "follow" button beneath our pictures. That will prompt Amazon to email you automatically whenever we release a new title.
3. Join the <u>Galaxy's Edge Newsletter</u>. You'll get emails directly from us—along with the short story "Tin Man," available only to newsletter subscribers.

Doing just one of these (**although doing all three is your best bet!**) will ensure you find out when the next *Galaxy's Edge* book releases. Please take a moment to do one of these so you can find yourself on patrol with Chhun, Wraith, and Exo for their next gritty firefight!

JOIN THE LEGION

You can find art, t-shirts, signed books and other merchandise on our website.

We also have a fantastic Facebook group called the Galaxy's Edge Fan Club that was created for readers and listeners of *Galaxy's Edge* to get together and share their lives, discuss the series, and have an avenue to talk directly with Jason Anspach and Nick Cole. Please check it out and say hello once you get there!

For updates about new releases, exclusive promotions, and sales, visit inthelegion.com and sign up for our VIP mailing list. Grab a spot in the nearest combat sled and get over there to receive your free copy of "Tin Man," a Galaxy's Edge short story available only to mailing list subscribers.

INTHELEGION.COM

GALAXYS
EDGE
TIN MAN

ANSPACH   COLE

GET A
FREE,
EXCLUSIVE
SHORT STORY

THE GALAXY
IS A DUMPSTER
FIRE...

ABOUT THE AUTHORS

Jason Anspach and Nick Cole are a pair of west coast authors teaming up to write their science fiction dream series, Galaxy's Edge.

Jason Anspach is a best-selling author living in Puyallup, Washington with his wife and their own legionnaire squad of seven (not a typo) children. Raised in a military family (Go Army!), he spent his formative years around Joint Base Lewis-McChord and is active in several pro-veteran charities. Jason enjoys hiking and camping throughout the beautiful Pacific Northwest. He remains undefeated at arm wrestling against his entire family.

Nick Cole is a Dragon Award winning author best known for *The Old Man and the Wasteland, CTRL ALT Revolt!,*and the Wyrd Saga. After serving in the United States Army, Nick moved to Hollywood to pursue a career in acting and writing. He resides with his wife, a professional opera singer, south of Los Angeles, California.

Honor Roll

We would like to give our most sincere thanks and recognition to those who helped make Galaxy's Edge: Legionnaire possible by subscribing to GalacticOutlaws.com.

Marlena Anspach
Robert Anspach
Steve Beaulieu
Wilfred Blood
Christopher Boore
Brent Brown
Rhett Bruno
Marion Buehring
Mary Ann Bulpitt
Nathan Davis
Richard Fox
Peter Francis
Chris Fried
Hank Garner
Michael Greenhill
Phillip Hall
Josh Hayes
Wendy Jacobson
Chris Kagawa
William Kravetz
Grant Lambert
Danyelle Leafty

Preston Leigh
Pawel Martin
Tao Mason
Simon Mayeski
Jim Mern
Alex Morstadt
Nate Osburn
Chris Pourteau
Maggie Reed
Karen Reese
Glenn Shotton
Maggie Stewart-Grant
Kevin Summers
Beverly Tierney
Scott Tucker
John Tuttle
Christopher Valin
Scot Washam
Justin Werth
Justyna Zawiejska
N. Zoss

Made in the USA
Monee, IL
02 October 2020